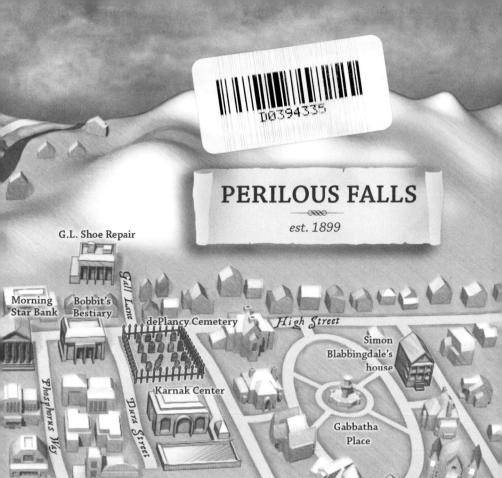

WILL WILDER
THE AMULET OF POWER

ALSO BY RAYMOND ARROYO

Will Wilder: The Relic of Perilous Falls

Will Wilder: The Lost Staff of Wonders

WILL WILDER
THE AMULET OF POWER

❖ BOOK III ❖

RAYMOND ARROYO

CROWN BOOKS
FOR YOUNG READERS

NEW YORK

Text copyright © 2019 by Raymond Arroyo
Jacket art and interior illustrations copyright © 2019 by Jeff Nentrup

All rights reserved. Published in the United States by Crown Books for Young Readers,
an imprint of Random House Children's Books,
a division of Penguin Random House LLC, New York.

Crown and the colophon are registered trademarks of Penguin Random House LLC.

Visit us on the Web! rhcbooks.com

Educators and librarians, for a variety of teaching tools,
visit us at RHTeachersLibrarians.com

Library of Congress Cataloging-in-Publication Data
Names: Arroyo, Raymond, author.
Title: The Amulet of Power / Raymond Arroyo.
Description: First edition. | New York: Crown Books for Young Readers, [2019] | Series: Will wilder; book 3 | Summary: When twelve-year-old Will Wilder uses the Amulet of Power to get on the Perilous Falls football team, he attracts dark forces that shadow townspeople, disturb graves, and lull many into a stupor.
Identifiers: LCCN 2018050334 | ISBN 978-0-553-53971-4 (hardback) |
ISBN 978-0-553-53973-8 (epub)
Subjects: CYAC: Supernatural—Fiction. | Demonology—Fiction. | Football—Fiction. | BISAC: JUVENILE FICTION / Action & Adventure / General. | JUVENILE FICTION / Family / General (see also headings under Social Issues). | JUVENILE FICTION / Religious / General.
Classification: LCC PZ7.A74352 Amu 2019 | DDC [Fic]—dc23

Printed in the United States of America
10 9 8 7 6 5 4 3 2 1
First Edition

For my three inspirations,
Mariella, Lorenzo, and Alexander

And for my adventurous readers,
the honorary citizens of Perilous Falls

Contents

It is excellent to have a giant's strength,
but it is tyrannous to use it like a giant.

—William Shakespeare,
Measure for Measure

WILL WILDER
THE AMULET OF POWER

THE HELMET AND THE LOCKS

Paris, France
The Louvre
November 3, 1940

W*hat have they gotten me into? Even the halls stink of demons. . . .*

Jacob Wilder's nose tingled uncontrollably as he pushed the canvas rolling cart through the abandoned Grande Galerie of the chilly museum. Though the Louvre was Paris's largest and most important temple of art, the art itself was hard to find.

The dying sun scarcely broke through the skylights overhead as Wilder passed a succession of bare walls. They held nothing but dusty outlines of frames no longer present. Chalk graffiti now marked the places where the art had once hung: Murillo 1, Delacroix 4, Fra Angelico 3. Like so much of Paris since the arrival of the Nazis, the best and brightest had gone into hiding.

Out of the corner of his right eye, Jacob saw something dark scamper across the wall, heading upward. His eyes narrowed as he studied the ceiling. Black shadows like mold collected at the corners of the room, but he saw nothing more. Still, his nose stung—always an early warning that evil was present or approaching.

Pushing past a series of marble columns into the next section of the hall, his glance casually drifted overhead. What he spotted paralyzed him. Hunchbacked creatures like small, dark monkeys frantically crawled across the ceiling. Defying gravity, hundreds of the slick beasts leapt over one another—scratching, clawing upside down to the far end of the hall.

Leave it to me to walk into a Fomorii *infestation,* Jacob thought. *It's a Legion, but what are they running toward? Something big is down there. A marquis of hell? A prince maybe?*

At that moment, a few of the minor demons pointed directly at Jacob, covering their mouths or baring their teeth at him. Wilder silenced his thoughts (which he knew the creatures could read), ignored the diabolic ceiling display, and resumed pushing his cart down the endless corridor. *Fomorii* came with the territory. Minor demons always swarmed near the major ones. He had a job to do, and being sidetracked by *Fomorii* was not part of it. Wilder's pace didn't slow until he reached rows of gestapo soldiers in shiny helmets and boots near the end of the hall.

"Something big" was in the Louvre after all.

Barking in German-accented French, the officer nearest Jacob blocked his path and demanded to see identification. Jacob produced the same documents he had flashed at Nazi checkpoints all over Paris, falsified papers provided by Brethren members of the French Resistance. The documents claimed that Wilder was a "curator of special collections" at the Louvre Museum. The officer sneered at the papers and shoved them back into his hands. Jacob nodded obediently and continued on between the rows of Nazis lining the walls.

He labored to hold back a sneeze. From the open door on his right, the metallic tinkling of a music box, laughter, and soft German voices spilled into the hallway. An enormously fat man wearing a camel coat and a purple scarf sat on a sofa inside, sipping champagne. A towering Nazi officer and a small bespectacled man in a brown suit presented paintings to the big man. He jabbed a chunky finger at a particular canvas.

"That one is for my collection," the fat man said merrily, spilling champagne on his lap. "The Vermeer—*The Astronomer*—we will offer to the führer." Two huge cats on the couch suddenly stood at attention and stared at Jacob. But he paid them no mind. He was too distracted by the sea of pint-sized black demons surrounding the three men and the sofa. The creatures' faces were pressed to the ground, their tiny wings extended to heaven.

Who are they bowing to?

AH-CHOO! Jacob's sneeze exploded in the hall, drawing the eyes of everyone in the room. The fat man lowered his cigar in disgust, glaring at Jacob as if he had just dropped a piece of china.

"You oaf. What are you doing here?" a young woman hissed in French, stepping into the doorway. Her ocean-blue eyes fell on the cart Jacob pushed. "Those were to go to the *other* gallery, *fool.*" She turned back to the room, dropping her head slightly. "Reich Marshal Goering, dear colonel, please excuse my absence. I must redirect my colleague."

The fat man's attention had already wandered back to the art before him. He waved her away, keeping time with the tune of the lacquered music box on an end table. Oblivious to his hostile cats, he continued greedily surveying his favorite artworks, like a wolf in a shepherd's field.

It took everything for Jacob to tear his eyes away from the room. He alone could see the small three-headed demon with pinched faces and long white horns perched on the shoulder of the Nazi officer. Turning away, he silently followed the irate woman in the black pencil skirt down the hall. Moving past the gestapo battalion, he pushed the cart after her for blocks.

Turning into a side hall off the Grande Galerie, the young woman continued to berate him, her auburn hair shaking.

"You must be more attentive. It is an embarrassment to Monsieur Jaujard and all of us when you . . ." Then as they moved beyond a pair of double doors, into a stairwell, she grabbed Jacob Wilder by the shoulders, spun him around, searched his eyes, and kissed him.

"I've missed you, *mon seul et unique*," she said under her breath. "Where have you been?"

He held her close, whispering. "I came as quickly as I could, Sarah. The Brethren sent me on a mission to Orleans—to protect an artifact. It was at the Abbey of St. Denis. Then as I left, the Nazis invaded the place. I couldn't leave this relic there." He released her and ran to the cart, shoving aside the stacked canvases inside. "I need your help." Beneath the paintings lay a rusted, conical metal helmet. It came to a point at the crown, which was adorned with a few links of hanging chain.

Sarah gasped, her full lips parting. "That's not . . . Is that the helmet of *the Maiden*?"

"One and the same. They say when Joan of Arc wore it in battle, she heard divine voices and received messages— even saw visions. The wearer who is pure of heart can supposedly receive similar messages—and hear the voices. I can tell you the Nazis think it's true. They rounded up a few of the Brethren at the Abbey trying to find it. But I had already smuggled it out in a wine barrel." He tossed the helmet to Sarah. "Make sure this gets to your friend at the Metropolitan Museum. I've got to return to Monte Cassino, but I'll be back—"

"You just arrived."

Jacob kissed her gently on the cheek, almost as an apology, and took her hand.

"I know." Sarah Vaillant sighed, looking away. "You must fight the *other* war. I'll show you the way, though I need a favor before you leave." She began to pull him from the room.

"One second." He plucked his battered pith helmet from the cart.

"You're still wearing my father's helmet." She smirked, touching the brim with her index finger.

"In a war, you take all the protection you can get." The pair raced downstairs, carrying their respective helmets into a dark gallery cluttered with broken statues and immense draped paintings.

Sarah chattered intensely. "All the art in the room upstairs—everything the Germans are rifling through— belongs to Jews all over Paris. Their homes have been raided and their belongings looted." She pressed a small leather journal into Jacob's hand. "This is a listing of all the items the Nazis have stolen and shipped out of Paris so far. Protect this, Jacob."

He nodded sharply, slipping the journal into his hip pocket. Sarah walked to the corner of the vast room and yanked back a sheet, revealing a white marble sarcophagus. Twisting grapevines and a carved seal with a large *P* covering an *X* decorated the front. "This is the only way back to

Monte Cassino now. The other two sarcophagi were taken to Austria."

The Brethren routinely used stone coffins to travel between far-flung locations. Though they had to recite a formula to transport via (what they called) *sarcophagal peregrination,* there was one other requirement: the sarcophagi at both the beginning and the end of the voyage had to be identical.

"I'll return before you can miss me." He hugged Sarah and threw his pith helmet into the sarcophagus. It landed softly on a burgundy velvet sack covered in gold Hebrew letters with a pair of wooden handles protruding from the top and bottom.

"Take that with you. It may be the last Torah in Paris. I hid it there the other day. When these monsters are gone, perhaps we can return it to its rightful owners," Sarah said, her face uncharacteristically flushing. "But you can't leave yet. We've found something downstairs: a Keep that the abbot would like you to inspect."

"A Keep?" Jacob reluctantly retrieved his pith helmet, put it on, and followed Sarah through a heavy wooden door and down a medieval staircase. The winding catacombs at the bottom went on for what seemed like blocks. Sarah cradled St. Joan's metal helmet under one arm and stayed close to Jacob as he lit their way with his flashlight. It was comforting to be near him again. "The big man upstairs is Hermann Goering. He's the highest-ranking Nazi officer under Hitler. The horrible man is filling trains with looted art and antiquities. He's seeking relics too. Colonel Von Groll—the tall officer—is not all bad. Though he's only been here a few days, he seems like a charming man."

"You should have seen Colonel Charming's *friends* hanging from the ceiling of the Grande Galerie." Jacob turned the light on Sarah's porcelain face.

"Don't be jealous. I said he seems charming. But he's not you." She slipped her arm under his and playfully pulled him along the tight, stoned hall. "We're going just up here around the—" She suddenly cried out. Jacob shoved her behind him and shone the light to the ground. A stream of brown dried blood issued from an open chamber.

"What is this place?"

"I don't know. The Nazis come down here every few days for officer meetings," Sarah sputtered. "They're into all manner of occult things. . . ."

"Stay here." Jacob ventured in alone. He stood on the highest level in the room, which encircled a sunken center. His flashlight found a lifeless body slumped against the wall. The dead man's slicked black hair and hard features were strangely familiar. One blue eye stared ahead, and the other—hazel and glazed—turned off to the side. A deep, thick red gash ran from the man's head clear down to his left kneecap. Three lighter slashes of similar length bordered it. *What in blazes cut this fellow open?* Jacob searched the room for answers. He found a gold saucer of thickened blood in the middle of the room, scrawlings in the dirt, and toppled candelabras. *Necromancy maybe—some type of blood ritual. What were they trying to do?*

"There is a dead man in here. We've got to go," Jacob yelled to Sarah, joining her in the hallway.

"Who is he?"

"No telling. Where is the Keep?"

"It's just here." Sarah worriedly led him to a rounded wall of pocked stone. A huge block jutted from the Keep. Three sculptures carved onto the side of the structure arrested Jacob's attention.

Upstairs, in the side room of the Grande Galerie, Reich Marshal Goering's ice-blue eyes fell on a tray of jewelry presented to him by the small groveling man in brown. The rings, brooches, even the assorted gems were not worth sending on to Germany. His thin lips turned downward.

"Trash," he pronounced before pawing a handful of the items and slipping them into his coat pocket. The eyebrow of the man in brown rose slightly, but when Goering met his eyes, he fearfully turned away. Dark creatures invisible to those in the room perched on the back edge of the sofa. One sloppy demon, with a Buddha-like belly and ram's horns, shuffled sideways and whispered into the Reich Marshal's ear.

"Colonel Von Groll," Goering muttered, as if he'd just been struck by a thought. The Nazi officer near the sofa clicked his heels. "I miss your lovely assistant. She had such a refreshing air about her." He scratched a piece of cigar paper from his bloated tongue and rubbed it on the sofa cushion. "Where has the dear girl gotten to? She is needed here."

"As you wish, Reich Marshal," the colonel said stiffly. On his way out of the room, Von Groll's good blue eye caught the Reich Marshal stuffing a small jade figurine from a side table into his pocket. The colonel's other eye, the hazel-colored glass one, wandered slightly, seeing nothing.

Jacob studied the three crude sculptures on the side of the Keep: a lion with gaping jaws, a honeycomb with a hole up top, and an open flower with nothing at its center. Each sculpture featured an opening big enough to accommodate a hand.

"The abbot is confused by the Keep. There is no door or entryway." Sarah gesticulated with the rusted helmet of St. Joan. "The Latin inscription on the big block there reads: 'The righteous Judge—'"

"The righteous Judge finds sweetness within," Jacob said, flashing his green eyes at her. "I did pretty well in Latin."

"So what does it mean?" She lit a torch on the wall behind them.

"Samson. The strong man in the Old Testament." Jacob

squatted, peering into the holes of the three carvings. "He was one of the Judges of Israel—one of their great leaders."

"And how does that help us open the Keep?" Sarah asked. She put the rusted helmet on her head, smiling. "Maybe I should try to contact one of Joan's voices."

"I wouldn't toy with that." Jacob turned back to the three carvings. "Where would the righteous Judge find 'sweetness within'?" He quickly shoved his hand into the gaping mouth of the lion and pulled at the lever inside. "Samson tore a lion apart and later found honey in its jaws."

The huge square block that seemed to be part of the Keep slid sideways, revealing an entryway.

"I would have guessed the honeycomb," Sarah said.

"You would have lost a hand."

Jacob cleared the dusty cobwebs with his flashlight and entered the dank stronghold. On a stone column in the center of the room sat an aged box with a greened copper latch. Jacob flipped back the latch. Inside he found a silver amulet with a glass face on a chain. His nose started to itch.

"What is it?" Sarah asked, stepping into the doorway, the metal helmet still atop her head.

"The locks of Samson's hair, I'd guess. He had superhuman strength, until a wicked woman learned his secret. His enemies chopped off his curls and stole his power."

"I'm familiar with the story. A reminder that you should always protect your hair." Sarah tapped the helmet of St. Joan and laughed.

"Frau Vaillant," a German voice called from outside.

"It's Von Groll," she whispered to Jacob.

The colonel blocked the entrance, diminishing the light. "Your assistance is needed upstairs," he said smoothly, limping into sight. He stared at Jacob with his blue eye. "What are you doing, young man?"

"He's cataloguing some new acquisitions," Sarah explained.

"Very well. Come, Sarah, dear." Von Groll grabbed her hard by the arm, yanking her from the Keep. "We shall let the young curator continue his work."

With his shoulder, the colonel began to force the great stone block over the entryway. Jacob lunged for the exit. But he barely caught a glimpse of the colonel's dead hazel eye before the sliding block killed the light, imprisoning him within the chamber.

"He is not what he appears. Escape this evil one," a young female voice echoed inside the metal helmet on Sarah's head. She wrinkled her brow, searching for the speaker. *"Use the helmet if necessary! Escape him."* For a moment Sarah thought she was losing her mind. The sight of the colonel sealing Jacob inside the Keep shocked her back into the crisis at hand.

Trapped behind the stone, Jacob turned his flashlight to the corners, looking for something to pry the cube of granite away. *How could the Nazi have moved that block so easily? He's either possessed by a demon or he IS a demon.*

Save for the old box and the amulet holding Samson's locks, there was not a thing in the chamber. Jacob grabbed the amulet and slipped its chain around his neck. His breath immediately shortened and a jolt of energy surged through his body. His muscles twitched and tightened. In the glow of the flashlight, he watched his shoulders balloon. His jacket sleeves strained to contain his bulging arms. Even his legs swelled with a heat he had never felt before.

Jacob ran at the stone block with all the power he could muster. It shifted only slightly. He drew back his fists and unleashed them on the stone. Chunks of the block crumbled under his assault. He ran back to the middle of the room and with a yell charged at the barrier again. This time the sheer force of his effort split the stone in two, sending the two halves tumbling into the hallway. Jacob stumbled out behind them.

A few yards away, Sarah, holding St. Joan's helmet in her hands, crouched over the colonel, who was splayed out on the floor.

"Sometimes a girl has to fend for herself. I couldn't wait for you," she said, throwing her hair back into place. Then getting a good look at Jacob, she blinked in disbelief. "I knew you were muscular but . . . what happened in there?"

Jacob Wilder's shoulders were broader, his legs and arms

much thicker than before. Long, wild hair poked from beneath his pith helmet. "I'll explain later. You're coming with me." As he stepped over the colonel, something caught his attention. "Sarah, look at his face. Come here." He took her to the side room where the dead man lay against the wall and shone the flashlight on the corpse's face.

"Oh my," Sarah expelled. "They're identical. He looks exactly like the colonel. Are they twins?"

"I'm not sure, but the shape of their faces and the eyes—"

"We borrowed his body. Made it stronger," Colonel Von Groll snarled, staggering into the room.

Jacob was the first to realize that the colonel's left shoe was missing. Instead of a foot, four enormous claws, like those of a giant rooster, protruded from beneath his pant leg.

"He was a willing sacrifice," the colonel said, eyeing the dead man. "Our spirit can assume the outer form of the victim. We absorb their strength. Once he summoned me, I had to take him—as I will take you now."

The colonel ran toward them, lifting his left leg. Brandishing lethal claws and a sharp spur on the backside of the leg, he hurtled toward them. Before he could make contact, Jacob touched his thumbs and forefingers together. A red and white ray blasted from the triangle of his digits, hitting the colonel in the chest. The Nazi was thrown into the hallway. A hole in the center of his body opened up, swallowing his arms, his head, and finally the twitching rooster leg until it resolved into a foul green mist.

"Still think he's charming?" Jacob asked, taking Sarah's trembling hand. "You need to come with me. Assuming I can still fit, it's time to get to the sarcophagus." He glanced admiringly at his swollen arms. "I may want to stay like this."

"You were perfectly fine before." Sarah pulled him back, a crooked smile on her face. She reached around his neck and grasped the chain that held Samson's locks. "Things we want can at times distract us from the things we need." For a moment he tried to stop her, but finally permitted Sarah to remove the locket.

"Don't lose that or Joan's helmet." Jacob gave her a quick peck on the cheek and they raced into the darkness of the Louvre. As they ran, Sarah hummed the lilting tune of the music box upstairs. With each step, Jacob felt his body contracting to its normal size. His nose started to tingle.

Had he returned to the strange sunken room near the Keep, he would have discovered that the dead man was no longer reclining against the wall. The colonel's slashed twin was now on his feet, shambling into the hallway, searching for Jacob and Sarah and the relic they now possessed.

CHAPTER 1

BIGGER AND STRONGER

Like an unloved potted plant, Will Wilder's legs protruded at odd angles from a trash can in the center of the Perilous Falls Middle School locker room. How he got there was only a mystery to those who knew nothing of Will's relationship with his classmate, Caleb Gibbar.

Caleb sat across the row from Will in the back of their homeroom. He was a big kid with a jutting forehead and a hairline that started just above his thick, yellow eyebrows. Some of the kids, especially those jealous of his size, called him "the blond ape." Since grunting was Caleb's preferred means of communication, he and Will rarely spoke. Though they did share a friend in Andrew Stout, their only interactions were when their teacher, Mrs. Belcher, questioned the class about history.

Will was a B student, but time spent at the museum

founded by his great-grandfather, Jacob Wilder, had sparked a love of history within him. From the start of the school year, Will had devoured his history textbook and occasionally conducted independent research in the museum library. With all that knowledge, Will's philosophy was: *What's the good of knowing something if you keep it to yourself?*

"Who led the French forces to victory in the Siege of Orléans? This person was injured and still continued to fight." Mrs. Belcher's eyes roved over her students on that day. "Caleb? Any guesses? I mentioned this in class just last week. Remember our 'Unlikely Heroes' chapter? French leader? Battle of Orléans?"

From Caleb's panicked expression, it was obvious he didn't know the Siege of Orléans from the Siege of Gondor. Not that he cared. He remembered the things he needed to remember. Caleb was quarterback of the Perilous Falls Middle School football team, not a *Jeopardy!* contestant. No one in the entire school could throw a ball farther than him. No one could execute a pass plan like him. But when it came to unexpected questions like this one—with the whole class staring at him—the pressure caused Caleb to freeze. He wiped the perspiration away from his upper lip.

"George Washington?" Caleb mumbled.

A restrained chortle sounded from across the aisle. He turned to find Will Wilder, hand up in the air trying to get the teacher's attention. Exactly like the year before, every time Caleb blundered in class, every time he whiffed on a question, he felt Will was there, waiting to humiliate him.

"Yes, Will?" Mrs. Belcher asked, nodding toward the back of the room.

"Wasn't it Joan of Arc who won the Siege of Orléans?" Will asked. At the teacher's affirmation, a self-satisfied smile broke across Will's face. It wasn't spiteful. He just liked being right once in a while. "Oh, and I think Joan was hit by an arrow during the battle. She yanked it out, got up, and led the soldiers to beat the English. My friend Mr. Bartimaeus told me that story before I read it in the textbook. He's from New Orleans and they have this thing for Joan of Arc there."

Had the teacher not been in the room, Caleb would have knocked Will right out of his chair. Instead, he tightly folded his arms and shot Will a hostile look. Over and over, in class after class, this pattern repeated. Caleb took it personally. Will barely noticed.

So it only stood to reason that when Will Wilder ventured onto the football field that fall Friday afternoon to try out for the team, Caleb Gibbar was ready for him.

Gangly and tallish, Will was not exactly built for football. His friend Andrew, who was a lineman on the team, warned Will that football might not be the best after-school activity for his talents.

"What about chess club or debate, Will-man?" Andrew suggested in the locker room as they got into their gear. Will's friend Simon Blabbingdale had urged him to "rejoin the Scouts," which he lost interest in and didn't have time for, given his training at Peniel. Simon, being a five-star, triple-badged Falcon scout, was relentless. He missed having one of his closest friends along for campouts and hiking trips and did his best to stoke Will's sense of adventure.

Unmoved, Will ignored his pals' advice and signed up for the second (and last) round of football tryouts anyway.

From the moment he walked onto the field that day, Will's nose burned. He cautiously checked the stands and the edges of the field for anything fishy: a shadow or a creature waiting to pounce on him. It wasn't allergies or a cold. It was the same sensation he felt any time demonic activity was present. But nothing out of the ordinary presented itself.

"Wilder! Join the guys on that scrimmage line and let's see what you can do," Coach Runyon barked in Will's direction, adjusting the PF-emblazoned hat on his head.

The oversized shoulder pads and helmet swallowed Will as he ran. From the stands, it looked as if a jumble of football gear was floating onto the field of its own volition. Coach Runyon ran a thumbnail across his forehead. "Wilder, you run long. Practice that move we discussed. Caleb, you know what to do."

"Got it, Coach," Caleb said. He licked his fingers and awaited the snap.

The moment the ball hit Caleb's hands, Will ran the figure-eight pattern that the coach had asked him to execute. He blew past all the other guys. Finishing the figure eight, he looked up just in time for the ball to hit him in the face mask.

"Wilder! Keep your head up. You've got to search for the ball, son," the coach yelled.

As Will reached down to pick up the pigskin, four guys landed on top of him. He ached everywhere—and his nose was tingling worse than ever. A whistle sounded and someone pulled at the back of his shirt. "Get up, Joan of Arc!" His helmet had turned sideways from the impact and now blocked one of Will's eyes. "Can't wait to see how you lead this army." It was Caleb lifting him from the turf, and he was not smiling.

Everyone reassembled on the scrimmage line. At the snap, Will sped to the backfield in another uncoordinated figure eight. But this time, he kept his head up as he ran. Caleb threw him a spiral pass. The ball was so fast, it slipped through his hands. But he jammed his legs together and caught it between his knees. The reception might not have passed muster in the NFL, but he had caught his first ball. When he looked up, four big guys were coming at him.

Will shuffled to the left as the opposing team rushed him. He knew he could outmaneuver them. Just as they closed in, he faked them out and dashed off to the right, running for the end zone. He was really moving now. No one in sight, nobody even close. He looked back to find the other boys just staring at him. *Take that, dudes,* Will thought as he chugged along. They were in obvious shock. The coach's whistle went off as he crossed the goal line— his nose burning. *Touchdown. First time I've played the game and I already scored a touchdown!*

Will held the ball overhead and did an awkward chicken dance in the end zone.

"Wilder!" the coach barked from the sideline. "What are you doing?"

"I made a touchdown, right?" Will unfastened his helmet.

"Yes, you did." The coach suddenly broke into a big grin. "You made it for the other team. Your end zone is over there, Wilder!" The coach poked a finger toward the opposite side of the field. Raucous laughter burst out of the guys in uniform, with the sole exception of Andrew. No one laughed longer or louder than Caleb Gibbar.

"Can I try again? I understand it now," Will begged the coach, his nose causing his eyes to water.

"Monday," the coach said, adjusting his cap. "We'll have final tryouts on Monday, Wilder. You can have another go at it then. But"—the coach's flat mouth and raised eyebrows said it all—"nobody's good at everything, son." Will had bungled the tryout badly. Over the coach's shoulder, Caleb ran a hand through his blond hair and smiled the way a fox cornering a newborn rabbit might.

Will removed his oversized helmet and glumly shuffled toward the locker room. A pale boy in the first row of the aluminum bleachers next to the tunnel called out to him. "You sure do move fast." The kid had a scratchy voice and a scrawny body, lost in what looked to be his dad's sweater. He leaned over the railing. Due to his turned-up nose, his nostrils were the most prominent features on his face.

"Thanks," Will said, closing in on the locker room.

"Don't let 'em get you down. Guys like us are stronger than we look." He guffawed. "And a whole lot smarter."

"Yeah." Will nodded and smiled to himself as he walked on. The kid in the bleachers was so pasty, he made Will's pale friend, Simon, look like a sun worshipper.

In the locker room, Will quickly changed out of the uniform and into his blue button-up shirt and khakis. While lacing up his red high-tops, he heard a commotion in the hallway. It was Caleb yelling.

"Back off, runt!"

Will's nose started stinging again. Then, from the edge of the locker room, something like a small dog scampered across the floor. Only it was walking on two feet. *What is THAT?* Will tilted his head around the lockers, trying to see what the thing was. That's when Caleb burst through the locker room's swinging doors.

"There's little Will of Arc." He threw his helmet down and pounded toward Will. "Let's get something straight. Forget being on the team. You're a lousy player."

"I had a bad day, Caleb, but . . ."

"You're going to have a bad year if you're on *my* team. You'll drag us all down. Just drop it." The much bigger boy closed in on Will. "You're weak, Wilder. None of us want you here."

Will looked toward the doors, hoping one of the other players would interrupt.

Caleb glanced back at the swinging doors, then smiled at

Will. "I told the coach I needed to hit the bathroom. Nobody else is comin'."

"I've got to get going. I have an appointment." Will checked his watch and noticed the ring on his finger. A worried expression washed over his face. His great-aunt Lucille had given him the ring a few months back. The ring's tiny glass dome held the dried blood of a saint. Whenever either he or his great-aunt Lucille were in danger, the blood would liquefy and bubble beneath the glass—as it was doing right now. Will couldn't stop staring at it.

"What's wrong with you?" Caleb asked.

"Nothing." Will quickly put the ringed hand in his pocket and grabbed his backpack. "I've gotta run. See you Monday. You can't stop me from being on the team, Caleb."

"Really?" Caleb blocked Will, grabbing him by his belt and his shirt collar. He hoisted Will into the air like a rag doll. "You might have all the answers in class, but I'll always be bigger and stronger than you—and there's nothing you can do about it." He carried Will across the room and dumped him face-first into a slatted metal trash can. "I better not see you on that field Monday. Don't come back."

Through the trash can's slats, Will watched Caleb lumber out of the locker room. The small black creature skittered after him before the doors closed. "I'll be there, Caleb. You watch me," Will yelled, pathetically trying to keep the surrounding trash out of his mouth. He helplessly kicked back and forth, trying to free himself from the can. Throwing his weight to one side, he capsized the trash bin and wiggled free. His nose was on fire. He wiped it in disgust.

There is no way I'm letting that big oaf scare me away. I've squared off with demons; I can take Caleb Gibbar. I'll get on that team if it's the last thing I do. . . .

The soft bleating coming from the hall stopped Will's inner monologue. He grabbed his pith helmet from his locker and ventured toward the sound in the hallway.

"Help," the voice whimpered in the hall. "Somebody help me . . ."

CHAPTER 2

AFRAID?

As Will pushed through the swinging doors of the locker room, the mournful cries grew louder. He carefully edged toward the noise. From a side hallway leading to a maintenance room, a scratchy voice cried, "Can you help me get down from here?"

In the shadows, squeezed onto a high metal shelf, was the pale, bony boy who had been on the bleachers. Gray tape bound his ankles and wrists.

"How'd you get up there?" Will asked, grabbing a pair of garden shears hanging nearby.

"The same way you got roughed up in the locker room. I told the quarterback that I heard everything that went on in there. He grabbed me, shoved me up here, and told me to shut my mouth."

"Caleb's a bully," Will said, cutting the tape around the

boy's ankles and wrists. "And maybe something more." He wiped his nose with the back of his hand, looking down the hallway. No˙sign of the small black creature or Caleb anywhere.

The kid jumped down with Will's help. He swept the mousy brown hair off his brow and offered an embarrassed "Thank you." His moist eyes avoided Will's glance, though his nostrils were well represented. "I'm Renny Bertolf. This is my first year. I'm a transfer from Sorec Middle School. Should we tell somebody what happened? The coach?"

"Nah," Will said, collecting his backpack. "That'll only make things worse. I'm Will Wilder." He offered a hand, which the boy awkwardly accepted. His skin was clammy to the touch.

Renny followed Will toward the back exit, his hands shoved in his pockets. "So you're going to let Caleb get away with this? You're not going to get even with him?"

"There are lots of ways to get even, Renny," Will said.

"Like getting on the team?" Renny's eyes danced in anticipation, but Will said nothing. "Are you afraid of him?"

"See you later," Will barked over his shoulder. He put his pith helmet on and burst through the rear exit. He didn't want to talk about Caleb or think about how small Caleb made him feel. With vengeful thoughts bubbling up in his mind, Will ran toward Peniel, the museum founded by his great-grandfather.

Everyone in Perilous Falls knew it as "the museum." The Jacob Wilder Reliquarium and Antiquities Collection was too long a name to remember. Though Will thought it a mistake to call it a museum since the items inside were more lively (and unpredictable) than the people ogling them.

His great-aunt Lucille, who ran the cluster of castle-like buildings at the high end of Main Street, always referred to the place as Peniel since that's what her father had called it (for reasons Will had yet to discover). The public wrote the place off as a curiosity erected by their town's founder. They knew nothing of the secret community that lived within the walls of Peniel. To them it was like a small village from another age at the edge of town separated from the present by a high, black wrought-iron fence. Will ran along the front of that fence and headed inside.

On certain Fridays after school, Cami Meriwether, her brother Max, and Will would join his great-aunt Lucille at Peniel to tidy up and explore the place. Peniel was a constant adventure for the kids, especially the secret passages, spiral staircases, and twisting stone hallways. Will sped through the expansive Bethel Hall, dodging the exhibit cases, and headed toward the door marked PRIVATE at the far end of the room.

"Wait awhile. Wait awhile," Bartimaeus Johnson, Aunt Lucille's assistant, bellowed at Will's approach. The gray-haired black man balanced on a pair of wooden crutches, fishing keys out of his tweed coat pocket. "Ya know, when you're on time, you don't have to run." Bartimaeus slid the key into the door, grinning.

"Guess that's why I'm always running." Will laughed, patting Mr. Bartimaeus on the arm.

"And that's why they're always waitin' for ya. Get ya butt upstairs. Your aunt took ya friends up already." He shook his head and returned to a King David exhibit he was arranging. Will darted up the winding staircase to his great-grandfather's office. He walked in on Aunt Lucille, who was midsentence.

"Anyway, that is how we acquired the locks of Samson," Lucille Wilder told Cami and Max, dangling a silver amulet from its chain between her fingers. "Oh, thank goodness," she said to Will with a slight sharpness. "I'm glad you made it." Aunt Lucille returned the amulet to the freshly dusted glass case in the corner of her father's office. "I was just telling your friends that this amulet and that helmet up there on the top shelf are the only artifacts in all of Peniel that both my mother and father had a hand in securing. Isn't that something?"

"Why are you so late?" Cami Meriwether asked Will, cutting right to the chase.

"I was trying out for the football team and got"— he rubbed the side of his forehead, which suddenly hurt— "a little delayed."

"You're bruised there," Cami said, moving closer for a look.

"This jerk on the team threw me into a— It's a long story. It doesn't matter."

"It does matter. I was worried," Aunt Lucille said, pointing to the brooch on the lapel of her light blue jacket. The liquid inside was boiling like tomato soup on a high flame. "I wondered why this was so active all afternoon. And Max has been telling me about a dream he's been having."

Will checked the ring he wore, the companion to his great-aunt's brooch. He held it out for his friends to see. The blood inside was still churning away.

"It wouldn't be agitated unless one of us were in danger—supernatural danger, dear." Aunt Lucille folded her arms across her chest. "Did you see anything out of the ordinary today, Will?"

He hesitated and then spoke quickly. "My nose was burning all afternoon. Before this kid Caleb came into the locker room, I saw a little black thing. Like a small monkey."

"Caleb Gibbar? From our class?" Cami asked.

"Yep." Just the thought of Caleb dumping him into the trash can made Will hot with anger. Feeling his ears warming and jaw tightening, he said nothing more.

"Describe the 'black thing,'" Aunt Lucille urged him.

"It was about this big." Will extended his hands nearly two feet apart. "A little hunched . . . I'm not even sure I saw it. It was there for like a split second and then it was gone."

"An imp. It might have been an imp," Aunt Lucille mused gravely. "Similar to your dream, Max."

For weeks, Max Meriwether had been telling Will and his sister about a recurring dream that woke him in the night. He often received glimpses, warnings of things yet to unfold. Max rolled his motorized wheelchair from the corner of the room toward Will. The Duchenne muscular dystrophy had weakened his muscles, but not his mind or his spirit. Max's head lay off to the side, held erect by a leather pillow attached to the chair. "Last night I dreamed that you were running very quickly. Running. Running."

"You told me that before," Will said.

"I know, but last night you were screaming for help and no one could hear you. Everyone was shaking and ignoring you. Then I saw what you were running from."

"Well, what was it?" Will lowered himself to face Max.

"Tiny, hunchy black devils. Little devils. There were hundreds of them. Then a big one showed up and the little ones ran away. They were all so scared. The face of the big one kept changing, like pictures flipping on a TV screen."

The boy seemed to be reliving the dream as he shared it. Aunt Lucille laid a hand on Max's shoulder to calm him.

"And then what happened?" Will asked.

"You dove into a pool . . . a dark, dark pool of water. That's when I woke up."

Will turned to his great-aunt Lucille. "So what am I supposed to do?"

"What you must always do, dear: take note of what he says, remain on guard, and continue your training."

Cami had heard Max speak about his dream so often that she occupied herself studying the artifacts on the bookcase on the side wall of the office. There were twisted knives, a bottle with a swirling blue substance inside, a pair of shriveled eyeballs under a domed glass. But for all of that, it was a framed picture at the edge of the cluttered, middle shelf that attracted Cami's attention. The young man in the black-and-white photo had slick hair and high cheekbones and wore a leather jacket.

"Miss Lucille, who is this? I don't remember seeing him before," Cami asked.

"Oh, I just found that last week in an old box and put it . . ." Lucille was uncharacteristically flustered. "He was an old beau, a friend—a long time ago. Cosmo Doheney was his name. We were close"—her voice fell into a regretful register—"until we weren't."

Cami picked up the photo, smiling as she studied it. "Was he your *boyfriend*?"

Aunt Lucille puckered her lips, her wide blue eyes scanning the ceiling. "Why don't you give me that?" She took the photo, deposited it in a drawer of her father's big mahogany desk, and slowly shut it.

"I didn't know you had a boyfriend, Aunt Lucille," Will said playfully.

"There's rather a lot you don't know, Will." She tried to shake away whatever she was thinking. "An old song Cosmo used to hum came back to me the same day I found the photo and, well, I just put it up. Cosmo always fascinated me. He was funny and tough. He taught me something, though: Love is more than fascination. Sooner or later love requires honesty and sacrifice." She clapped her hands and moved about the room with her usual gusto. "Well, that was a loooong time ago and it's all in the past now."

Will didn't budge. "Weren't you the one who told me 'the present is always in dialogue with the past' so 'we should never forget'?"

"You're a very impertinent boy, Will Wilder." She placed her arms around Cami and Max. "Now, why don't you two take your friend here down to help Bartimaeus with that David exhibit. He could use a hand."

Cami followed instructions and held the door for Max and Will. "Come on, guys. That's Miss Lucille's nice way of saying 'get out.'" She giggled to herself, training her green eyes on Will, who lingered.

"Aunt Lucille," he whispered, "what exactly is an imp?"

"What you are at times!" she said in her husky tone. "It's a minor demon, a *Fomorii*. One invisible to everyone but a *Seer*. Perhaps that's what set your ring off."

"Where do they come from?"

"They're dark spirits that literally come out of those enchanted by evil. They're like a rapidly spreading virus. The imps tempt and harass the spirits of the pure. Imagine a shadow cast by a person caught in evil's sway. Now imagine that the shadow had a mind of its own and you pretty much have an imp."

"What should I do if I see one again?"

"Run and call us for help." Aunt Lucille clapped him on his shoulder. "Keep your eyes open and do be careful in town. Now, go on downstairs. There should be no imps there. Bartimaeus could use your assistance."

Will for once followed her instructions to the letter.

Lucille Wilder found herself suddenly humming that tune from so long ago, the one Cosmo Doheney would hum during long drives or while they were walking hand in hand along the Perilous River. It was a catchy thing, a bewitching melody. She yanked at the drawer of her father's desk and stole a glimpse of the picture of Cosmo at the bottom. Her face hardened. *"What are you afraid of, Lucille?"* That's *what he'd be saying if he were here. I should have been more afraid.* Then with disgust, she slammed the drawer shut and busied herself with paperwork, trying to put the melody Cosmo never tired of humming out of her mind.

CHAPTER 3

THE FLOATING AUNT

In the warm back room of the Burnt Offerings Café, with its bowed wooden floors and low ceiling beams, Simon Blabbingdale and Andrew Stout fought over a muffin basket. Cami, Max, and Will tried to continue their conversation through the melee. The kids regularly met at the restaurant, owned by Simon's cousin Rhonda Blabbingdale, for their Saturday-morning brunches. And they always sat in "their room": the small dining room in the rear.

"You can have anything in the kitchen. But those are *my* organic, gluten-free, non-peanut muffins. Rhonda sent them out for *me.* I don't need any more allergic episodes, lummox." Simon's slender fingers held his side of the basket as if his very life were in danger of being snatched away from him.

Andrew clung just as fiercely to the other side of the basket. "It's a muffin. I know it's one of your tasteless muffins. But since I don't see no others, that's the one I want."

"Well, you're not getting this one." Still holding his side of the basket, Simon reached in with his other hand and shoved the whole muffin in his mouth. "Yaaa caaah allwaah haa whaat yaaa waaan. . . ." Bits of the muffin sprayed all over the table.

Cami, who really wanted Will to finish his Caleb story, glared at the boys. "Can you all just chill for a minute? Andrew, you're on like your third breakfast and there's still food on your plate. And, Simon, could you for once just calm down?" she asked. "We don't even know what you're saying."

A quaking Simon pointed to the water pitcher in the center of the table and made a pouring motion. Andrew dropped the muffin basket and filled the boy's water glass. After he downed it, Simon heaved, "I said, you can't always have what you want—and you can't."

Will and Cami instinctively reached for Andrew's shoulders. The beefy boy was already jumping at Simon, but under the grip of his friends, quickly calmed himself and took his revenge out on the eggs before him. "I'm trying to listen to Will's story." Andrew's face was nearly as red as his hair. "If you touch my food, I'll break your finger." He jammed a forkful of eggs and sausage into his mouth.

"I don't make it a habit to take other people's food," Simon muttered in his nasal tone.

"Listen to the story!" Cami and Andrew said at nearly the same time.

Max rolled his eyes and took a sip from the straw in the orange juice on his wheelchair's tray.

"Go ahead, Will," Cami urged, turning her attention back to him. She played with the end of her ponytail, focused on Will as if they were alone.

"There isn't much more to tell. He threatened me and warned me not to come back to the field. He said none of the guys wanted me on the team." Will eyed Andrew. "Is that true?"

"Nah. Most of the guys don't care." Andrew was a lineman and got along with everybody. "Caleb and his friends don't want you there. You know why that is, Will-man: You make him look bad in class. He's not too bright."

"That's why I plan on being at the tryout on Monday. I'm a lot smarter and quicker than he is."

"That's true." Andrew put his fork down and folded his arms in front of him. "But he's also a lot bigger than you—and angrier. His mom died a few years ago and he lives with his uncle, I think. Anyway, he's one tough dude. I've seen him smash guys bigger than me like LEGO figures."

"So I should give up and let him win?" Will asked.

Andrew stabbed a sausage. "What's he winning?"

Cami sighed and put on her take-charge voice. "You're a really talented guy. You see things none of us do. You're smart, sort of good-looking, and brave when it counts. But, and I mean this in the nicest way, you're not exactly football player material, William."

"If you go to that field on Monday, Caleb'll slaughter you. He and Harlan and Boyd will put a hurt on you—bad. I've seen 'em do it," Andrew said ominously. "Will-man, I've got your back no matter what you do. I just don't think it's worth it. Cami's right. Some people ain't supposed to play contact sports."

"You're too skinny for that stuff anyway," Simon announced. "Come back to the Scouts. Our big campout's in a few weeks and who is better at exploring than you? We'll have a great—"

"No Scouts. Unless I'm going to be a netmaker or an undertaker, I don't need to learn any more about knots or ditch digging."

"Actually"—Max dropped the straw from his mouth and looked sideways across the table at Will—"ditchdigging might come in handy for you."

"Huh?" Will asked, half irritated, half bewildered.

"Here comes the dream," Cami said, drum-rolling with her fingers on the table. "Go ahead, tell him."

"The little devils chased you in my last dream; then you dove into the dark water," Max said through gritted teeth. "Well, last night I had the same dream again. After you dove into the water, something weird happened. Dead people started rising from graves. Dead people!"

"Wait a minute. A lot of dead people?"

"I could only see about seven or eight in the dream. They were dead and they came out of the ground."

"Nobody has cheery dreams like you, Max," Will said nervously.

"The dead people were walking."

Simon stopped eating. "So you're thinking real dead people are going to rise? Dead . . . dead people?"

"Dead until they crawl out of the ground," Max said calmly. "They looked pretty alive once they were up and moving. They left empty holes in the graveyard."

Will swallowed hard and suddenly reached for his backpack and pith helmet, breaking the spooky silence. "I gotta go, guys. Training session at Peniel. I'll check in with you all later."

"Think about what I told you, Will-man. Football might not be for you this year," Andrew added quietly.

"I don't know whether I should be more worried about Caleb or the zombies in Max's dream." Will slipped on his pith helmet and hastily headed out. "Later, guys."

"He took that well, I thought," Cami said to Max once Will disappeared down the hall. Max nodded.

"You know that Caleb has a punchable face," Simon said.

"A what?" Andrew muttered.

"A punchable face. You know, a face ideal for punching. I mean, I'm not usually moved to violence—"

"No, you move the rest of us to violence," Andrew added without looking up from his meal. "Just finish eating so we can get on with the day, tough guy."

As Will began to cross High Street to enter the gates of Peniel, a familiar tune struck his ear. The melody was blaring from speakers in Perilous Falls Park, a couple of blocks away. There was an insistent beat to the music and every so often he heard a crowd cheer. Will ignored the sound at first. But there was something about the music and the "oohs and aahs" drifting down the block that demanded his attention. He knew his mom was recording a story for her *Supernatural Secrets* TV show at the park that morning. She had mentioned that she was taking his brother and sister to Peniel for their training and then doing a story on some DJ. She said "amazing things" reportedly happened through the power of his music.

Though Will was running fifteen minutes late for his Use and Care of Relics training, curiosity got the best of him. *It'll only take a few minutes. I can see what all the fuss is about—and check on Mom,* Will reasoned. He hightailed it down Main Street until he hit the park.

The music spilling into the street was like audio cotton candy. It was sweet and made him feel warm inside. Where had he heard that tune before? The haunting melody slithered in and out of the pounding remix groove. Was it from some TV show? Did his mom sing it to him when he was little? The heavily female crowd, swaying as one organism, gathered near the bandstand. Arms shot up from the crowd, punctuating the beat. It almost looked choreographed. Will ran alongside the throbbing mob, searching for his mother.

Near the front of the bandstand, he found Deborah Wilder, speaking to the camera, in midsentence.

"—similar to what we've seen of his work nationwide and in Europe, DJ Cassian certainly has this crowd in the palm of his hand."

A tanned man with a coal-black ponytail worked the turntables inside the bandstand. He was huge, like a wrestler, and wore a T-shirt covered by a floor-length leather coat. Light brown sunglasses covered his eyes, but not his dazzling smile or the stubble surrounding it. On either side of the turntables was what might have been the most beautiful cheerleading squad Will had ever laid eyes on. They were covered in shiny, brightly colored outfits, grooving in unison to the music.

Will tore his eyes away and refocused on his mom. She had finished her on-camera read, so Will knew it was okay to approach her.

"Mom! Mom!" he yelled. But Deborah Wilder continued swaying like the rest of the crowd, oblivious to his cries. In frustration, he pushed his way through the sea of people, inching toward her. "Mom!" he yelled again. Just then a whoop of laughter rose to his left.

He couldn't believe what he saw. A heavyset woman with a cyclone of blond hair literally floated up above the crowd. Just as she descended, disappearing behind the dancing throng, she fluttered upward even higher.

"It's just like the other Cassian concerts," one woman yelped with laughter. "His music is so incredible. You just feel light as air." Applause and more laughter followed. The crowd made space for the floating woman, watching her in amazement.

Wait! Will knew this woman. It was his mom's aunt Freda. He pressed through the mob for a closer look but couldn't reach the front. He couldn't see how Aunt Freda was managing to float upward. He bent down and peered through the legs before him, but he could only make out a smudge of shadows. Will's nose began to sting, and then came the sneezes. Something was wrong—very wrong.

Each time Aunt Freda neared the ground, vanishing behind the crowd before him, she would fly skyward again like a very large rubber ball.

None of us should be here—she can't be flying, Will thought. He tried to warn his aunt. "Aunt Freda! Aunt Freda!" But she was lost in the giddy thrill of defying gravity. Will ran over to his mom, who was still gyrating along with the rest of the crowd; the same tune, remixed, played over and over.

"Mom! SOMETHING'S WRONG! MY NOSE IS . . . I don't think she's flying. Something's really wrong," Will sputtered.

"It's amazing, Will," Deborah said flatly in a blissful trance. "They're so happy. The music is . . . enchanting . . . freeing." She continued swaying as she spoke.

"Mom! Do you hear me? Mom—" Suddenly, other ladies took flight over the heads of the people around him. Through the shifting legs and wriggling bodies, Will could see something dark moving on the ground. Were they

shadows cast by the dancing crowd? Or were the shadows moving on their own?

What is happening? Will pushed past the gyrating spectators, searching the ground for some explanation. Reaching the front of the crowd, he found it. All expression drained from his face.

AH-CHOO! AH-CHOO! Overcome by intense sneezes, Will made a snap decision. *If Mom won't listen to me, I know Aunt Lucille will.* He turned heel and ran toward Peniel, confused and scared by what he had witnessed.

CHAPTER 4

DEPLOYING THE RELICS

In the north tower of Peniel, Aunt Lucille pressed her hands together and knelt before Leo and Marin Wilder. With mixed success, they attempted to copy her posture. "Breathe in slowly now. You too, Marin. When you're very still, there's a stirring you can sometimes feel—a warmth. It might be small at first, hardly perceptible. That's where your gift resides. Focus on where you feel that warmth. I've always felt mine in my heart. But it may be different for you."

Over the last few months, Will's brother and sister had manifested what Aunt Lucille was convinced were supernatural gifts. She knew from experience that Leo was a *Candor* with the ability to emit light from his pores. His glow could scatter minor demons and dispel the *Darkness*.

Marin possessed abilities altogether different. Her touch could heal. Once, she even brought some dead animals back to life in her front yard. She was surely a *Healer* but also a *Summoner*—one who could, with only a cry, call down angels. Aunt Lucille had talked Will's mother into letting her conduct occasional training sessions so the kids could develop their unique gifts. Their dad, Dan Wilder, knew nothing of the secret lessons and would not have approved.

"So where are you feeling a sensation?" Aunt Lucille asked.

"In my belly," Leo whispered. "I feel it in my belly."

"That could just be hunger growls," little Marin said, her eyes tight.

"Shut up and find your own gift," Leo spat out.

"Mine's up higher, Aunt Lucille," Marin lisped. "In my noggin."

"Well, there's no telling where a gift will reside. Now, let's focus on those individual locations and breathe right into that spot."

Instantly, Leo's face and hands burst into a hot, white light. Neither Aunt Lucille nor Marin could look at him directly.

"Leo, remember how we restrained the light before," Aunt Lucille instructed, looking away. "Hold your breath and see the light dimming in your mind's eye."

"I'm doing it," Leo murmured.

"Don't talk. Hold your breath aaaaaaand . . . very good."

The brightness of the boy's sweaty, round face decreased, as did the light spilling from between his palms.

"We'll keep working on that—"

Just then, Will bounced into the training room. "Aunt Lucille, there are imps all over the park—at the concert that Mom's covering."

"Imps?" Lucille jumped to her feet. "Are you sure? How many did you see?"

"A bunch of them. They were tossing ladies around in the park. Aunt Freda was flying around like a blimp losing air."

"Be respectful, Will."

The memory of the imps scuttling on the grass at the park rattled him. "I'm sorry, it's like I'm going crazy. Nobody sees what I'm seeing. The imps, I mean. Mom wouldn't even listen to me."

"I'm sure your mother was listening." Aunt Lucille pulled Will's hands away from his face. "Never doubt your vision. Reality is not based on others' ability to see it. There are times we must stand alone and call out what others cannot see."

"I wish I couldn't see them. Mom was in some kind of daze. She kept dancing with all the others."

"And the imps were throwing people around the park?"

"Bouncing them in the air. I think they were invisible to everybody else. The ladies thought people were floating."

"That's very curious," Aunt Lucille said, tugging at the silken collar of her blouse. "Tobias and the abbot have been waiting for you in Parlor Five. I'll send Bart down to the park to look into your imps and flying ladies. Come up to my father's office after your session and we'll sort it all out."

She pushed Will into the hall.

"But shouldn't we sort it out now? The imps were all over the park."

"I've got to finish up with Leo and Marin. We'll look into it. Go to your training." And with that, Aunt Lucille closed the door on him as the kids giggled.

Will reluctantly stomped down the hall and yanked at the round metal ring on one of the doors. Inside, Abbot Athanasius impatiently tapped his fingertips together. He sat at a long table, covered with objects, on the far end of the room.

"Come in. There is no time to waste—though apparently you think there is," Abbot Athanasius said, rising from the table. Dressed in his jet-black robes, he came to the center of the room. Tobias Shen lifted a small gold reliquary from the table.

"Mr. Wilder, it is time to train you in the care and use of relics. For a *Seer*, such as yourself, this knowledge—this responsibility—could not be more critical." Tobias held the reliquary out to Will. "Take, take, take."

Will threw down his backpack and tossed his pith helmet atop it. He grasped the reliquary with one hand. "Being late wasn't my fault. I was at the park—"

"Silence, William," Abbot Athanasius advised. "We are training now. Whatever went on at the park or at home is irrelevant. Stay in this present moment."

"What is it?" Will whispered, looking down at the gold box with images of three men in crowns carved onto the side.

"The present moment is the time we occupy now. It's all the duties and responsibilities—"

"No, not that. This! This relic. What is it?"

"Close your eyes. Don't open them until you see the light," Tobias said quietly.

Will followed Mr. Shen's instructions. He had learned to trust the old Chinese man. Even under pressure, Mr. Shen had an air of tranquility about him, a quiet power that he unleashed only when absolutely necessary. Will strained to keep his eyes shut. He wanted to tell the abbot and Mr. Shen about the mist he saw coming out of some of the people's ears at the park, the imps, and Aunt Freda. Maybe they could help him figure out what was happening back there.

Wow. What a light.

"What am I seeing?" Will said, his eyes still shut.

"Keep watching," the abbot said.

Thoughts of the imps, his fear, even his annoyance over his mother's unwillingness to talk were all burned away by this light. It stood in the distance, hovering, demanding his full attention. He bathed in the calming clarity of its glow.

Suddenly the relic was yanked from his hands. "What was that?" Will's eyes snapped open. "I feel really alert, like I just ran around the block a few times."

"Those were the relics of Balthasar, Gaspar, and Melchior—better known to you as the Three Wise Men,"

Athanasius said, returning the golden casket to the weathered table near the wall. "Most of the Three Kings' bones are in a reliquary in the Cologne Cathedral. But we store a few of their remains here for safekeeping."

"You saw the star? The bright, bright star?" Mr. Shen asked.

Will nodded.

"The Wise Men followed a star to find the newborn king. The Promised One. They were single-minded in their pursuit. The star became their guide," Shen said with a smile. "Many, many miracles have been attributed to their relics, but clarity of mind, a renewal of purpose is the most common."

Will did feel better, suddenly relieved of the worries that had filled his head.

"As you know, these relics are not some sort of magic," Abbot Athanasius said, gently lifting a rope from the table. "They are the remains of good people. We honor their example by preserving these articles—instruments of great wonders, surely. But the power they possess—the power that remains—is divine. Protecting these bones or clothes or sacred items from harm is part of our mission. And at times they must be deployed in our fight against the *Darkness*."

Mr. Shen raised a finger of caution. "However, not every relic should be used, or even touched, Mr. Wilder. Powerful channels of grace are best used for good purposes and only for the benefit of others."

Will wrinkled his nose, thinking of the saint's finger bone he snatched for his own reasons earlier that year. When he lost it, monsters and floodwaters were unleashed all over town. Then the Staff of Moses fell into the hands of a demon, which could have really ended badly.

"Here in the walls of Peniel, we are safe. But using a relic in the outside world requires the utmost caution. As you have learned, Mr. Wilder, it can attract the attention of the *Darkness*. A relic emits something like a floodlight of goodness. The *Sinestri* feel its power and are compelled to destroy it." Mr. Shen clapped his hands together for effect. "They will work to snuff out any light."

The abbot held a tattered cord out to Will. "Now it takes some coordination and a firm sense of purpose to properly utilize a relic. Like this one, for instance. It was once the cincture—the rope belt—of St. Joseph of Cupertino."

"Who?" Will asked.

"Joseph of Cupertino. He too saw things others could not. He would gape, slack-jawed, at the visions before him. His fellow Franciscan friars thought Joseph was out of his mind or slow. This was the sixteen hundreds after all. Occasionally while in prayer, and once while hearing Christmas carols, he levitated into the air. He would simply take flight and hover there."

Will took the rope in hand with great reverence. "This is his actual belt?"

"It is indeed," the abbot said. "I want you to tie it around your waist."

A lock bolt shot back from a small door along the wall, startling Will. When the door flew open, there stood a great barrel-chested man with a plume of thinning blond hair. Brother Baldwin was the second in command at Peniel and an endless source of annoyance to Will. Baldwin had been reprimanded by the abbot for pushing the boy too hard in the past. Whatever Will did, the vicar was always there to criticize, correct, or ratchet up the challenge. And though he intimidated Will and anyone else who crossed his path, he was one of the Brethren's best teachers of defensive tactics. Baldwin looked down his great hook nose at the boy, who held the cord loosely, as if he were about to jump rope with it.

"Is that Joseph of Cupertino's cincture?" Baldwin asked indignantly. "You're not going to let him blunder around with that, are you, Abbot?"

"It's best to allow Will to feel his way—"

"Feel his way?! With all due respect, Abbot, without instruction he'll soon be feeling his way to the emergency unit."

Abbot Athanasius stroked his beard and kept his attention on Will. "Proceed."

Will puffed up his cheeks and struggled to knot the rope. He hated Baldwin staring at him like that.

"Mr. Wilder," Tobias said gently. "Push all distractions aside. Think of that star you saw earlier. Just kick the earth away—let it go and fly."

Will bent his whole mind to letting go of the earth. After

several seconds, he jumped as if laying up a basketball in the gym. Will Wilder suddenly floated in midair. He was twelve inches off the ground—and he remained there.

"I'm doing it. I'm doing it." He was too afraid to look down.

"It is a start, William," the abbot said, glancing at the sour-faced Baldwin. "Now breathe out and return to the ground."

Will's landing was less than graceful. Like he was stepping off an out-of-control escalator, he stumbled forward into Baldwin's hard torso.

"Deeply unimpressive," Baldwin huffed under his breath. "If I may?" In one move, he whipped the rope from Will's waist and began tying it around his own. "The use of this relic requires control and a certain amount of physical strength."

Will's face began to flush. Mr. Shen raised a hand to quiet him before he said anything he'd regret.

Baldwin walked to the center of the room. "The mind must be clear and . . ." He leapt with great force, hovering for barely a moment, inches from the ground. He abruptly dropped to his knees with a thud seconds later.

Will puckered his lips to hide a laugh.

"Vicar, to take flight certainly, the mind must be clear," Tobias said, "and the heart should be pure."

"Maybe you're just too bulky," Will said sharply.

"And maybe you are too flippant." Baldwin struggled to his feet, tore at the rope's knot, and threw it at Will. "Your lack of experience and strength will cost you. I have seen you struggle to master basic skills, Will Wilder. You're easily distracted and weak. Weak!"

Will started to protest, but the abbot intervened. "That is enough, Baldwin. We are here to train him, not crush his spirit. At Defensive Tactics next week, you can build his strength. He is making progress."

"Progress?" Baldwin laced his fingers together over his stomach and moved close to the abbot. "You coddle him and put us all at risk. Every time you look at him, you see another Jacob. Athanasius . . . he is nothing like his great-grandfather. Not even close." He exhaled and without regarding anyone further, marched out the door leading to the hallway.

"Do you think I'm weak?" Will asked the abbot.

"Strength is found in self-control, William," the abbot said.

"Do not be deceived." Tobias moved the relics on the table to side chairs. "Power is not strength. Force is not strength." He lifted a flat hand, bladelike, in front of his nose, then in a precise move struck his fingertips on the tabletop. The wood groaned and ever so slowly a crack opened in the center of the table where his fingers had landed. "Intention is strength, faith is strength, Mr. Wilder. The truly strong use force for a noble end." The two sides of the table crashed to the ground as if on cue.

Will shuddered a bit at the sound. "How can I get strong like that? I need to be ready for whatever is coming."

Thoughts of the imps raced through his mind once more. "And then there's football. I need to be stronger on the football field."

"Football? Focus on your training. There is no time for meaningless sports," the abbot said, checking his watch. "Our time is up."

Will gathered his things and raced for the door. "Maybe Brother Baldwin's right. I might not be strong enough for what you're asking me to do."

"Mr. Wilder, strength comes from here," Tobias said, pointing to his heart. Then, indicating his flexed biceps, added, "Not from here. Go. Go to your aunt Lucille."

CHAPTER 5

A FAMILIAR TUNE

Will ran up the spiral staircase of Peniel's highest tower until he reached the open door of Jacob Wilder's office. Bartimaeus's voice ricocheted in the tight stairwell.

". . . sure he's right. They're flipping and floatin' all over that park. I could feel the evil vibrations all the way down the block. Somethin' bad's goin' on down there, Lucille." Bartimaeus dropped into a chair in front of Jacob Wilder's huge desk as Will entered.

Aunt Lucille greeted him from her seat behind the desk. "I propped the door downstairs so you could make your way up. Your mother was just here to fetch Leo and Marin. She's not herself today, a bit distant . . ."

"That's what I was telling you." Will closed the door behind him. "She was kind of spacey this morning. She barely talked to me at the park. All she did was sway and tell me

how freeing Cassian's music was. I don't know what's gotten into her."

"Bart visited the park. It's worse than we thought," Aunt
Lucille said, turning on the small TV on a corner table.

"Folks were flyin' all over the place—just laughing and
cutting up," Bartimaeus reported. "It was chilly too, with
a sweet stink in the air. *Fomorii* all the way if you ask me. I
saw your mama packin' up her TV equipment. She paid me
about as much attention as the grass did."

"Shhh," Aunt Lucille hissed, focused on the television.
"Deb's report is coming up. Look."

Within a few moments, Deborah Wilder's segment
began. She was standing before a group of excited women
in the park. "They have come from miles around to see a DJ
who has taken the music world by storm." There were shots
of people swaying in unison as Cassian smiled like a mannequin. He slid his hands over the turntables before him.

"I don't know about you all, but that *music* sounds repetitive to me," Bartimaeus said. "It's like the stuff you hear
in the elevator at one of those hip hotels where it's so dark
you can't see the door in front of ya."

Aunt Lucille was bothered by what she saw on the TV.
She rose and stared hard at the picture tube. "I think I know
him. He looks like . . . what did Deb say his name was?"

"DJ Cassian has this crowd in the palm of his hand,"
Deborah breathlessly announced, as if in response. "He
electrified this crowd in Perilous Falls as he has excited au-
diences in Europe and beyond."

"They didn't look electrified to me. Those people seemed zombified. Look at their faces," Will said, pointing at the screen.

"Shhh. I'm trying to listen." Aunt Lucille tilted her ear toward the TV. "That tune . . . La-dee-dah-dee-dee-dah. It's like the one Cosmo Doheney used to sing." She quieted for a moment, listening to the pulsing beat coming from the TV. "It's definitely Cosmo's song."

"I knew I'd heard it before. You were humming it the other day," Will said.

Bartimaeus rose to his feet. "Sarah Lucille, that man ain't been around since we were kids. There's no way that's the same song."

"It's the same. I'm sure of it." Aunt Lucille set her jaw and leaned toward the TV screen, her brow wrinkled. "This Cassian character even favors Cosmo."

"Come on, Lucille. Cosmo was nowhere near that dude's size," Bartimaeus said.

"It's his gestures. His strong jaw. Those lips—he's bigger than Cosmo, but there's something about him that's so familiar. I wish he didn't have those sunglasses on; then I'd know for sure," Lucille said excitedly, her hands holding the edges of the screen.

"This guy is thirty years old, tops. Cosmo would be at least double that," Bartimaeus said.

"I've got to see this Cassian fellow in person. The song, even his posture is identical."

"Oh Lord, here we go—Lucille, it's not the same man,"

Bartimaeus said, trying to calm her. But she would not be calmed.

"I know that song and . . . and it's got to be him." There was a look of loss and longing in her blue eyes. Then she turned to Will. "If your mother was in fighting shape, I'd call her. But given the circumstances, I'll have to do my own homework on this DJ Cassian." She headed to the door and left without so much as a goodbye. All the way down the stairs, Aunt Lucille hummed the haunting, melodic lullaby they heard on TV.

"She always was nuts about Cosmo Doheney." Bartimaeus shook his head. "Sometimes people see what they want to see. Ya aunt's chasing ghosts. Cosmo's been gone since your great-granddaddy Jacob died. It ain't the same man. I'm more worried about those imps running around town. See, they usually serve major demons. They swarm like hornets around the really big, bad dudes." Bartimaeus moved his crutches across the floor to Will. "How'd your Care and Use of Relics session go today?"

"Pretty good actually. Even flew around a little bit. I put Saint . . . somebody's cord around my waist and I floated for a minute or two."

"St. Joseph of Cupertino."

"That's right. Brother Baldwin said I was too weak to use the cord. Then he tried and almost fell flat on his face."

Bart smirked. "Will, don't worry about Baldwin. The vicar's hung up on strength. Do ya know he used to be a boxer?"

"I didn't."

"Sure was. Golden Gloves, one of the best. But ya see, that kind of power wanes."

"The vicar thinks I'm too scrawny for this. I've been hearing that a lot lately."

"Just keep your mind on your training. You want to develop the kind of strength that lasts a lifetime: inner strength. And that takes time." Bartimaeus pointed a crutch toward the glass display holding the amulet in the corner. "Even ya boy Samson over there didn't possess true strength. He had muscle, but no sense. Real strength comes from consistent habit and training. Take it easy. You'll have all the strength you need when the time is right."

Bartimaeus walked past Will. "Close the door behind ya and come see this new item I pulled out of storage this morning. It's a beautiful piece—once belonged to King David."

Will started to follow him. But as he went to extinguish the wall lamps and turn the TV off, his eyes lit on the talisman holding Samson's locks in the corner case. He sauntered over to the case and studied the coiled braid of hair inside the silver locket. "Wonder what it could do?" Will whispered to himself. He lifted the glass top of the case and extended a hand toward the silver amulet. Then he stopped.

I'd better not touch it. Though Samson was a pretty strong guy . . . I wonder if it could give me a little strength boost. That could be cool. How do you learn to use a relic or know what it can do unless you try it? I mean, the abbot let me try the cord of

St. Joseph of . . . Cappuccino, with no prep at all. They WANT me to try out the relics.

He reached his hand toward the locket again before pulling it back.

Taking a tiny relic like this out of Peniel is probably not that big a risk. It's not like the finger bone of St. Thomas—in that enormous reliquary—or the Staff of Moses, which was huuuge. This one's so small. You can barely see it. It could fit in my pocket.

Will pinched the chain and felt how light the amulet was. He lifted it up and down as if weighing it—like a decision.

Mr. Shen said relics should be "used for good purposes and only for the benefit of others." Winning a few games for my school is a "good purpose." I might be able to protect that Renny kid with it—and maybe myself. I'll bet it could help me even up the score with Caleb. And if those imps get out of control, I could use the extra power to help those people at the park. Or my mom.

With that, he snatched up the locket and threw it into the secure part of his backpack. He'd decide what to do with it later.

"Will, you comin'?" Bartimaeus yelled from the bottom of the stairwell.

"Yes, sir." Will flipped the switch, killing the wall lamps. But he had forgotten to turn the TV off.

On-screen, Herb Lassiter, the veteran WPF Channel 4 reporter with a bushy mustache and a solemn demeanor, stood in the middle of the de Plancy Cemetery. A pile of freshly turned soil was at his feet, with a hole beside it.

"Authorities received a call from a groundsman who stumbled across this disturbed grave earlier today. With only a few letters visible, the weathered gravestone makes it impossible to determine whose grave this is. And worse, the body is missing." The camera tilted down into the hole to find a busted open, empty coffin. "The Perilous Falls Police Department is searching for leads in the case. If you have any information about the grave robbers or the missing body, you are urged to contact local authorities."

CHAPTER 6

THE WOMEN OF WORMWOOD

His head covered by the hood of a black cloak, Brother Baldwin stepped into a flat-bottomed boat along the shoreline of the Perilous River. He jammed an oar into the muck and launched the vessel over the swirling waters. He was not far from Lucille Wilder's house and could see her baby-blue Victorian beyond the pier as he drifted farther into the unsettled river. He checked over his shoulder a few times to make sure that neither Lucille nor anyone else saw him rowing against the current toward the far shore. The purple dusk of that Sunday evening cast an eerie light on the overgrowth of the swiftly approaching riverbank. The arms of enormous trees reached down into the swampy water. As he rowed closer, it looked as if their twisted limbs had created a tunnel, welcoming him.

Baldwin hated the reek of the place. It smelled like dead

rats trapped in a wall for too long. He pulled the edge of his cloak over his nose as he maneuvered the boat onto the spongy land. Wormwood was the perfect name for this godforsaken place, he thought. Had it not been for the old woman who lived in the decaying forest and the knowledge she possessed, he would never have left Peniel.

Stepping from the boat, he wandered through the blackened marsh, searching the rotted trees for the dilapidated cabin he had visited weeks before. The woman inside had told him things that consumed him. He had earned the right to lead the Brethren at Peniel, she said. But he had to "smite" Will Wilder first. "While he is bewildered and preoccupied," she told him, "use your strength to *smite* him." But how? When? For weeks he had pondered the meaning of her words. He knew he was a born leader. He had put his time in—faced the enemy and won every battle. He had proven himself. A runt like Will was not about to stand in his way—prophecy or not. This woman had some secret knowledge. She would know what he needed to do and when.

Dark mold covered the shanty nestled among gnarled vines and withered trees. This was the place. He gathered up the bottom of his habit and trudged toward the crooked door.

"Lost, are you?" a woman's voice called out. From the corner of his eye, he spotted the only green thing in the diseased wood, about twelve yards away: an older woman in a green shawl, her eyes bright.

"I wouldn't go there," the woman said.

Baldwin clumsily yanked at the cloak to conceal his face and called out, "Who are you?"

"One who knows what lies in that place." The woman had short, thick, white hair and a leashed golden retriever at her side. She held her ground and watched him warily. "Go back to your community. There's nothing here for you."

"I have been here before."

"Oh, I know you have." She smiled. "I'm wondering why you came back?"

"Are you *her*? The woman who lives here?" Baldwin moved closer for a better look. He had never actually seen the face of the woman who lived in the cabin. During their one visit, her face had been hidden by a hood.

"No. I'm as far away from her as a human can be—and I don't cut my visitors."

Baldwin's mind raced back to his last visit to the cabin, when the old woman sliced his hand open with a knife. She'd collected the blood that spilled from his hand in a saucer. At least he thought she had. When he pulled away, the wound on the fatty part of his hand had healed and no scar ever appeared. Baldwin doubted his memory of the visit. Details were hard to recall. Standing outside the cabin that night, he absently looked down at the palm of his hand. Beneath the thumb, an ugly scar rose up.

"How do you know about that?" Baldwin yelled, lifting his great beak nose toward the woman in the woods.

"I know her ways," the white-haired woman said. "She

has a hold on you, Baldwin. You're still free enough to go now. But it won't always be so." The large yellow dog at the woman's feet growled. "Think quick. She's coming for you."

The rickety door clattered behind Baldwin. When he turned, the woman he sought stood in the doorway of her hovel, a hood once again masking her face. "Why are you standing out here? Come in, honey. Come in."

"I was just speaking with—" When Baldwin turned to the white-haired woman and her dog, they had vanished. "I thought I saw a woman. . . ."

"These woods—the shadows—play tricks on us all. No matter, come in. You're home now." The old biddy held the door open for him.

Following her inside, he glanced down at his hand. The scar he saw only moments earlier had faded as quickly as the woman and her dog.

It was dark and smoky inside the shack, like the last time. The woman squatted on a stool near the fireplace, dim embers providing the only light.

"I have been thinking about what you said during our last visit," Baldwin started uncertainly. "You said to smite him. Surely you don't mean . . . to kill him."

The woman turned her shadowy face toward him. "Now, Baldwin, you already know what you must do."

"I don't. I . . . I couldn't kill the boy. What must I—"

"Do you want to be leader of the community or not? Do you want to take orders from a child? Is he *your* chosen one, Baldwin?" She stabbed a poker into the flickering glow of a collapsed log in the fireplace and squinted at him. "I didn't think so."

"When is the most opportune moment? What must I do?"

A guttural chuckle escaped from the woman. "You don't listen well, do you, sweetie? There is a *master* among us who will confuse the boy. Once that happens, your moment will come." She turned her shadowed face toward him. "Look at you. I didn't even mention the boy's name and your hatred comes right to the surface."

Baldwin grunted. Folding his great hands over his knees, he leaned in and whispered intensely, "Tell me how, woman. Tell me how to smite the boy. Be specific."

She handed him a rounded jar of powder. "Take this black powder. Spread it on the boy's belongings or his shoes at one of his training sessions. It will alarm the Brethren and furnish you with a chance to accelerate his training against the dark ways. Of course, it's practically harmless. But they'll see the powder as a threat from the *Darkness*, which is for the best. Over there, by the door, is a spear." Its sleek steel surface caught the firelight, making it appear as if lava ran through it. "Throwing and catching spears are part of your training at Peniel, idn't it? Oh, I've seen Lucille Wilder across the river during her exercise sessions in the woods. She thinks she's being secretive. But I see her. I know all her tricks. Introduce little Will to spear throwing and when the time is right, hurl that one at the boy with all your might. Hit him squarely in the chest. The spear has special properties."

"I can't kill him. I won't."

"Did I say kill him? Or did you? You'll do what needs doing. You've been given strength by the *master* and your contribution won't be forgotten."

"Master?" Baldwin's forehead knotted in concern. "I want no part of your 'master.' What are you talking about?"

"Don't play innocent with me, honey." She grabbed the spear and walked toward him. "You came here of your own free will. You gave your blood. The *master* is already within you. And you're within him." He could see a crooked, thin smile on the lower part of her face, which was lit for a split second as she passed the fireplace. "Take the spear. Run the boy through when you feel the time is right. You'll know the moment."

He handled the spear, almost without thinking. "What if I refuse to smite him? I'm not some killer. I'm the second in command of my community, the vicar. I just can't—"

"Then you'll never be the first in command. Maybe you're not up to it. Maybe the best thing for you is to let that impetuous, disrespectful brat lead you. Get in your boat and go follow the child. Go on. He's like all the Wilders, so high and mighty. Grovel to the Wilders all your days."

"I grovel to no one. I only want what is in the best interest of the community and myself," Baldwin muttered.

"Honey, you don't understand. You'll either embrace

your destiny or live out your days serving the *chosen one*—another slave to that idiot prophecy your community so reveres. Do you ever wonder why only the Wilders get to see what's in that old Book of Prophecy?"

"I have wondered that." Then conscious that he had said too much, he retreated to formalities. "How do you know about the prophecy? Who are you?" The woman clucked her tongue and retreated to the fireplace, saying nothing. Baldwin tossed the spear against the doorjamb in disgust, as if it were suddenly on fire, and pulled at the cabin door. "I can't hurt the boy."

"Then you hurt yourself. Imagine where Will Wilder will take your community. Let your mind wander to the troubles he will bring as he grows."

His head aching, Baldwin grit his teeth and yanked again at the door, which refused to yield to him.

"Have it your way," the woman said quietly. "You're free. Perhaps I'll take my own trip across the river someday soon—let your *Brethren* know about our little visits. They'd be fascinated to learn how their noble vicar spends his free time. Or I could always have a chat with little Will Wilder. Tell him all about Baldwin's visits with the Witch of Wormwood."

The door flipped open. Baldwin glared at the shadowy figure in the corner of the smoky hovel. He snatched the spear and bolted from the cabin without another word.

In the Peniel community room, Abbot Athanasius intently read a column in the *Perilous Times,* surrounded by his fellow brethren playing board games, reading, or in the case of the rotund Brother Amalric, arranging stamps in a thick leather binder. Athanasius adjusted the half-glasses at the end of his nose and cleared his throat in a way that let the others know he was concerned about something.

"What's up, Abbot?" Brother Ugo Pagani honked in his best Bronx library whisper. He was pinning rare insects to an absolutely frightening shadow box. "You've been clearing your throat for about ten minutes, so it's either postnasal drip or a beast's in your bonnet. I'm guessing it's the latter."

Snapping the paper, the abbot shot Ugo an irritated look. He carefully refolded the newspaper and hung it on a wooden dowel in the corner. "There was a grave robbery at the de Plancy Cemetery. I suppose these things happen. But usually there are missing articles, not missing bodies."

"Maybe somebody wanted a couple of gold fillings and left their pliers at home. Popped the carcass in the car and made a house call."

"Have some respect for the dead, Ugo."

"You know I'm kiddin'," Ugo said, driving a pin through a hard gray insect with two talons and eyes like red marbles. "The body snatching is weird."

"I'm glad you think so," the abbot said. "Why don't you and Tobias go down there and investigate. You're the scientist of the community. Let me know what you discover. And lie low."

Ugo closed the lid of his shadow box. "Lie low? It's a cemetery, Abbot. The residents probably won't be paying us much mind. Do we have to go now or can we go tomorrow?"

"Tomorrow will be fine. But don't make assumptions about the residents there. Someone is disturbing graves and stealing bodies. I'd like to know why."

"Can't you just wait for the next news report like everybody else?" Ugo asked. The abbot shook his head slightly and vacated the community room.

Squatting behind some brush along the riverside of Wormwood, the white-haired woman in green and her dog silently watched Baldwin place the spear in his flat boat and paddle back toward Peniel. The golden growled from the back of his throat. She scratched behind the dog's ear.

"I worry about going back to the other side too. But we may have to, Raphe. This one's up to no good. We'll have to watch him—and keep tabs on that old hag." She didn't dare say anything more. In silence, she checked the rotten roots and dead branches surrounding her for any movement and listened for the dangerous clicks and growls she knew all too well.

CHAPTER 7

THE POWER OF THE AMULET

Will shut the door to his room and stared at the book bag in the center of the carpet. He paced around it the way a starved mouse might consider a hunk of cheese on a trap. He had been wanting to touch the relic in the bag since he got home, but between dinner and homework, he hadn't had a moment.

The football tryouts on Monday afternoon weighed heavily on Will that night. He barely picked at the taco and rice dinner that his mom had made just for him. The idea of confronting Caleb and his crew on the field ruined his appetite and actually made him a little nauseous. His only consolation was the thought that he might be able to balance the scales with a little supernatural assistance.

Will threw himself on the floor and unzipped the side compartment of the backpack. He carefully pulled out the chain attached to the silver locket. It glimmered as it came into the light. He didn't want to touch the talisman holding Samson's curled locks for fear that it might blow up his fingers or something. The hair looked so ordinary under the glass, he wasn't even sure it still possessed any real power. For a brief second, he thought of putting it down. But curiosity, as it often did, got the best of Will and in an explosion of confidence, he pulled the chain over his head. Crouching on the floor of his room, he waited for some surge of power, some sensation to confirm the potency of Samson's locks. His wait lasted about thirty seconds.

Will's heart suddenly felt as if it were enlarging. Heat filled his chest. The blue button-up shirt he wore tightened around his torso and arms. He ran over to the mirror in his bathroom. He wasn't the Hulk, but he was a little beefier than he had been seconds earlier. Will undid the strained top button of his oxford and peered inside. His chest was ripped. Wide-eyed and eager to test his strength, he reached down for the metal trash can in the corner. It was stainless steel with a hard bottom. He held it in his two hands and applied the lightest pressure. CRUNCH. The thing collapsed like a paper cup. Tugging at the sides, he tried to return the can to its original shape, but his adjustments only made it worse.

"I've got to be careful with this," he said, delicately placing the warped can back in the corner. He ran into his room and tried to think of another way to test his power. *I could lift my bed or the dresser. That's it. I'll try the dresser. What could go wrong?* As he reached under the chest of drawers, shattering plates and yelling from downstairs stopped him.

Opening the door to the hallway, Will leaned on the door frame and listened.

"What is wrong with you, Deb?" his father, Dan, shouted uncharacteristically. "Those were my mother's dishes. I'm trying to help."

"You're not trying to help. You're trying to *control*. That's what you do. You have to *control* everything," Deborah Wilder ranted.

"Most people would welcome their husbands helping with the dishes."

"Not when their husbands turn their music off." The music blared again. It was the incessant beat of Cassian that Will had heard at the park and that his mother had played throughout dinner. "I am more than capable of stacking dishes without your help—and don't touch my music."

"You . . . you broke that dish on purpose," Dan stammered.

"Now you know how it feels when someone takes it upon themselves to ruin something you cherish."

"I turned down a song. What is wrong with you?"

"Nothing is wrong with me."

Will scurried down the staircase and poked his head in the kitchen just in time to see his mother slam the dishwasher shut. "It's all yours. Stack them to your heart's content," Deb spat at Dan. "I have some work to do." She stamped down the hall into the den and without looking back added, "Don't touch the music volume, Dan. I'm listening. Leave it alone."

Will's dad stood beside the counter looking as if he had been punched in the belly. He was clearly thrown by Deb's change of mood. Her explosive anger and sharpness were out of character. She had taken to yelling in recent days, something she rarely did before—and then only in extreme circumstances.

"What's going on, Dad?" Will asked.

"Your mother is under stress or . . . I don't know, son."

"She was in a daze yesterday too. At the concert in the park she was totally out of it." Will had an idea. He reached for the volume knob on the speaker beneath the kitchen cabinet and turned it off.

"Turn it back on!" Deb bellowed from the den. "What did I just say?!"

Will quickly turned the volume up.

"That's weird, Dad."

"I know." Dan removed his glasses and rubbed his eyes. "She's attached to this Cassian guy's music for whatever reason," he whispered. "She's been talking about him since Friday. She says it's calming and freeing."

"Doesn't look too calm or free to me," Will said, surveying the dish fragments on the kitchen tile.

"Just give your mother some space. She'll be back to her old self in a day or two." Dan squatted and began picking up the broken dishware. Then having caught sight of Will, he stopped. "You could use a haircut, son. Getting a little shaggy."

Will hadn't realized that his hair had grown by half an inch and his formerly straight hair had a touch of curl to it. "I guess you're right," Will said guiltily, catching his reflection in the kitchen window.

Dan resumed his glass collection and said quietly, "Is this the worst music or what?"

"I can hear you, Dan!" Deb yelled from the other room.

Will nodded his head without a sound and quickly raced up the stairs. Marin's and Leo's heads were protruding from their bedrooms.

"What's wrong with Mommy?" Marin whispered in a way that could be heard down the block.

"She's fine. Just needs some alone time probably," Will said unconvincingly.

Leo frowned at his brother. "If she keeps screaming like that, we'll all need some alone time."

In class on Monday morning, Caleb Gibbar gripped the desk across the row from Will with quaking hands. Without much prodding, he could have ripped the desktop off its metal base and flattened Will with it.

Mrs. Belcher had sprung one of her pop quizzes on the class. Her question was straightforward: "What were the events that started World War I and II? This is for extra points."

When no one raised their hand, Will did.

He was in the middle of discussing the assassination of Archduke Ferdinand of Austria when Caleb snarked beneath his breath, "You talk like you were there, Wilder."

Will's friend Andrew, who sat behind him, whispered, "Let it go, Will-man. Just keep doing your thing."

But Will refused, and for a split second glared at Caleb. He then turned to Mrs. Belcher and in the sweetest voice said, "I don't want to hog all the time. I think Caleb wants to finish the story. Go ahead, Caleb. I'm sorry. I didn't mean to take over." He smiled a syrupy smile at Caleb.

Andrew sat back in his chair and smacked a palm on his forehead. "Here we go again."

That's when Caleb white knuckled the desk. "Uh . . . uh . . . I don't have nothing else to say," he muttered.

Mrs. Belcher, a thin woman with probing gray eyes, walked down the aisle to Caleb's desk. "You might have more to say if you did your home reading. See me after class, Caleb."

The bell rang and the room exploded with the clamor of books slamming and bags zipping.

"See you on the field, big guy," Will said, bolting down the aisle.

"Oh, you'll see me," Caleb said to himself, watching Will leave. "You won't be able to miss me."

CHAPTER 8

GAME CHANGER

"Why did you have to set Caleb up like that, Will-man?" Andrew asked, catching up to Will in the hallway. "That was not cool."

"You didn't hear what he said. He's a jerk." Will headed toward the locker room.

"This isn't going to help you with the guys on the team."

"Ask me if I care," Will said, pulling the pith helmet brim over his eyes.

Cami and Simon dodged classmates until they reached Will and Andrew.

"Are you trying to get yourself killed?" Cami asked, grabbing Will by the arm. "You know Caleb didn't have a clue about those wars."

"And what's going on with your hair there, Curly?" Simon

asked, tilting his glasses for a better view of the curls beneath the pith helmet.

"It's growing, okay?" Will stopped and faced his friends in the hallway. "Back off, guys. Caleb jabbed me and I jabbed back. It was nothing. He deserves to be embarrassed."

"Maybe it'd be best if you didn't try out for the team today," Andrew warned. "Caleb's going to be good and ticked after talking to Mrs. Belcher. It could get ugly on the field."

"You're right"—Will smiled—"ugly for him. See you later, guys." With that, he pushed the bar on the metal door and exited the school.

Cami remained behind with Andrew and Simon. "Will is losing it. He's delusional."

"For a kid who's about to get slaughtered, you've got to give him points for confidence," Simon squawked in his high-pitched way.

"I can't stay to watch the tryouts. Text me what happens, Simon. The only thing I'm happy about is: you'll be out there with him," Cami said to Andrew. "He'll need some friends on the field."

"He'll need an ambulance," said Andrew before breaking into a sprint for the door.

"Wait up, Lummox," Simon said in gangly pursuit. "Should I get some bandages from the school nurse?"

As Will closed in on the locker room, a vaguely familiar voice called out to him. It was Renny Bertolf, pasty as ever, waving a bony hand in the air. "Today's the big day, huh? Are you ready? Do you think you'll make the team?"

"I think I might. We'll see." Will stopped for a second. He felt sorry for the scrawny kid, who was all alone. Glancing over Renny's sweatered shoulder, Will checked for the approach of Caleb or his pals. "How are your classes going? Are you making friends?"

"Nope. I don't think the kids here like me." He stared at the ground, pushing long, weedy hair from his eyes. "I'm trying. I'm kinda—you know—shy. I'll be watching your tryout. I really hope you make the team."

"Me too."

"Is that bully Caleb going to be there?"

"He'll be there." Will smiled at the boy. "Make sure you stay for the whole tryout. It'll be fun for us."

"For us?" Renny asked, brightening.

"Just watch." Will winked at him and ran into the locker room.

Most of the team had assembled on the field while Will quickly changed into uniform. Andrew yelled into the locker room: "Will-man. The coach has already called your name. I told him I wasn't sure you were trying out, kinda hoping that you'd drop—"

"Oh no, I'm ready," Will said, snapping his helmet into place.

Somehow Andrew thought the uniform seemed to fit

him better. "I'll try to stay close to you in case there's trouble or anything."

"It's okay, big guy. I've got a plan." Will had that look in his hazel eyes and the mischievous grin that usually preceded buildings crumbling, water rising, or monsters appearing from nowhere. Before Andrew could recover from the look or muster a response, Will clapped him on the shoulder and marched out the locker room doors. Even with the pads on, Andrew felt the sting of the friendly blow. He rolled his shoulder a few times, grimaced, and followed Will onto the field.

"Gentlemen, those are the two teams. Caleb, you'll be quarterback of the A team. Sam, you'll be quarterback of the B team," Coach Runyon barked at the boys on the field. "Mr. Wilder. B team. When I call roll, you'd better be on this field in uniform, son."

Several members of the A team (including Caleb) and a few of the Bs sniggered.

"It won't happen again, Coach," Will said, rushing to join his B teammates.

"Better not." The coach blew the whistle, and the teams separated for stretching and then the kickoff.

The kick to the B team was high and Andrew easily caught the ball. He ran about three yards before a tidal wave of opponents smashed him to the ground. Will was shocked by the power and aggression of the opposing team. "You all right?" Will asked Andrew as the pile atop him scattered.

"After I find my right leg, I'll be fine."

"I thought I told you not to come back, Wilder?" Caleb called out as the lines re-formed, his nostrils flaring. "Last warning."

Will said nothing and looked away.

After the spike, Will ran into the backfield. The ball came sailing his way. He reached up and . . . nabbed it before running as if he were on fire. "Guys!" Caleb yelled, pointing to the boys nearest Will. Suddenly three huge boys closed in on him. Will didn't change course; he didn't duck to the right or the left, but ran straight toward the rushing players.

They extended their arms and prepared to knock the much smaller boy down. This coordinated approach had stopped guys four times Will's size.

Will pulled the ball to his chest and went straight at them. The first opponent leapt at Will, arms open. Before the kid knew what had happened, he was on his back near the sideline. The second and third boys flanked Will, hoping to tackle him from both sides. Will threw his right shoulder toward one guy and his left to the other. The boys went flying backward like they had ropes tied to their torsos. He didn't stop to check for damages. Will ran all the way into the end zone until he heard the whistle blow. Coach Runyon was beaming, scratching notes on his clipboard.

"Go get 'em! Whoo-hoo!" Renny Bertolf yelled in his raspy voice from the bleachers. Andrew, like the rest of the team, was slack-jawed. Even Caleb watched the scene in shock. He tore his helmet off for a clear view of just what the heck took out his three strongest teammates. They were still splayed out on the field, rubbing their respective backsides, elbows, and shoulders.

Coach Runyon clapped. "Come on. Come on. Let's go, guys. Kickoff to A team. Harlan, Boyd, Wicker—off the ground. Let's go. Couldn't have been that hard a hit. Good hustle out there, Wilder."

Will smirked, strutting back to his teammates, who were still amazed by what he had done.

"Great job, Will-man. You tossed those guys out of the way like they were pillows," Andrew said. Then he whispered, "What's going on?"

"Training, I guess," Will deadpanned.

> **Cami, You would not believe this. Will just flattened three guys—huge guys—in the second play here. It happened so fast I almost missed it. One of them—Harlan I think—is still trying to get up. We'll see if Will survives the next down. Are you praying? LOL. More soon.**

Simon finished tapping on his cell phone and set it down. He sat on the edge of the bleacher as the snap happened.

"Can you believe how amazing Will is doing?" Renny asked Simon. "I've seen you all at lunch and stuff. You must be friends. I'm Renny Bertolf."

"Pleased to make your acquaintance." Simon found it

hard to stop focusing on Renny's turned-up nostrils but smiled as best he could. "Will mentioned you the other day."

"He did? Caleb roughed us both up last week. When Will came in, he—"

"Let's talk later," Simon said, trying to focus on the game. "I really need to watch this."

"Oh sure," Renny said apologetically, studying Simon. Simon quickly turned back toward the field just in time to see Caleb gripping the ball behind his head, looking for an open receiver. Will danced around the midfield, shadowing one of the A team members. Caleb fired the ball to Phil Nance, who was to Will's left. Will sprinted toward the boy and dove for the ball. Before Phil knew where the ball was, Will was off and running to the opposing goal line.

Caleb smacked his hands on his helmet as Will, unbelievably, ran in his direction. Fire flashed in Caleb's eyes. The quarterback became a Mack Truck, rolling forward, determined to stop Will Wilder at all costs.

"You might be bigger," Will shouted as he pressed forward. "But I *can* do something about it." And with that he collided with Caleb's helmet.

Simon and Renny winced in the bleachers, sure their friend would need major medical care. But when Simon managed to open one eye to survey the damage, it was Caleb not Will backflipping across the field.

"What the . . . ? He's like Superman," Simon howled. Renny was too busy beating his fists on the bleachers to say anything.

Will passed the 20-yard line, then the 10, then the 5.

With no opposition in sight, he scored his second touchdown of the day.

Caleb shook his head, trying to process his current state: flat on his back in the middle of the field. How did Will Wilder manage to knock him down? How did it happen? *I must have slipped and hit my head,* Caleb thought. *Maybe I was moving so fast I lost my balance. Wilder was coming at me and . . .* Whatever the explanation, Caleb's anger bubbled over. Wilder had shamed him in the classroom and now he had disgraced him on the field. His field. Before he could get to his feet, the voice of the coach startled him.

"Easy, Caleb. That was quite a tumble. Take your time getting up." The coach gently raised Caleb off the ground. "Have you ever seen a little guy do something like that? He's incredible. With your arm and him as a receiver, we'll take the state championship. Go ahead and change."

Caleb grunted without so much as a word. He jerked his arm away from the coach and sullenly headed for the lockers. He purposely walked right by Will.

"This isn't over," Caleb said, looking back half in defiance, half in shame. A few of the bigger guys on the team followed him.

Will tried to ignore the threat. He kept his cool and patted his chest to ensure that the Samson amulet was where it was supposed to be. *No worries,* he thought. And he went right on glorying in the backslaps and adulation of the B team.

The coach interrupted their celebrations. "Wilder, you're

in, son. Nineteen years as a coach, I've never seen a scrapper like you do anything like that. You're fast. Strong. I'm very impressed, Wilder. Welcome to the Perilous Falls Middle School team."

Even though a tiny part of him felt guilty for wearing the amulet to tryouts, he wasn't guilty enough to fess up or refuse the offer. "Thanks a lot, Coach Runyon," he said. "I'll try to make you proud."

Dreading being caught in the locker room with Caleb or his crowd, Will made small talk with Simon once Andrew headed to the showers.

"I have to give it to you, Will. You were like a superhero out there," said Simon.

"When you focus hard on something, anything is possible."

"So that was mind over matter?"

"Exactly!" Will nodded. "Mind over matter."

"No vitamins? No tricks? Those guys went flying for yards. Don't your arms hurt?"

"I feel great. Just doing what I had to do to make the touchdown."

"Why don't I entirely believe this story?"

"Stop being so suspicious." Seeing Caleb and his gang leave the locker room, Will figured the coast was clear. "I'll see you in a little bit, Simon."

Will was all alone inside the fragrant, fluorescent-lit room. He hastily changed out of the team uniform and put on his khaki pants and blue shirt. As he reached for the pith helmet on the top shelf of the locker, a roar shook the room. He froze in place. This was not the bark or yowl of a dog, but the type of rumbling roar that could only come from a creature with a sizable chest cavity and an even bigger mouth. The sound cut through him. He made no sudden moves for fear of attracting the thing. It seemed to be coming from the band room. His first thought was to run outside onto the field. But then his nose began to itch.

That isn't good. Will slowly put the pith helmet on his head, summoning his courage. He rubbed the amulet at his chest and ventured down the dimly lit hallway that led to the band room and the growls.

CHAPTER 9

A Lion in the Hall

When the next roar sounded, the air in the hallway turned sticky. It reeked the way food does when left in the sun for too long. Breath, Will thought. It had to be the heinously stinky breath of whatever was roaring.

Will held his nostrils together to keep a developing sneeze from drawing the attention of the creature lurking in the shadows. He flattened himself against the wall, hoping for a better view of the thing. Another roar shook the hallway.

Worried that he had gotten too close, Will started creeping backward along the wall, toward the lockers. A sudden whimpering wafted in from the band room. "Will! Will? I'm hurt."

It was Renny Bertolf.

"Are you okay?" Will whispered.

"Not really."

"I'm coming," Will said, stepping into the middle of the hall.

Two red eyes glowed near the end of the hall. *RAAAAAAAAAHHHHH!* In the faint light coming from behind him, Will could just make out what the two eyes were attached to. A gargantuan creature, like a prehistoric lion, scratched its claws into the concrete floor and defiantly roared at him. A tangle of glistening quills served as its mane, like a porcupine had exploded around the thing's face.

Will blinked hard. This was no illusion, but a massive monster whose attention was now trained on him. Then it charged. For a split second Will considered running back into the locker room. But how far would he really get? There was nowhere to hide. He touched the amulet at his chest and felt a mighty power surge through him. Then Will did the unthinkable: he ran at the lion.

The creature leapt into the air with both claws extended, its jaws wide. Drawing back a fist, Will jumped up to meet the thing and popped the beast squarely on the chin. The evil cat flew sideways, smashing into a trophy case. Panting, the monster tried to right itself onto floppy legs and struggled to rise. It managed to steady the front two legs, but the rear haunches were wobbly. The creature trembled with anger, the quills of its mane stood straight out. It unleashed a terrible growl, sticky spittle landing on Will's arm.

"Renny. Just hold on a second," Will shouted down the hall. "I'll be there soon."

"It's okay. A friend is here with me," Renny responded weakly.

The lion turned its great head toward Renny's voice, echoing from the band room. Sensing a weaker target, the monster spun away from Will and headed in Renny's direction. Its killer claws dug into the polished concrete, dragging the weakened back legs along the hall. It quickly closed in on the band room.

"Oh no you don't," Will said.

He ran forward and grabbed the lion thing by the tail. In response, two claws viciously slashed at his face. He yanked his head back just in time to save it. The creature reared up on its back legs and disengaged its jaws to reveal a mouthful of enameled daggers. Impulsively, Will reached for the dullest teeth up front—between the huge fangs. He clutched the lion's upper and lower jaw and began to yank it apart.

The monster's red eyes went vacant as it absorbed what was happening. A choked wail of fear came out of the beast. The huge body flailed on the floor, but it no longer offered much resistance. Only the quills, like a hundred angry snakes, strained to poke Will.

He continued to pry open the foul mouth as if it were a clamshell. The muscles across his chest and arms ached from the effort. He knew he couldn't keep this up for much longer. But if he let go, he'd lose more than his hands, and a few of the pulsating quills were only inches from his arms. Will shut his eyes and with all his might, ripped the teeth apart and twisted. The lion's jaw separated like hot taffy.

When he opened his eyes to check the carcass, the teeth dissolved in his hands along with the entire body. A sickly sweet, purple mist exploded into the air before him. Aside from the scent of honey, nothing of the lion creature remained. Will stood there, shell-shocked, his arms still fully extended. *A Fomorii, it must have been a* Fomorii. But before he could consider what had happened, the cries of Renny from the band room needed his attention.

Will rushed in to find Renny on the floor, in the corner of the room, broken concrete blocks all around him. A girl—a really beautiful cheerleader with jet-black hair and startling green eyes—knelt next to him. She was pressing a band T-shirt to his head.

"What happened?" Will asked, trying not to be distracted by the cheerleader, who smiled at him in a weird, but kind of neat, way.

"It was Caleb . . . ," Renny wheezed, his right eye swollen and bleeding. "I came in here to congratulate you and he knocked me down."

"What the . . . What happened to *the wall*?" Something had obviously punched through the back of the band room, creating a five-foot-high gaping hole.

Renny gestured for Will to come closer. He was woozy and paler than usual. "Caleb did it. He didn't look like himself. He was big—like a monster. He asked me if I had seen you. When I told him I hadn't, he threw me up against the wall . . . slapped me hard. He was looking for you! He said he had a little surprise for you if you came back here. Then he pounded the wall and ran out."

Will stared at the open hole into the dusky schoolyard, trying to make sense of it all.

"You were great out there," the beautiful cheerleader said in a voice like honey.

"Thanks." Will blushed a little.

"I mean it. I've never seen anyone do *that* and I've cheered at a lot of games." She lightly touched his arm. "I'm Lilith Lorcan."

"Lilith's a friend of mine from Sorec Middle School. We were going to go out for ice cream, but . . ."

"I told Renny I'd meet him after my cheer squad. Then I didn't see him on the bleachers. After the tryouts I went looking for him and he was in here."

"I can't believe that Caleb would— I'm Will," he said suddenly, offering his hand. She had the most glittery eyes he had ever seen. "I should get help," he said, rising to his feet and heading for the hole in the wall.

Lilith smirked and took his arm. "It's okay. My dad's a doctor. He's on his way. And I know how to tend wounds pretty well." She yanked at the bottom of her short black and red skirt as she stood.

"Will-man?" It was Andrew, followed by Simon. They stuck their heads in the room.

"Did somebody set off a bomb? What happened in here?" Simon asked.

"I'll tell you on the walk home," Will said. "Renny, are you sure you'll be okay until Lilith's dad gets here?"

"Oh he'll be fine. The bleeding's stopped and everything," Lilith said. "It was great meeting you, Will." She played with her ear in the cutest way. "Maybe we can grab an ice cream or something, after a game?"

Will could only stare at her, his mouth not quite closed. He couldn't think of a thing to say. She smiled a crooked smile that only encouraged him to continue staring.

Lilith pulled a card from her little purse and pointed at it. "My number is right there. I wish you'd been here before that Caleb kid came through. Maybe Renny would be in better shape. He needs a strong friend to look out for him at school."

"Oh, I'll look out for him. We're friends. Right, Renny?" Will's voice went higher than he intended.

"I hoped we'd be friends. I'd like that."

Andrew and Simon frowned at each other. "Can we go now?" Simon squawked to Will. "Or are you two going to sing a duet?"

Will walked toward the door. "Okay, I'll check on you tomorrow, Renny. And Lilith, we'll talk . . . soon. . . . I'll call so we can talk and . . . see each . . . well, I'll see you and . . . you know." He pinched the brim of his pith helmet and pushed Simon and Andrew back into the hall.

"Smooth, Romeo. Real smooth," Simon said, guffawing once they were down the hall.

Will kept walking, keeping it cool. "She's nice."

"She's gotta be in high school. What is she, sixteen or something?" Andrew asked.

"I don't know. I just met her. She's cool, though. Pretty." Will looked to the boys for confirmation.

"I suppose," Simon said, rolling his eyes. "Andrew's right, though—she is a little old. Forget that, the real question is: How did you manage to knock those big players down like toy soldiers?"

"I told you. It's focus—mind over matter."

"I get all that," Andrew said. "But your mind isn't that strong. Harlan and Caleb were limping after you hit them."

"Don't even mention his name. He's lucky he went home at all. Did you see what he did to Renny?"

"Caleb did that?" Simon asked.

"Yes. He was looking for me but decided to take it out on that poor little kid."

"I saw," Andrew said gravely. "Where'd this Renny come from?"

"He's a transfer student from Sorec Middle—but that doesn't matter now. What matters is taking Caleb down. He needs to be taught a lesson."

"Oh, now you're the enforcer of Perilous Falls? Give me a break." Simon flipped his hand in the air, dismissing the whole idea. "You're half Caleb's size. It's a miracle you survived out there today. You proved your point. Why don't you just return to the Eagle Scouts and forget this vendetta, tough guy."

"You all don't understand. Somebody has to teach Caleb

a lesson." Will pulled them close to him and whispered, "And I'm starting to think he's more than meets the eye."

"What do you mean by that?" Simon asked.

"Did you see the wall in the band room? Kids can't do that. Even strong kids. I think he's a demon, or possessed by one."

"Possessed! You think he's POSSESSED?" Simon squealed.

"Why don't you announce it over the loudspeaker?" Andrew nudged him.

"Something's not right, and I haven't even told you all about the demonic lion in the hallway. Normal people don't bust through walls and turn into monsters."

"Normal people don't throw guys who've been playing for years across the field either." Andrew turned Will around by the shoulders. "Level with us, Will-man. What's going on?"

As he formulated a response, Will's eyes drifted to the floor beyond Andrew and Simon. Three hunched imps scampered out of the band room, running right past his friends. Will tracked them with worried eyes.

"Will? What is it? What do you see?" Simon asked, checking the floor all around him.

"Nothing. It's nothing." Will couldn't put all the pieces together and feared telling his friends anything further— especially anything about the relic that might be attracting the demon's attention. "I just have to figure this out. Everything's going to be fine."

Andrew didn't believe him for a second.

CHAPTER 10

THE THIRD CLAW RISES

Inside Peniel's north tower on that late Tuesday morning, Tobias Shen and Ugo Pagani shared their discoveries at the de Plancy Cemetery. Abbot Athanasius sat behind the desk in his office, listening intently, while Aunt Lucille watched from a leather side chair.

"There were two open graves. One in the front and one in the rear section," Ugo reported, flipping through his notes. "The dirt from the graves wasn't piled up in mounds—which was strange. It was spread all over the place, like twelve guys had dug them up at once, throwing the dirt in all directions."

"I thought there was only one disturbed grave," the abbot said.

"We did as well," Tobias said, "but this morning we found a second open grave—one that has not been reported—in the newer part of the cemetery."

"From the condition of the busted coffin in the hole, I'd say it's been open for two . . . three weeks. Rain washed a lotta dirt over the thing," Ugo added, his thick black eyebrows rising. "And tell 'em about the can-opening technique. Haaaa."

Bartimaeus and Will stood at the doorway, wary of entering given what they just heard.

Aunt Lucille invited them in and quickly brought them up to speed. Ugo interrupted. "Hey, shouldn't you be in school, young man?"

"It's a teacher planning day. I have football practice this afternoon, but no classes," Will said.

"Good thing. We don't need to be contributing to your delinquency any more than we already are." Ugo guffawed to himself, then noting Will's black curls added: "Maybe you can use the extra time to visit a barber."

Brushing him off, Aunt Lucille returned to the business at hand. "Go on, Tobias. I think we were at the 'can-opening technique.'" She shot a bothered look at Ugo. "Whatever that means."

"The coffins were both opened in a very, very peculiar way," Tobias continued, narrowing his eyes. "They were slashed. Ripped open by a big, big blade of some kind."

"Given the weathering around the casket cuts and dirt intrusion, the most recent grave has been open for a few days, I'd say. The other, several weeks." Ugo pinched at his bulbous nose. "No bodies at all. Someone—or more likely some*thing*—snatched the bodies. Now what would they do that for?"

The abbot folded his arms and checked the faces of those surrounding him. "Bartimaeus. Go on. You appear to have a thought."

"So, it does sound familiar." Bartimaeus tugged at the lapels of his tweed jacket and stepped forward. "Jacob sometimes talked about a demon that used the dead as vessels. This thing would collect dead folks and use 'em like puppets. The demon pulled all the strings, ya see. I don't recall the details, though."

"Would my great-grandfather's diaries tell us anything, Mr. Bart?" Will asked.

"Not the ones we have. I know all the diaries here backwards and forwards." Which made sense since Bartimaeus was the de facto librarian of Peniel and had worked with Jacob Wilder as a young man. "Jacob wrangled with this demon early on, during the war." He turned to his side. "When he was courting your mama, Sarah Lucille."

Aunt Lucille nodded with concern.

"Yeah, he mentioned it a few times. There were imps running around then too . . . What was that thing's name? It was a marquis, as I recall." Seeing that Will was confused, Bartimaeus clarified: "One of the top demons. A Marquis of Hell is a bad dude. Your great-grandfather discovered a way to immobilize this particular demon." He scratched at the back of his gray head. "But darned if I can remember how he did it. The diaries with all a dat are probably still at Monte Cassino in Italy. That's where he was based during World War II."

"I'm still seeing imps around town," Will blurted out. "Saw them at practice yesterday."

Aunt Lucille swallowed hard and locked her blue eyes on him. "Where? Tell us everything."

Will did—mostly. He told them about Renny getting beaten by the "monster," the punctured wall of the band room, and the imps. He didn't mention the lion creature, or the fact that he ripped it apart thanks to the amulet of Samson's locks.

"Will, I think it's time you looked at the Book of Prophecy," Aunt Lucille said solemnly. "The grave robbing, the events at your school, the imps—there's no doubt it's diabolic activity. We need to figure out where this is headed and which demon is causing all of this."

Abbot Athanasius rose, hiding his hands beneath the scapular of his long black habit. "If you think it's warranted, Lucille, consult the prophecy. Assuming it opens, we should all remember—especially you, William—that reading it will only hasten whatever is coming. Let's not lose sight of the most important thing: strengthening your gifts so we can battle the *Sinestri* together. We all rely on you, William, and you can rely on us."

"I get it. But I'd feel better if I knew what we were dealing with. Then at least I'd know what to be on the lookout for." Will lifted his backpack from the floor to leave.

Aunt Lucille and Bartimaeus started to follow him out.

The abbot barked suddenly, "William!" He dramatically pointed his index finger toward Will. "Don't move." No one did. The abbot flew over to Will and snatched the backpack by its straps. He held it high in the air, scrunching up his nose.

"Lucille. Ugo. What do you see there? On the bottom of the bag?" the abbot asked.

"Pepper, maybe some kind of soot." Ugo licked his finger and went to touch the base of the bag.

"I wouldn't do that, Ugo dear," Aunt Lucille said, clutching his wrist hard. "I've seen this before. It isn't pepper. I believe it's black powder."

"Black powder?" Will asked, perplexed.

"Witches sometimes use things like this to commit *Maleficia*—vicious acts against people they hate or want to wound."

Ugo pulled a plastic bag and a small brush from his habit. "I'll break down the powder and let you know what we have in a little bit." He collected a sample and started to lumber toward the door and his laboratory.

"This could explain the missing corpses, no?" Tobias asked, craning his neck for a glimpse of the powder.

"How would powder explain missing bodies?" Will asked.

"Witches have been known to use dead bodies to create their ointments and powders. Very, very dangerous, Mr. Wilder." Tobias reached for the bag straps. "If you allow me, Abbot, I will purify the bag." The abbot released it to him. Without another word, Tobias carried the backpack at arm's length out of the office.

"You haven't had a playdate with a witch, have you, Willy boy?" Ugo chuckled as he sauntered out.

Will grew defensive. "I don't know where that came from," he shouted to the absent Ugo.

"Lucille, we'll have to accelerate his Defensive Tactics training." The abbot stroked his beard and stared at Will. "The *Darkness* may be targeting him. Let Baldwin know what we found on the bag. You are seeing the vicar this afternoon, correct, William?"

"Yes, sir."

"Follow directions and focus on your training. It could be critical in the days ahead." The abbot walked behind his desk and stared out the big cathedral window there.

Will, Bartimaeus, and Aunt Lucille navigated stairs and corridors, walking through multiple buildings, to reach the public part of Peniel. Once in the expansive Bethel Hall, they pushed through the door marked PRIVATE and up the tight spiral staircase to Jacob Wilder's private office. Aunt Lucille negotiated the ornate door with her special gold key. Once inside the rounded room, she went to the stone fireplace behind the heavy desk. She twisted the heads on the angels carved into the mantel and a panel slid away to reveal the olive-colored book they had come for.

It was a great, aged volume with seven sculpted metal locks wrapped around the outer edge of the thing. All but one of the hinged claws nestled inside various leaves of the book. Only the "chosen one" could gain access to the prophecy within. On two occasions, Will's touch caused the first couple of locks to snap back, revealing a timely prophecy. Will stared down at the cover of the book, decorated with copper curlicues surrounding a leather panel. On it, etched in gold calligraphy, was the prologue of the prophecy, which Will could practically recite by heart.

The Prophecy of Abbot Anthony the Wise

The Lord came to me upon the waters and said:
Take thee a great book and write upon it as I instruct thee.
My spirit trembled, for the visions He placed in my head
*   frightened me.*
Still, I write in obedience:
In those days, when the people have grown hard of heart
and belief has dwindled;
when wickedness has become commonplace; and the Brethren
*   have broken their unity;*
then shall I raise up a young one to lead them.
He shall be the firstborn of the root of Wilder.
He shall have the sight of the angels
and perceive darkness from light.
Behold, when his time is ripe, he shall come riding on a colt,
*   the foal of a donkey, and his blood shall spill.*
This shall be the sign that the battle is near

and all must prepare.

For in those days the beasts shall rise from the pit

to test my people . . .

Will held his breath and laid his hands on the volume, eager to discover who or what the next beast to "test" the people might be. The first lock with carved reptilian scales sprang back, then the second, which looked like the paw of a wolf. Finally, the metal rooster claw retracted and the book opened to a page Will had never seen before. He read swiftly as Aunt Lucille and Bartimaeus leaned over his shoulders for a view.

The waters were greatly agitated and the Lord spoke:

Woe to those seduced by the sounds and visions of the wicked.

Their ears itch for the melodies of hell and their eyes delight in

   dark delusions.

Shades rise up to greet them,

And restrain them from the light.

In their bewilderment, the third of SEVEN beasts shall arise.

For behold, when my children are amused to distraction,

and the Amulet of Power has been exposed,

a Marquis of Impurity shall ascend.

This commander of legions wears many masks

and desires power it should never possess.

Sowing seeds of madness and calamity,

false desires and empty cravings,

this clawed hellion severs even the closest of relations.
It will bewitch innocent maidens and devour those they love.
There is one particular maiden who must be protected;
For she may in turn protect my chosen one.
Hear these words, firstborn of the house of Wilder:
Let not the desire for beauty conquer you;
do not be ensnared by your eyes:
captivated by the surface, but blind to the reality beneath.
Your gifts exist not for yourself, but for others.
Like a roaring lion, your adversary prowls everywhere looking to
    destroy you.
My chosen must resist the beast, steadfast in purity.
For only in weakness shall he find his strength
and only in self-giving shall he vanquish ASMODEUS.

"Wait awhile," Bartimaeus said, his milky eyes wide. "That's the name of the demon Jacob did battle with during the war. That's the one he paralyzed." He snapped his finger repeatedly. "How the heck did he do it?"

"If you think one of my father's diaries in Monte Cassino holds the answer, you should go there," Aunt Lucille said, her eyes sparkling. "You and Will. Why not go today?"

"I . . . I can't go today," Will sputtered. "I have my training and football practice. But maybe I could go with Mr. Bart on . . . Thursday."

Will was still trying to make sense of the confusing prophecy. Though some parts were less confusing than others.

"Like a roaring lion, your adversary prowls everywhere looking to destroy you." He sure tried, Will thought. *Maybe I should tell Aunt Lucille about the lion. But then I'd have to fess up to using—*

"'The Amulet of Power has been exposed.' Now, what could that be referring to?" Lucille studied the prophecy on the desk. "There are all sorts of powerful relics here. Could be anything. And how would it have been *exposed*?"

Will guiltily decided to keep the talisman he wore beneath his shirt to himself. "What about the end here," he said, trying to change the subject, "where it reads 'only in weakness shall he find his strength'?"

"I can attest, you have weakness down to a science," Baldwin intoned from the doorway, a silver spear in his hand. "I am sorry to intrude." He entered slowly, surveying the desk with his beady eyes. Will slammed the Book of Prophecy shut. Baldwin, raising his strong chin, glanced at Lucille and Bartimaeus.

"I guess you're here to collect Will for his Defense Training, Vicar," Bartimaeus said, blocking Baldwin's view of the desk.

"Good guess," Baldwin murmured.

Aunt Lucille came around the front of the mahogany desk. "Baldwin, you need to know that—"

The vicar closed his eyes and raised two hands. "I'm already informed. I saw Tobias and the black-powdered book bag on my way over. We have much work ahead of us, William. This is troubling business." He pointed the spear at

Will. "Dangers surround you." He turned. "I've prepared a new course for us today. Come." And he started down the stairs.

"Hide the prophecy—even though I can't figure it out," Will confided through gritted teeth to Aunt Lucille as he left. Then he doubled back. "Who do you think the innocent maiden who must be protected is?"

"Your guess is better than mine, dear." Aunt Lucille tucked the book back into its concealed nook above the fireplace. "Could be anyone at all. Who do you think it is?"

CHAPTER 11

LEERS AND SPEARS

Cami Meriwether walked her brother to his bus stop that morning, several blocks from their home. Due to his special needs, the bus service offered to pick him up at his door, but Max preferred to join the other kids at the area bus stop. He enjoyed making the trip up Main Street each day. With Cami off from school that day, she made the trip with him.

While they passed familiar storefronts, something was decidedly unfamiliar about the people Max greeted each morning.

Miss Rosie, the usually bubbly black lady that owned the Milk and Honey Bistro, completely ignored Max as he rolled in front of her shop. She was placing a sign near the curb, gently swaying to whatever her earphones were pumping out. "Good morning, Miss Rosie," Max offered as he approached. Miss Rosie didn't even look up when he sped right by her.

Max stopped his wheelchair and spun it around.

"What are you doing?" Cami asked as Max backtracked toward the bistro. "We're going to miss your bus."

"That's strange. Miss Rosie always tells me hello." Max rolled right into the woman's line of vision. She continued sashaying, stepped inside the glass front door, and slammed it behind her.

Max turned his motorized chair around so he could see the establishments across the street. "Notice anything?" he asked Cami.

"People getting ready for business and a kid who's going to miss his bus."

Max continued up the street. Mr. Bonaventure, the owner of the used bookstore, pushed a rolling shelf of books in front of his big shop windows.

"Good morning, Mr. Bonaventure," Max sang out, his head pressed onto the pillow that held it up.

The stooped man had a big smile on his face but completely ignored Max. He wandered into his store and cranked up the music. DJ Cassian's music.

A few moments later Mrs. Bonaventure, a chipper woman with her hair up in a bun, came out of her shop, hands over her ears.

"Is everything okay, Mrs. Bonaventure?" Max asked.

Her face changed from a frown to a smile and back again; then she blurted out, "It's Mr. Bonaventure. He's acting very odd." The woman seemed to be on the verge of tears and her voice quaked as she spoke quietly. "We have stacked books together for thirty-five years. He's always kidded me about being so slow, because I like to take my time and ensure that the books are properly shelved—as you know, Max. About a week ago, a friend of mine gave us a CD by this DJ Cassian man. Well, you can hear it yourself. He plays it all day long—loudly." She folded her arms, rubbing at her elbows. "Can't stand that music—but he says it's 'wooonderful.' Out of the blue, he tells me the other day to go home early, and maybe I shouldn't work in the store any longer. He says he can do everything faster by himself. I told him, 'Victor, there is no way you can stack all this inventory alone.' He said, 'Go home and you'll see.' So yesterday afternoon I had enough of his lip and went home. But around six o'clock I got worried and came to check on him. Well, as I looked through the window—and you kids will think I'm a crazy old lady—the books were flying off the floor up to the shelves. Flying! Hundreds of books shelving themselves all over the shop. I saw it with my own eyes."

Max and Cami exchanged concerned looks.

"When he got home, I asked him what happened at the shop and he cut his eyes at me. 'Work is what happened. Work. If you weren't so lazy, maybe we'd get more of it done,' he said. I was so upset I didn't speak to him all last night." She rearranged the sticks in her bun, pulling in the stray hairs. "He was just as moody this morning. All he wants to do is listen to that ridiculous music—the 'music of miracles' he calls it—"

"Caroline." It was Mr. Bonaventure, standing in the doorway of the shop. "Are you going to do the paperwork, or should I do that myself too?"

Max tried to say hello to Mr. Bonaventure again. The stooped man flattened his barely there gray hair to the side, his leg absently keeping time with the music. "Shouldn't you children be in school?" he grumped, and returned to the store.

"Cami has the day off, but I'm going to my school," Max yelled after him.

"Sorry to have burdened you children with all of this. You have a good day," Mrs. Bonaventure whispered, patting Max on the back before scurrying in after her husband.

Max locked Cami in a glare. "My dream's coming true. Remember, I said Will would be in trouble, and everyone would shake and ignore him. It's happening the way I said. See?" Max looked up the street. Cami turned and followed his stare.

Sally Dagon, who owned Dagon's Hair Cuttery, tried to hold three bags in her arms while she slid her key into the aquamarine door of her salon.

"Hello, Miss Dagon," Max said, deliberately stopping in front of her.

"Hey." The woman never looked over at him. She too was listening intently to the sound coming from her earphones and tapping her feet rhythmically—completely preoccupied.

Frustrated for her brother, and doubtful of his theory, Cami put her foot in the door and raised her voice. "Miss Dagon. Hi. Hey!"

The woman turned indignant. "What do you want? Do you have an appointment?"

"No, ma'am. Just saying hi. My brother—"

"Can't you see I'm busy here. I haven't time for you or your brother." There was a note of unwarranted viciousness in her speech.

"Okay. I'm leaving." Cami backed toward the doorway. "By the way, Miss Dagon, what are you listening to?"

"Music. It relaxes me. Unlike this conversation." She angrily flipped the lights on at the cutting stations. "It's Cassian," she said with a quick, eerie calm. "You should listen to his music. He's so gifted. When I hear his music, I feel complete relaxation. . . . I could just float away." She widened her arms and rose several feet off the floor.

Cami grabbed her mouth in panic. She had heard stories of people "flying" at Cassian's concerts, but the sudden vision of a grown-up she knew levitating freaked her out.

With Sally Dagon still hanging in the air, Cami backed out of the hair salon and ran to her brother on the sidewalk. "Did you see? She was floating."

"I saw. Something's very wrong," Max said, rolling up the street in the direction of Peniel.

"She was floating in midair, Max. Didn't you find her odd? She seemed very odd to me. Kind of zombified."

"Miss Lucille wants us to be her eyes and ears. You have to go tell her what we saw. They're all zombified."

Cami looked over her shoulder. "I feel we should be doing something," she said, clutching her fingers nervously.

"We are doing something. You're going to the museum, and I'm going to catch my school bus." And he sped to the corner where his bus had just arrived.

Baldwin led Will to a building at the back end of Peniel that he had visited only once. It was eight stories tall and the bars on the windows of the upper two floors distinguished the tower from the structures surrounding it. A domed black slate roof with sharp metallic daggered ornaments on the overhang gave the building a menacing air.

They entered a dark cavernous space. The far wall of the room hid a rounded staircase. During the climb up many flights of stairs, Will began to sneeze.

"You must learn to contain that unfortunate habit," Baldwin said dismissively, looking back at Will. "You might also consider a haircut." Will apologetically tucked a few of his untamed curls beneath the pith helmet as he stomped up the last of the stairs. The sneezes made him a little jumpy.

Baldwin leaned the metallic spear he carried against a

corner near the black metal door before them. There were three locks: one at the bottom, one in the middle, and one near the top of the door. The vicar disarmed all three with an oversized key from his habit and turned the door's braided metal handle.

"This is the community attic. We rarely use it today," Baldwin whispered. "But I've taken some liberties for your Defensive Tactics training. Step in quickly. Go on."

Will hesitated, never really trusting Baldwin. But he did as he was told.

The room contained aisles of stacked chairs, metal pots, sculptures, old lamps, and mirrors. Lots of mirrors. Crisscrossing beneath the dome overhead, carved exposed beams wore webs coated in dust. The barred windows, hidden by piles of bric-a-brac, permitted little light inside. Will eagerly walked down the main aisle to explore the room.

"Why are there bars on the windows?" he asked.

"To keep the things here—here."

Will stopped walking. "What things?"

"The belongings of the community, I suppose." Baldwin locked the door they entered through. "There are also *Fomorii* scattered about."

"*Fomorii?!*" Now Will understood why he continued to sneeze.

"I've placed a few *Fomorii* in the room. Don't fear. They are restrained. Some are leashed. Others are in cages." He had Will's full attention. "There will also be a few projected delusions. You will have to distinguish the true *Fomorii* from the delusions. As a *Seer,* this should be second nature to you. The task is quite simple: Clear each of the aisles. When you see a *Fomorii,* spear it. And please avoid breaking the mirrors." He slowly tossed the metallic spear back and forth in his large hands. Will reached for it.

"No, not this one," Baldwin said, placing it aside. He pulled two wooden spears from a storage cabinet. "Use these. They're lighter. They'll handle better."

AH-CHOO! AH-CHOO! Will struggled to talk over the sneezes. "I've only trained with spears once—with Aunt Lucille. Do we have to use spears?"

"Yes, William, we do."

Will shrugged. "Any other instructions?" *AH-CHOO!* "Or is that it?"

Baldwin turned his hawk nose up at the boy. Will noticed that the vicar's brow was moist. "The *Darkness* uses the black arts to distort reality. To make you believe you are seeing one thing, when you are seeing something quite another. Look deeply before you throw the spear; try to see with your heart. Otherwise you'll be easily deceived and lose your way."

Will frowned in confusion, but nodded anyway. He stepped into the main aisle, a spear in each hand. There was a faint scratching on the wooden planks past the piles of gold chairs. Will carefully padded forward, on the lookout for anything out of the ordinary. The scratching on the floorboard grew louder. He took a right turn down an aisle canopied with big hanging lanterns.

"Vicar!" Will yelled. "What if one of these things gets loose or hurts me?"

"That's why I am here, William," Baldwin responded loudly. "I have your back. It's a controlled environment. What are you afraid of?"

Will decided not to answer him. He pushed aside a dangling lamp and pursued the scratching noise. A few feet away, a small dog furiously pawed at the floor. It was white and fluffy—obviously scared. The dog began to whimper. It kept looking to the left, nervously, and loosing those high-pitched barks that only an animal in distress can summon. Will peered closely at the dog. He lowered his spears. *Poor little thing.*

Will squatted low. "What's wrong, fella?" He crept forward to try to see what the dog was reacting to. As he got closer and stared into the darkness, the dog stopped barking. When he looked back at the animal, it wasn't a dog any longer. Inches from Will's face was a small dragon-like creature, with oozing red eyes and small, sharp teeth.

Will threw himself backward. But not fast enough. The dragon beast leapt onto his chest and spread its tiny arms wide. The balled-up black paws sprang open and talons almost as long as the arms shot out. Will didn't even see the leash around its neck. He instinctively dropped the spears and punched the thing in the face. It tumbled into the darkness.

Will got to his feet and picked up one of the spears. The disoriented creature wobbled into the dim light. The thing's neck was now bulging just above the leash, which stretched to the breaking point. Will had apparently punched the *Fomorii*'s head into its throat. Not knowing what the creature was capable of, Will shot it with the spear.

His throw was so intense that the creature, like a missile, snapped its leash, overturned chairs, and a pile of swords and finally lodged onto the leg of a table full of old goblets. In seconds the dragon beast evaporated in a haze of green mist.

"Did you survive?" Baldwin intoned from somewhere in the room.

"I'm fine," Will said, snatching the other spear from the floor.

Baldwin reached for the metal spear. He gripped it near the center, and then as if he were hunting something, started down the right aisle, along the attic wall.

Will had been deceived by the *Fomorii*'s puppy routine. He would be sure to look closer next time. Jumping around the corner, he spied only a canyon of stacked trunks leading to a barred window. The trunks to the left jostled, which startled Will. He lifted the spear and stood stone still. He didn't even breathe. Then something moved behind the trunks to his right. He silently widened his stance and heaved the spear at the sound, even though a trunk blocked his view. The whole wall of luggage tumbled down on top of Baldwin, who began shouting. "You are a complete disaster. You have failed, William. Failed."

Will looked over the top of the trunk rubble, where

Baldwin crouched, pinned to the bottom of the wall. The spear had pierced the wide sleeve of his habit, immobilizing the vicar. Baldwin fought to loosen the spear, which had lodged nearly two feet into the wall. "I am not a *Fomorii*, William Wilder. Come remove this spear, instantly." At his feet, the silver spear he had carried earlier rolled across the floor.

"I'll be right there." Will ran to the end of his aisle. Turning the corner, he could hear Baldwin hollering and thrashing about.

From afar, Will saw two toddlers crawling slowly toward Baldwin—which made him laugh. But the vicar kicked his feet at them, anxiously yanking at the spear that still held him fast to the wall.

As Will approached, the infants faded from view and he saw them clearly for what they were: two huge grubs inching toward Baldwin. Their white translucent bodies pulsed with gray fluids and their pinchers snapped along the sides of their oval mouths.

"I thought the *Fomorii* couldn't get loose," Will whispered.

"They must have eaten through the tethers," Baldwin hissed. The grubs closed in on him. "Stop them," he pleaded. "William! Stop them."

Will ran forward and kicked each of the grubs like footballs. One exploded into a gray mist on the domed ceiling; the other hit the far wall, meeting an identical fate.

Baldwin relaxed for a moment and exhaled. "That's

sufficient training for today." He tugged at the spear, which refused to leave the wall despite his efforts. Will knelt next to him and with one hand pulled the spear from the wall, releasing the vicar's sleeve.

"Quite the sudden display of strength, William. You must be training continuously. Who is working with you?"

"Nobody," Will said, taking the wooden spear with him. He headed for the door, keeping a sharp eye on the sides of the aisle, watchful for any *Fomorii* that might leap out at him.

Baldwin clutched the metal spear on the floor and started to stand. He gripped the weapon and raised it above his shoulder, feeling its weight for a moment.

Will turned. "Could be my football workouts. I've been training with the team. I just joined. In fact, I have to go to a practice in a little bit."

Baldwin lowered the spear and nodded. "Physical discipline is necessary. It will sharpen your reflexes. Those reflexes could save your life one day. Next time we'll devise a course with that in mind, William."

Will mumbled an "okay," even though the odd look in Baldwin's eye and his steady, calm voice gave him the creeps.

"Hold on to that spear. In fact, take it. It's time you learned proper handling." His thin lips curved into a smile. "I think you'll do very well with a spear."

CHAPTER 12

THE WARNING

The sun burned Will's eyes as he ran from Peniel to meet his friends at Bub's Treats and Sweets. Exiting the main gate of the fence that surrounded the complex, he lifted a hand to fend off the sun's glare. While crossing onto Main Street at the corner, a voice called out to him.

"Will Wilder? Will?"

He squinted to make out the owner of the voice. It was a woman he had never seen before: a sturdy white-haired older lady with apple cheeks. She wore a green shawl over a simple brown dress; a beautiful golden retriever lay at her feet. The woman stood in the shade of a weeping willow.

"You *are* Will Wilder?" she asked.

"Yes." Though after what he'd just been through, he was wary of the stranger.

"Oh, I knew it." Her eyes crinkled and she smiled a satisfied smile. As she stared with a piercing glance, all the warmth and kindness she radiated turned to a sudden look of concern. She uneasily checked the faces of the people walking up the street and to her left. "I know you don't know me—which is hardly important—but I ask you to listen. There is a woman—uh, people—who mean you harm, Will."

"Do I know you, ma'am?" Will asked, trying to remember if he'd seen her before.

The woman exhaled and patted her dog's head. "That wouldn't change a thing." She shook her head from side to side as if she had made some decision. "There is a woman across the river in Wormwood who means you harm. She's a witch." She pointed toward Peniel. "A member of the community there—one of the Brethren—knows this witch. He could hurt you if you aren't careful."

"Who? How do you know the Brethren?"

She went to say something, then shook her head again and pressed on: "It's the vicar, Baldwin. Be mindful of him. He's under her control."

"A witch's control?"

"That's right."

"Where is she?" Now Will was the one looking up and down the block, searching the faces of the people swaying along the street, headphones fixed in their ears.

"She came to Perilous Falls the other day. I followed after her, but I can't say where she is now. Once she docked her boat, I lost her."

"She has a boat?"

The woman took Will by the arm. "Tell your family that you're in danger. They'll help you. It's no good keeping secrets from them. You'll live to regret those. If I've learned one thing, it's the importance of being honest with your family."

"What about the witch? Why are you telling me this?"

"Because I've seen Baldwin and the witch together—in Wormwood. Don't you worry, now, I'll find the old hag. She's here somewhere. But we must keep you safe."

The mysterious woman made Will nervous. "And why do *we* have to do that?"

"Because you're important, Will." She leaned into his ear. "I know who you are." She smelled of lavender and powder.

From across the street, Cami yelled, "William! William! We're waiting!"

Will broke away from the kindly old lady. "I've got to go. Thank you—I think."

"Remember what I said. Stay clear of Baldwin and put your family on guard. They'll protect you." She smiled wistfully after Will as she watched him cross the street.

"Who's that?" Cami asked, shooing the flies that constantly surrounded Bub's Treats and Sweets, like the sugary smell in the air.

"Some weird lady. She was warning me about Baldwin and a witch."

"Really?!" Cami looked back to the spot where the old woman had stood. She was gone.

"She's probably crazy," Will said, patting the heads of a few of the animals lining the front of Bub's. They were always hovering around the shop, drawn by the food and water put out for them. He opened the door for Cami and checked the street one last time. What he saw disquieted him. Will rushed to the metal table in the corner by the front window, where Simon and Andrew were already chomping on doughnuts and a slice of cake.

"Guys, look outside. What do you see?" Will asked in a hush.

Simon put down his fat paperback of *The Once and Future King* and his doughnut and started to giggle. "You do know you do this all the time. Don't ask us what we see. You're the one who sees what others can't. Let's just save time. What do you see?"

"All the people are in a daze. Look at them. They're lost in their own worlds," Will said.

"Aaaaand?" Cami said, taking in the zoned-out passersby.

Will could think only of the prophecy:

Their ears itch for the melodies of hell and their eyes delight in
*   dark delusions.*
Shades rise up to greet them,
And restrain them from the light.

"Well!" Simon quipped. "Snap out of it. What do you see?"

Will frowned, never taking his eyes off the citizens slowly walking down Main Street. "There are little black

demons—imps—all around them. They're following everyone on that street. It's like an invasion."

"Didn't Max mention something about 'black devils'
chasing you down, Will-man? In his dream?" Andrew added
with a full mouth.

"He did," Cami said. "Are these just like the ones you saw
at the park?"

"Identical. They also look like the one trailing Caleb in
the locker room." A look of hatred washed over Will's face.
"That kid is possessed, I'm telling you. And I'm going to
stop him today."

"Whoa, there, Dark Knight. Who made you leader of the
Justice League?" Andrew said, poking Will on the shoulder. Then he checked his watch. "If we don't head over to
practice soon, we're going to be late. But I'd lay off the ven-
geance thing."

"Might does not make right," Simon said, waving his
paperback at Will. "Just ask King Arthur."

"Caleb's not going to bully everybody—especially me.
And after what he did to Renny Bertolf and the band room,
somebody needs to smash him back."

"You were great on the field the other day, but don't get
a swelled head," Simon warned. "Just because you can run a
ball a few yards doesn't mean you can take down a guy like
Caleb."

"You don't understand, Simon," Will said, grabbing his
backpack. "I read the prophecy today and I think Caleb is
part of it. Let's go, Andrew. See you later, Cami."

Cami watched them exit and shoot past the front window. She waved her fingers at them as they passed. "I went to see Miss Lucille at Peniel this morning. Max and I saw some pretty wigged-out people on the way to his bus. There are flying books at Mr. Bonaventure's and Miss Dagon was floating in the air, totally out of it," she shared with Simon, her attention on the street. "You gotta admit, they do look zombified. Miss Lucille believes that DJ Cassian is at the center of this. She also thinks Will is in big trouble. I told her we'd keep an eye on him."

"He's acting like a real jerk," Simon said, swallowing the allergy pill he always took after eating chocolate.

"I know. But he's also our friend. Come with me to the practice."

Simon called Miss Ravinia, the waitress, over and paid the bill.

"Okay, I'll come, but if he says one more jerky thing, you're on your own," Simon huffed.

Cami smiled and thanked him. As they got up, Miss Ravinia, the portly woman with the pile of fire-engine-red hair and a lace doily atop her head, called out to them. "Would you all be sweeties and make sure you close that door right quick when you leave? One of the customers left that door open earlier and we had a dog and three cats makin' an awful ruckus in here." She turned back toward the cutout that led to the kitchen. "Took us all morning till we got 'em under control, right, Bub? Anyway, thank you, kids. Have fun out there, okay?"

Cami and Simon looked at each other for a brief second, smiled awkwardly, and bolted from the shop, closing the door firmly behind them.

On the other side of Main Street, inside the chambers of the Perilous Falls City Council, Mayor Ava Lynch was bringing the daily council meeting to a close.

Her helmet of black hair, reminiscent of a very large skunk, given the white streak running up the middle, bobbed slightly as she spoke. "Before we close out, just two quick matters of business. As some of you know, there have been a rash of graveyard robberies of late, which I find very disturbing. After consulting with our police department, we've made some most interesting discoveries." She patted a bony hand on a red folder before her.

Dan Wilder, at the end of the dais, ran a hand through his salt-and-pepper hair and stared down the table at the mayor. Her tone dripped with malice, as if she was about to deliver a lethal blow. Then it came.

"These photos show two men wandering around the cemetery." She waved several photos in each hand and passed them down the dais to the council members on her right and left. "It's just awful that people think they can disturb the dead and escape punishment. We have to make sure these two pay a hefty price."

The council members studied the photographs handed

down the row. Dan Wilder licked his lips uncomfortably when he realized that a very fuzzy Tobias Shen and Ugo Pagani were meandering among the headstones in the cemetery photos.

"Dan, sugar," the mayor sang out in her happy voice. "Do those men look at all familiar to you?"

Dan removed his glasses and shook his head. "No . . . they're . . . they're . . . out of focus. Tobi—the guys could be . . . the . . . the people in the shots are hard to make out. Do . . . do . . . you know them?"

"That is peculiar." The mayor leaned back in the leather high-backed chair, her heavily made-up eyes peering at Dan. "These two men were seen making their way to the museum—your granddaddy's museum, Dan. They could be just visitors . . . or perhaps they're employees of some kind." She dropped her voice into a low register, purring, "I wonder if your dear aunt Lucille might be able to identify these scoundrels?"

Perspiration dotted Dan's hairline. "Unlikely," he muttered, looking down.

"Weeeeeell, in any event"—the mayor theatrically threw open her hands and returned to full bellow—"if any of you know these men, or can offer any leads, I'm sure the sheriff's office would appreciate it. Oooh, one final bit of business . . ." She held a hand out to Heinrich Crinshaw, the chairman of the city council. He handed her an official-looking document, which she fluttered in one hand. "This is a project that I am more than sure you will all join me in

supporting. Bowled over by the reaction of our citizens—
particularly the ladies—to the arrival of Cassian Modo,
Heinrich and I had a notion." She kicked Crinshaw under
the table, inspiring him to nod enthusiastically.

"So many seem captivated by Cassian's music, we
thought, wouldn't it be clever if we used that music to draw
patrons to Main Street? He's like the Pied Piper of Perilous Falls," she said, laughing. Only Dan did not return the
laugh.

"Earlier today, we secured agreements from almost
every shop and store on Main Street to install speakers outside their places of business. And Mr. Modo has agreed, at
no cost to the city, to allow us to exclusively play his music
throughout the day and early evening up and down Main
Street. By our calculations, this could draw forty to fifty
percent more young shoppers to the businesses on Main
Street—shoppers that spend big dollars. We only need to
approve the cost to install the speakers, a mere twenty
thousand dollars." Once again, the mayor kicked Heinrich
Crinshaw's ankle beneath the table.

"Uh, let's call the vote," Crinshaw said, stroking his
pencil-thin mustache, gavel in hand. After a quick show of
hands and a sputtering objection from Dan Wilder, the city
council voted five to one to approve the speaker installation.

"How wonderful," Mayor Lynch said, sliding the document into the folder before her. "Perilous Falls is so pleased
to have DJ Cassian as our official musician. Close the
meeting out," she whispered to Crinshaw under her breath.

He did as commanded, and the council members began to disperse.

Mayor Lynch walked toward Dan Wilder's chair at the far end of the dais. He rose as she approached. "Ava, can't the businesses on Main Street install their own speakers and decide what music their customers want to hear? Why are we giving special treatment to this DJ? Do we know anything about this Cassian? The people at his concert were acting . . . very strange."

"All I know is the young people and many others seem captivated by him. Your wife even did a flattering piece about Cassian the other night on TV. We have plenty of money in the discretionary fund for the speakers. That's good enough for me."

"Well, it might not be good for the city. Why not play other music on these public speakers?"

"Oh, Dan"—she struck his arm lightly with the folder— "we have to give the people what they want, not what we want, honey."

"Now you're a music expert. You should go run a radio station or buy a record company, Ava."

"That is a right fine idea, Dan." She began to step off the dais and then turned back to him. "I didn't want to mention it in front of the whole council, but I have authorized an independent investigation of the destruction of our jailhouse and the Karnak Center. Terrible the way they both burned."

"Half the city nearly burned. There was fiery hail falling from the—"

"Oh, I know. I was there. But idn't it odd that your aunt Lucille was in the jailhouse as it burned to the ground, yet she escaped. Then she's over at the Karnak Center, and it burned to the ground. That's my property, Dan. You'll remember that I allowed Pothinus Sab to build that eyesore on my land." The mayor raised one carefully drawn eyebrow, awaiting an answer.

"I hope you're not trying to pin those fires on Lucille." He leaned in to the mayor's face, his voice shaky. "She told me you and Sab tried to kill her in the jail that night. You forgot that detail, Ava."

The mayor's mouth flattened along with her eyes. "She's out of her mind and Pothinus Sab is dead and gone."

"My aunt said there was a deputy on guard that night. I wonder if he saw anything?"

The mayor shook her head sadly, filled with sympathy. "Oh, that poor, poor man. Deputy Stevens, I think his name was. He went across the river on some investigation and just disappeared. They haven't found hide nor hair of him since a few days after the fire. Ask your friend Sheriff Stout. He'll tell you."

Dan, lost in his imaginings of the deputy's fate, couldn't think of a response.

"Tell Lucille to keep herself available," the mayor said with a threatening edge. "Where is dear, old Lucille anyway?"

CHAPTER 13

DIS

"It's like another world up here. This I didn't expect," Lucille said, gazing at the evenly spaced palm trees and lush manicured lawns blurring past the car window. It was a jarring scene given what they had just witnessed on the way up the mountain. Brother Philip, the community gadget master and former spy, drove Lucille about an hour outside of Perilous Falls to the exclusive town of Dis. Once they started up the twisting mountain, a barren landscape of rock and bramble surrounded them, until they reached Dis.

"Why are you surprised? The Modo family owns casinos and resorts in four states. Pretty lawns are their specialty," Brother Philip said out of the side of his mouth. "It's what they do on the other side of the landscaping that bothers me," he said conspiratorially.

They pulled through an open gate with the word MODO

emblazoned in gold on the archway overhead. An immense white structure with marbled columns, hundreds of windows, and glittering golden balconies rose up before them. Lagoons with dancing fountains and sculpted topiaries fanned out around the mansion. A team of uniformed gardeners tended to the flower beds while young women sunned themselves in the lagoons on either side of the main entrance.

"I hope I don't offend, and I'm not complaining, but does anything strike you as odd?" Brother Philip turned a squinty eye on Lucille and then looked out the window.

"No men," Lucille said, yanking at the silk collar of her jacket. "Ever since we pulled onto the Modo property: the guards, the groundskeepers, the sunbathers—all women. Every one of them." She faced Brother Philip. "Cassian has some unusual power over women."

"Do you want me to come in with you?" Philip said as they pulled to the front of the residence. "He won't have any unusual power over me, I can promise you that."

"No, no, I'll be fine. The prophecy said something about the demon Asmodeus: 'It will bewitch innocent maidens and devour those they love.'"

"Maybe we should come back with the abbot, Brother James, or another exorcist."

"We're here. I have to see what we're dealing with. I can't shake the feeling that I've met this Cassian before." Lucille looked at her hands, which were trembling slightly.

"How would you have known him?"

"He's a dead ringer for Cosmo Doheney, a boy I dated back when we lost Father and . . ."

Brother Philip looked past Lucille, out the driver's side window. "Will you look at these two." A pair of statuesque women in gray uniforms, who could have been twins, exited the residence and approached the car.

Lucille eyed the two women. "I can handle this. If I'm not back in a half hour, come and get me." Lucille threw open the car door and sauntered up the glittering walkway toward the open front door like she owned the place. "Hello, ladies. I've come to see Cassian. Can you tell him Lucille Wilder is here."

The two women looked at each other without expression, turned toward the house, and reentered. Lucille stepped lively after them. Philip waited until Lucille was inside before peeling out in the driveway and racing away.

"Okay, gentlemen. I want to run pass formations. Caleb and"—Coach Runyon glanced at his clipboard—"Will. You'll rotate as quarterback. The rest of you, line up. I want to see everyone run the formations as we call them out."

Caleb was first up. He threw the ball to his teammates as they serpentined and crisscrossed midfield or ran deep into the back field. All but two of the passes were completions. Then Will stepped in.

The coach barked out a number. Vance Bonneux, a tall

boy with a crew cut that Will knew a bit, ran to the middle of the field. He cut hard to his left and opened his arms to receive Will's pass. Vance leapt to catch it. The ball came in so hard, it threw Vance to the ground as if he had just intercepted an asteroid.

"Why don't you throw the ball a little harder next time, Wilder?" Vance yelled, brushing the dirt off his arms.

Will ignored the comment, set his legs, and prepared to throw another ball. "Twenty-seven!" the coach hollered. Todd Ferguson, a tank of a kid, built to be a linebacker, blundered out onto the field. He took three steps, turned, and met Will's ball. It hit him squarely in the helmet, knocking him over.

"Caleb, you'd better get back in there," Coach Runyon said quietly from the sideline. "You're throwing missiles, son. Now we have to work on targeting them," he yelled to Will, motioning for him to come to the sideline.

Caleb reattached his helmet and kicked the bench where Harlan and Boyd were sitting. "Where did string bean get an arm like that? You know what it takes to knock a guy like Todd over." Will gently lobbed the football to Caleb as he came off the field. "What are you up to, Wilder? How do you throw like that?"

"Focus," Will said, not stopping.

Later in the practice, during their water break, the coach questioned the team about the "vandalism" in the band room. He removed his hat and got very serious. "It happened after our practice the other day when most of us were gone. But if you all have any knowledge about who busted out the back wall of the band room and destroyed one of the trophy cases, I need to know, gentlemen. We can't have this at Perilous Falls Middle."

Will stared at Caleb. He thought for a moment about telling the coach what he knew: how Caleb had rushed in, hit Renny, then punched a hole in the back wall of the band room. He even started to raise a hand to get the coach's attention. Then he thought: *I'd better handle this myself or bring the Brethren in—especially if he's possessed or a demon.*

Caleb stared at Will with pure disgust until the coach called the team to line up. Coach Runyon separated the players into specialties. Specific drills started all over the field.

"Wilder, come here for a minute," the coach bellowed. "Have you ever kicked before, son?"

"Not really," said Will.

"I want to see what you can do." The coach handed him a football and asked Sami Korah, the team's best kicker, to demonstrate a proper kickoff. Sami's ball landed squarely in the end zone. Will then carried his ball to the center of the green. He jogged for a couple of steps, dropped the ball onto his foot, and kicked it hard. It hurtled forward faster than he thought possible. The ball pinged one of the goalposts, bending it back upon impact. It then sailed into an aluminum storage shed, embedding itself in the indented wall.

The coach puffed up his cheeks and ran out to Will. "I've never . . ." He shook his head, laughing. "You've got a leg on you, I'll give you that. But I don't think we have enough goalposts for you to be our kicker. You'd better stick to receiving."

In the stands, Simon watched wide-eyed with amazement. "Did you see what he did to that shed? Look how he smashed in the wall," he screeched at Cami in his high nasal tone.

"He's not that strong, Simon," Cami said, leaning forward in the bleachers. "What do you think he's doing? Is it the training or a relic?"

"I have no idea."

"I don't like the way he's strutting around," Cami said, watching Will stick his chest out along the sideline. "That's so unlike Will."

"Let's talk to him after practice and see if he'll tell us anything."

Cami quickly spotted the explanation for the strutting. She spied a few cheerleaders from another school sitting in the bleachers near the sidelines. Will gave one of them a chin wave—the kind of thing guys who are too cool to actually wave with their hands do to acknowledge other human beings. "What has gotten into Will?" Cami asked, folding her arms. Several ideas came to mind.

In her march down the main hall of Cassian's residence, Lucille passed ornate rooms filled with pool tables, slot machines, and all manner of entertainments. Poker games were in full swing in one room. What appeared to be a dance club occupied another. There were two constants in every room she passed: no men and the incessant, pulsating beat of Cassian's strange melodic music. The whole place made her want to run. But she was determined to see Cassian in person and confirm or dispel her suspicions.

The two tall, uniformed women entered a twelve-foot double door at the end of the hallway, shutting it behind them. The gold MODO emblazoned across the surface of the two doors left no doubt as to who was within. After several seconds, one of the women emerged. "Miss Wilder, Cassian will see you now."

They ushered her into a bloodred room with heavy velvet curtains and wall-to-wall carpeting. Slick black couches, tables, and chairs filled the enormous space. Smack in the center of the room, with one of his bare feet resting atop a black lacquer desk, was Cassian. A woman massaged his shoulders while others lounged on the furniture throughout the room.

"Lucille Wilder. I don't believe we've met," Cassian said, sitting up and waving away the woman behind him.

"No? You're very familiar to me, Mr. Modo."

The DJ cinched his black floor-length silk robe over his chest and rose to his full height. "Cassian, please. Call me Cassian—I am humbled that you are 'familiar' with my music." He adjusted the brown sunglasses he wore and tied his long ponytail into a man bun. He limped as he approached.

"I've never listened to your music. Yet so many things about you are familiar, Mr. Modo." Lucille lifted her chin slightly and put her hands on her hips. "I once knew a young man. You remind me of him."

"Really? Was he handsome too? You should give my music a chance." Cassian's voice was like velvet—smooth and low. He tightened the belt of the robe and flashed a smile at her. Casually flipping his hands at his waist, all the women in the room began to rise and headed for the doors like trained pets. The sudden commotion disquieted Lucille.

"The beat is probably throwing you off," Cassian said, walking to a table near Lucille. She noticed that there was a collection of black onyx bull and ram figurines on the table. In the midst of them sat a weathered black-and-gold box. "The kids enjoy the beat. But it's unimportant, really. Melody is the thing that touches us. Melody is timeless. Don't you agree, Lucille?" He tilted his head and laid a hand on the large box. "Open it. Go on." He was playful, tapping his fingers on the lid. "Are you afraid, Lucille?"

She felt a chill. *That's exactly what Cosmo used to say: "Are you afraid, Lucille?"* She studied his face. He even smiled like Cosmo. The way he tilted his head, the earnest, boyish pleading . . .

"Well, ARE you afraid, Lucille?"

She defiantly flipped open the box's lid just to spite him. Soft, jangling music poured from the box, filling the room. It *was* Cosmo's tune! The same tune he would whistle or hum when they were together. She wanted to cry—and laugh. How often he sang that song on one of their long drives and even the last time she saw him.

"I knew if you gave the music a chance, you'd enjoy it." Cassian smiled, bobbing his head in time with the gentle melody. "Music is powerful. It can take us wherever we want to go and bring us the things we most desire."

"Where did you get that tune? That song?" Lucille was stone serious, a tremor in her voice. "Are you Cosmo Doheney? *Are* you?"

"I don't know who you're talking about."

"Cosmo was a boy I was very close to. The night my mother and father died, he picked me up for dinner. We were eating and laughing . . . During dinner he hummed that song. He was always humming that song."

"So you like it? I can tell you do." He laughed and spun around, almost dancing to the slow waltz.

"Where did you get that music box?"

"I don't know any Cosmo . . . whoever he is."

"Oh yes you do." She pursued him. "You move like him. You smile like him. And you are playing HIS song—selling it, recording it, spreading it. Either this is some grand trick or you are Cosmo Doheney." She got in his face. "Why have you come back?"

"Back? Easy, Lucille. Have a seat."

"I don't want to sit." She pushed her sleeves up her forearms.

He began humming the song from the music box.

"Please don't do that," Lucille said, shaking.

"I can't hum my own songs?" He gently opened his big hands. "Calm down. I've heard that song since I was a kid. The box has been in my family for generations."

"Take off your glasses. I want to see your eyes."

Cassian smirked. "All the girls want to see my eyes. A fellow has to retain a little mystery."

"You're a man of mystery all right, Mr. Modo. Please do me the favor of removing your glasses. Then I'll go," Lucille said, staring holes into him.

He slowly pulled the glasses down the bridge of his thin nose. "Are you satisfied now?" One steel-blue eye met her stare; the other, dull and hazel, drifted off to the left. "I told you I wasn't your man."

He was right; his eyes were nothing like Cosmo's. Maybe the song was a coincidence, but his fluid hand movements, his world-weary smirk, the way he tipped his head to the side were so like Cosmo. She could almost smell the musky fragrance of Cosmo's aftershave. There was something sweet about Cassian. He had a kindness about him that she thought . . .

In a sudden movement, Lucille slammed the music box shut to stop the music. She closed her eyes for a moment and whispered a few words of Latin to herself.

"What are you saying, Lucille?" Cassian asked, getting close to her.

"I'm very sorry to have troubled you, Mr. Modo."

"Well, you can't go now." Cassian laughed, pushing his sunglasses back into place. "Stay for a drink or maybe a round of poker?"

"I have to be going." Lucille stomped deliberately to the door.

"Would you like a CD? Or an album?" He held up one of each.

"No thank you, Mr. Modo. I've heard your tune before. I don't like how it ends."

She ripped open one of the double doors and walked out into the hall.

"La-dee-dah-dee-dee-dahhhh." Cassian sang the haunting tune from the music box at the top of his voice.

For a moment Lucille stopped walking. She turned back to see a parade of young women returning to the office, squeezing past a smiling Cassian. Once all the women were behind him, he clutched the knobs of the double doors and started to close them.

Leaning his body into the hall, tilting his head, in a stage whisper, he asked, "What are you afraid of, Lucille?" Before she could answer, he slammed the door shut and continued to sing the muffled melody to the women within.

THE AMBUSH

While he changed, Will could hear Caleb and his pals talking about him on the other side of the lockers. Much of it was hard to make out. Caleb angrily vented to his teammates in a harsh whisper about that "little runt Will." He called one of the boys "chicken" and then said something like "he might be able to take one of us down, but he can't take us all down." By the time Caleb mentioned "pounding him to teach him a lesson," Will had heard enough.

He wanted out of there as quickly as possible, so he ran out the side locker room exit without even telling Andrew goodbye. He could handle these guys individually on the field, but maybe Caleb had a point. Will wasn't sure how he would hold up against a squad of these big guys. He definitely wasn't looking for a fight. He just wanted to get home in one piece.

It was getting dark and the cool fall breeze moved with him as he walked along Main Street. He made it as far as Perilous Falls Elementary when he heard the sound of running feet behind him. In the lamplight he saw Caleb, Harlan, Boyd, and Todd racing his way.

He crossed Falls Road and ran into the shadowy cover of the Perilous Falls Elementary School playground. He had played there since he was a kid and knew it like his own backyard. Will ran up a slide and sheltered inside a playhouse at the top. He crouched there, quietly watching the guys on the street through a rounded opening.

Caleb motioned to the boys at his side, pointing toward the playground. They checked around the school building, among the stacked planks near a half-constructed fence, and then they surveyed the yard before moving near the play set.

"Where did he go?" Caleb asked his posse.

"Dunno," Harlan said, looking back at the street.

"Will! You here, Will?" Caleb shouted. "You scared now? We just want to talk, big man. Just want to get to know our new teammate a little better."

Two of the boys sniggered at that.

Will didn't move a muscle.

"Fan out, guys," Caleb whispered, huddling with his crew. "You go there. You check along the fence. I'll look over here. First one who sees him, holler. Then we pound him." The three boys nodded and spread out. Caleb walked around the play set, thinking Will might be hiding in the rear.

Will's nose started to itch. He snatched a look out of the plastic portal on the playhouse. Caleb stood nearby. The other three boys were out in the yard. Waiting was not an option. Better to face them one at a time than as a pack. Will jumped down from the play set right behind Caleb.

"You plan on doing to me what you did to Renny Bertolf?" Will asked, assuming a fighting posture.

"I never touched that kid. Hey, guys, he's over here," Caleb yelled. Without waiting for his friends, Caleb lunged at Will with everything he had. Despite the incredible force coming at him, the smaller boy didn't move an inch. It was as if Caleb had tried to push a house down.

Stunned, Caleb backed up and stared at Will, his mouth agape. Before he could formulate a sentence, Will grabbed him by the shirt and shoved him up the slide, cramming him into the playhouse.

By the time Will had finished, Harlan and Boyd were almost on top of him. He jumped down and planted his feet at the bottom of the slide. His attackers rushed him simultaneously. Using their shoulders to propel himself upward, Will leapfrogged over the players. They smashed, headfirst, into the slide and into each other. Will pushed the two disoriented boys up the slide as well, throwing them against Caleb in the playhouse.

Only Todd Ferguson remained in the yard. He was so big, it took him a few extra minutes to reach Will. But once he heard the other boys groaning inside the play set, he stopped short. "No hard feelings, Will," Todd said, backing away. "I always liked you. Caleb wanted to do this, not me. I can go now, okay?"

Will took two steps in Todd's direction and the hefty boy hightailed it all the way to the street. Caleb stuck his head from the opening at the top of the slide.

"Oh no you don't," Will crowed, running up the slide and pushing Caleb back into his two friends.

Thinking fast, he jumped off the slide and unlatched a couple of swings from the other end of the play set. He then collected a few fence planks. Jamming the planks over the two openings in the playhouse, he trapped the boys inside the plastic cubicle. To make sure they weren't going anywhere soon, he circled the entire structure with the swing chains, moving like a dervish. Knotting the chains, he yanked at them until the links began to fuse to one another. The boys beat on the planks, trying to get out of the improvised prison.

"Be quiet. Don't test me, guys," Will said, smacking the edge of the playhouse. He straightened his pith helmet and headed toward the street, fist punching the air cockily.

Behind a tree on Falls Road, Cami and Simon couldn't believe what they had witnessed. "We've got to ask him what's going on. This is ridiculous," Simon hissed. "He rounded those guys up like a bounty hunter. I'm going to—"

But as Simon went to leave their hiding spot, Cami yanked him back, pulling him to the ground. "Not yet," she said. "I want to see this. Black-haired cheerleader at nine o'clock." Sure enough, Lilith Lorcan walked into the school-yard in her red-and-black cheer uniform. She too had been watching Will's amazing display from afar.

"Impressive," she said. "I watched the whole thing from over there by the school entrance."

"You did?" Will swallowed.

"I sure did." She batted her long lashes and squeezed his arm. "You're really strong."

Will could say nothing.

"Can I ask you a favor?" She parted her long hair so he could see her green eyes. "Promise you'll tell me the truth?"

Will nodded. "Uh-huh."

"How did you get so strong?" She looked from side to side. "You can tell me. Whisper it if you want." She moved her ear inches from his mouth.

Will laid his hand over the amulet beneath his shirt. "Just a lot of working out, I guess," he said, louder than expected.

"It's gotta be something more than that. Every guy on that field—and those guys in the playhouse—works out. You're stronger than all of them. What is it? Can't you tell me?"

Will shrugged. "Focus. Mental focus, I guess."

"Let me ask you another way: Can anything stop you?"

Will began to giggle. "Well, I mean—if somebody threw chains on me, that would probably stop me, but I don't know. . . ."

Lilith turned to check on her three friends standing at

the bus stop up the street. "I'd better go join my girlfriends. Bus'll be here any minute."

"Sure. Yeah. I have to get home too." Will pointed lamely behind him with his thumbs.

Lilith gently pulled at one of the curls poking from beneath his pith helmet. "You're full of surprises, Will Wilder. Did anyone ever tell you that?"

"Not that I can . . . I don't . . . no."

From behind the tree across the street, Simon held Cami by the arm to keep her from running out. He placed a straight finger over his mouth to encourage her to keep quiet.

Just then a bus rumbled up Main Street. "Will I see you after the game on Friday? We're playing you all and, um, maybe we can get a milkshake or something afterward? At Bub's?"

"Sure thing," Will said, shoving his hands in his pockets.

Lilith sashayed away slowly and without turning back said, "Maybe you'll be ready to share your secret then." When she reached the bus, she spun around and shot Will a smile that made his knees buckle. He waved at her like a little kid, savoring every glimpse of her through the bus window until it pulled away. Once it was gone, he practically skipped home, punching at the air as if he had just won the Super Bowl.

Cami and Simon remained in hiding, even as Will passed just a few feet from them. "I don't like that girl," Cami said once Will was out of earshot.

"She seems to like Will," Simon said. "She's appealing. Kind of old, but appealing."

Cami swatted him on the shoulder. "You're no help at all. Something about her I don't like. She's sneaky. Let's go to my house. I'll have my father drive you home." Cami lived across the street from Perilous Falls Elementary. But with her various complaints about "that girl from Sorec," even the short walk was not a happy one for Simon.

The Wilder home was usually alive at dinnertime with the sounds of Will's brother and sister bickering, his mom trying to restore order, and his dad reading out news from his cell phone. But when Will walked in the house this night, there was only music playing. He ventured into the kitchen to find his mother listlessly putting food away. "Oh, hi, Will," she said with no enthusiasm. "Your food's there." She pointed to the tin foil wrapped plate. "We already ate."

Cassian's music filled the kitchen.

"Where is everybody?" Will asked, surprised by the empty room.

"I don't *know*, Will. I don't know where everyone is. I just cooked a meal, edited three pieces today, helped two children with their homework, and am now cleaning up dinner. Forgive me if I don't know the whereabouts of every member of the family," Deborah fumed.

"It's okay. I was just wondering."

"Wonder somewhere else. I need a moment of quiet here. Okay?" She turned up the Cassian melody. His ears actually hurt from the loud drumbeat.

Will threw his bag in the foyer and went upstairs. His brother Leo's head appeared in the narrow opening of his bedroom door. "Come in here," he said.

When Will entered the room, he found Marin doing cartwheels near the window. Leo closed the door and flopped onto his bed. "I have a question: What is up with Mom? She's been biting our heads off all afternoon."

"She made me do all my homework for tonight—and tomorrow," Marin groused, waving her small hands in the air. "She didn't even give me a snack when I got home."

"Okay, Marin. Go back to flipping," Leo said, looking over the lenses of his wire-frame glasses. "Seriously, what happened to our mom? And how do we get her back?"

"I think it has something to do with that music she's playing." Will took off his pith helmet and sat on the bed. "The whole town is acting crazy. That guy Cassian's music is weird. And there are imps, little black devils, running all over Perilous Falls. I saw them."

"So what should we do?" Marin lisped.

"I'm going to call Aunt Lucille." Will got up to leave. "Where's Dad?"

"He was in the kitchen with Mom, but after she screamed at him for the twelve-thousandth time, he got real quiet and went into the garage."

"You better go check on him," said Marin.

Will took up his pith helmet. "Do you guys want to come?"

"Nope-see," Marin said, her eyes wide with mock fear.

"Why do you think we're up here? Mom'll scream at us if we go downstairs. She's very grumpy." Leo pushed Will into the hall. "You're on your own," Leo said before swiftly shutting the door.

Will pulled out his cell phone and called Aunt Lucille. "Do you have a minute?" he asked her. "A lady came up to me today. It was very strange." He described what she looked like and told Aunt Lucille about the dog. "She said that Baldwin might harm me and that he was under the control of some witch. . . . Yeah, a witch, from across the river in Wormwood . . . No, I've never seen her before. . . . She was real insistent that I tell my family, so you all could 'be on guard.'"

"Whoever she is, the advice sounds wise, dear. When you come on Thursday, go to your training per usual. We'll be watching to make sure Baldwin is on his best behavior." Aunt Lucille alluded to her "odd encounter" that day with Cassian and promised to share more when they saw each other on Thursday. He agreed to see her then, quickly informed her of his mother's continuing behavior, hung up, and headed to the garage.

The repetitive melody was still playing in the kitchen.

Cracking open the garage door, Will could hardly believe what he walked in on. His father somersaulted forward across the length of the pristine garage. When he landed

on two feet, Dan pushed his two hands together, extend-
ing his palms forward. He stopped just inches from Will's
face.

"Son!" Dan Wilder assumed his normal ram-rod posture
and brushed his hands on his thighs, as if he'd been caught
dancing an illegal ballet.

"What are you doing?" Will asked.

"I . . . was . . . uh . . . working out. Some calisthenics. You
know."

"Looks very familiar," Will said. "I mean the flips and all.
Aunt Lucille showed me some moves like that. . . ."

Dan wiped the sweat from his brow and ignored the ob-
servation. "You need a haircut, Will. Have you seen your
mother?"

"I saw her."

"She's in some kind of . . . phase. I hope she's okay."

"Dad, it's not a phase. Look around. The whole town is
freaking out. Have you seen the people downtown?"

"Are they acting odd?"

"They're all acting like Mom! We have to help her—
and them. It's the music." Will pointed toward the house.
"There's something going on with that music."

"She has been listening to it a lot." Dan nervously stroked
the hair on the side of his head as he recalled Mayor Lynch's
plan to broadcast Cassian's music all over downtown.

"Why were you doing those flips?" Will said suddenly.
"I've never seen you move like that before."

Dan folded his arms. "I guess I'm worried. When you're

worried, you revert to the things you know. When I do that routine, I feel more in control—"

"Are you training for something?"

"Training? You mean for a marathon or something?" Dan definitively shook his head, walking toward the house. "No."

Will carefully watched his father's hasty retreat into the mudroom. "Whatever you say, Dad."

Before he turned the lights down in the garage, Will noticed that there were four toppled old barstools on the edges of the garage. One drew his attention. It had a perfect circular burn mark on the seat back. The spot of wood had turned ashen and was still smoking. *What was he doing out here?* Will wondered, standing the stool upright.

CHAPTER 15

THE BARREL BATTLE

The next day, Wednesday, Will dazzled on the practice field. He caught repeated passes and ran the plays with ease. Some of his teammates were so accustomed to getting knocked over by him during practice that they now just stepped aside, letting him pass unopposed whenever he came their way. Why add to their bruise collection?

With bad memories of the confrontation at the Perilous Falls Elementary play set, Caleb and his crew kept their distance. They grumbled to themselves that day but never approached Will. They were all too embarrassed to tell anyone what had actually happened or to explain how it took them a half hour to break out of the play set. After practice, Will and Andrew walked home without incident.

At home, Deb Wilder's general hostility toward her family increased. Each time Will's father attempted to lower or stop the steady flow of Cassian's music, a loud argument broke out. She refused to make dinner that night and Dan Wilder had to bring in bags of Ground Deliciousness Burgers for the children. He also spent his second night on the couch in the family room.

Peniel was all but empty Thursday afternoon when Lucille Wilder stepped out of the door marked PRIVATE on the back end of Bethel Hall. "Bart," she called over to her friend, who was slipping a typed card into an empty display case. "Let me know when Will arrives for his training. I neglected to share a conversation he had with me the other day. I want to make sure the abbot and I—"

"He's been here awhile," Bartimaeus said, locking the case.

"Will?"

"Yeah, Will. You just asked me to let you know when Will arrives for his lesson? Well, he got here about fifteen minutes ago. Now you know."

Panic washed over her face. "Where? Where is he now?"

"With Baldwin at his Defense Training. I think they went down to the cellar."

"The cellar!" She started running down the broad hallway. "Call the abbot and tell him to meet me there right away. He knows all about it. Right away."

"You knew he was coming today. We're supposed to go

to Monte Cassino later, remember?" Bartimaeus yelled after her. He walked over to the information kiosk and reached for the phone. Waiting for the abbot to pick up his call, he muttered to himself: "Asks me where the boy is, then I tell her and she runs off in a huff. Don't know why she's all excitable lately. One minute she's chasing after that 'Music Man'; next we're supposed to sound the alarm because Will walks through the door. Life's too short for this. . . ."

Ten spears stood at attention, side by side, near the middle of the rough-stoned cellar. Baldwin had placed them in holes cut into the floor. The wide cavern, deep in the recesses of Peniel's east wing, was hardly ever used. The barrels of wine along the walls had been emptied long ago. Jacob Wilder once used it as a training space.

Barrels hung from ropes and pulleys high above the ground. Against the rear wall, what appeared to be a hundred niches were filled with badly damaged barrels. They had holes all over them.

"William, this training should increase your agility and speed, if executed properly," Baldwin said, using a shimmering steel spear as a pointer. "When the *Darkness* deploys their black arts, they do so with great force and suddenness. This 'sequence'—your great-grandfather always called it a 'sequence'—will test your reflexes and challenge your ability to fight off multiple attacks at the same moment."

Will glanced up at the barrels in the niches with some anxiety. "How does this work exactly?"

Baldwin strode into the dead center of the room. "I trigger the pulley system." He indicated a brass hand wheel on the wall. "That will release the barrels. They'll come hurtling at you, unexpectedly from a variety of angles." Baldwin pointed behind him, to the rear wall. "I will be there throughout the exercise." He pulled one of the wooden spears from the floor and tossed it sideways at Will, who caught it clumsily. "You will defend yourself by throwing one spear at each barrel before it reaches you. The moment the spear strikes a barrel, it will fly up to the rafters. Ten spears. Ten barrels. It's a very simple exercise."

"And what if I miss a barrel?"

"It would likely pummel you. But, as I said, I will be posted behind you, there. If you're moving too slowly, I'll simply spear the barrel for you." Baldwin smiled supportively. "What is that phrase you young people use: I'll 'have your back,' William."

Will could feel his palms sweating. He kept thinking of the strange old woman on the street who warned him that Baldwin was under the control of a witch and meant him harm.

"Why don't we wait and do this with Aunt Lucille. She's really good at throwing spears and I'll bet she could give me some tips—"

"The *Darkness* will not wait and neither can we." Baldwin turned the wheel on the wall. "The sequence is beginning. Look sharp." He ran behind Will, steel spear at the ready.

Three barrels flew out of the niches on the back wall and sped toward him. Baldwin was right, they did come at unexpected angles. Will felt the talisman under his shirt, which gave him a bit of confidence. He chucked the spear at the nearest barrel. When it made contact, the barrel popped off the rope and shattered against the wall. With lightning speed, he made short shrift of the other two barrels, striking each one with the precision of a marksman. Four barrels peeled off the wall next.

As he reached for two more spears, Will looked back at Baldwin. The vicar was stone-faced, white-knuckling his steel spear.

Will discharged four spears, each hitting their targets. Splinters of wood showered down onto the cellar floor. The last three barrels flew at him now. He grabbed two more spears and readied his arm for the release.

Baldwin shook, a pained look on his face, his spear still firmly in hand.

Will exploded two of the barrels in seconds and awaited the approach of the last.

Shutting one eye, Baldwin threw his steel spear with all the force he possessed.

"You've got to admit, Vicar, for my first time, I'm doing pretty good." Will turned just in time to see the point of the steel spear closing in on him.

"*Will!*" Aunt Lucille yelled from a niche overhead.

From a dark opening on the side of the cellar, the abbot dove at Will in an attempt to knock him from the oncoming spear's path. But he was too late.

The steel point hit Will on the side of his chest. He stumbled back a few steps, then looked down in amazement. The spear lay at his feet, its tip crumpled. It had ripped his shirt, but aside from a faint bruise caused no other damage.

"Baldwin, what have you done?" the abbot asked.

"I was . . . training the boy. I thought the last barrel was going to injure him and I must have misjudged—"

"You didn't misjudge anything. Your aim was accurate. You meant to hit Will and you did," the abbot said, with some sadness.

"I saw the whole thing," Aunt Lucille said, appearing from a staircase on the other side of the cellar. She raced to Will and checked his chest. She too was astonished that he had not been injured and puzzled over the mangled spear on the floor. "Thank goodness you're all right, dear." She patted his chest and felt the metal locket beneath his shirt. It all suddenly made sense to her. Folding her arms, she trained her blue eyes on his. "We need to have a conversation, young man."

"I thought you'd say that," Will guiltily whispered.

The abbot took Baldwin by the arms and studied the big man's eyes. "Why would you target the chosen one? Who have you been with, Baldwin? There are rumors that you have been frequenting Wormwood. Is that true?"

The vicar opened his mouth and then closed it. He lowered his head and looked as if he were about to cry. "I've made just two trips there—only two, Athanasius. They were moments of weakness and—"

"You have seen the witch, then?"

"I have."

"What did she promise you?"

"Nothing. Nothing at all."

"Oh, Baldwin. She always promises something. It's how the *Darkness* operates: grand promises—miserable, empty outcomes. Tobias, Pedro," he yelled out. "Please escort the vicar to his cell. She has a hold on you, Baldwin. I can see it. Perhaps with candor and grace we can loosen her grip."

Tobias and Pedro, the muscular brother with the build and talents of a gymnast, stepped from the main entryway to the cellar. They stood on either side of the vicar. Baldwin avoided looking at either Lucille or Will, and belligerently walked ahead of the others.

Aunt Lucille urgently invited Will and the abbot to her office. Once there, she went straight to the case in the corner. There was nothing beneath the glass. "As I suspected," she said almost to herself. She turned to Will. "At least we now know which 'Amulet of Power' the prophecy was referencing."

"I was going to tell you—you all have been wanting me to work with relics. So I thought this would be a good one to start with." He pulled the amulet from inside his shirt and started to remove it.

"Uh-uh." Aunt Lucille shook her head. "I had thought of taking it from you downstairs, but it may be offering you some protection."

"The *Darkness* is already aware that he has used the relic of Samson. It will do no good to deprive him of its power now," the abbot said, sinking into one of the high-backed leather chairs near the desk. His long forehead was knotted with worry. "You must be very disciplined in the way you use the relic, Will. It is fine for defense or for the protection of others. But it mustn't be used for selfish ends or to feed your vanity. Remember, even with all his power, Samson was deceived and ultimately blinded by his selfishness."

"I am going to use the amulet to help people," Will protested. "There's a friend of mine who has been beaten up by this guy at school—and you can't see the imps running all over—"

"We're on the same wavelength, Abbot," Lucille said, disregarding Will. She removed a key from the top drawer of the desk and approached a slight metal door built into the wall. "I want to show you something, Will, and get your reaction."

She opened the metal door, revealing a storeroom of oddities. A gray hand on a table, a stuffed cat, bizarre weapons the likes of which Will had never seen. "Come here," Aunt Lucille instructed. "Do you see that mirror there?" It was a gold-framed, floor-to-ceiling mirror, half draped by a black cloth. "Look into it and tell me what you see."

Will cautiously approached the glass. He stared hard

into the dull reflection. It was cloudy and dark. "I just see my face. You know, me."

The abbot and Lucille stood in the doorway of the little room. "Nothing else?" the abbot asked.

"Nope." Will turned his head to the left, admiring this thick neck and slightly wider shoulders. "Just me." He flexed his muscles, smirking.

"Take him out of there, before we lose him to the glass," the abbot spat out, stepping away from the door.

Aunt Lucille ushered Will from the storage room and, once they were both out, locked the heavy metal door behind them. "Your vision is very dim, dear. You should have seen tormented spirits in the mirror. My father always did. He would use it from time to time to test his vision. We keep it locked away because the mirror is a portal, once used by wicked people to communicate with demons. They should have been obvious to you—to any *Seer*." She folded her arms and bit her lower lip, looking to the abbot for assistance.

"Describe exactly what you saw in the mirror, Will," Athanasius said.

Will half smiled. "Just a really handsome, buff guy."

"Illusion is the first of all pleasures, and the most ruinous," Athanasius said, stroking his beard with two hands. "Your vision is compromised and we are all weaker for it. Listen to me. This Asmodeus is prowling about, looking to destroy us—and you. I can appreciate your youth, but you are so wrapped up in yourself, you can't see anything else—"

Will tried to interrupt. But the abbot spoke over him. "This is not about you, boy. Don't ruin the gift you've been given by thinking it exists to serve you. It doesn't. Our gifts belong to others—we serve them—and the One who granted the gift."

"Should he still go to Monte Cassino with Bartimaeus?" Aunt Lucille asked as if Will weren't there.

"Without a doubt. Jacob's notebooks may provide us with a way to restrain this demon and Will could learn a thing or two from Abbot Gamaliel." Athanasius looked directly at Will, half smiling.

"Who is Abbot Gam-hay-leel?" Will asked.

"A very old master. Strengthening your sight alone would make the trip worthwhile. Go to the sarcophagus in the main hall of the north tower. The one near the stained glass window. I'll fetch Bartimaeus and meet you there."

Will whispered to his Aunt Lucille, "How long will it take to get to Monte Cassino and back?"

"As long as it takes, dear." She walked ahead of him out of the cellar. "You'll be back by dinnertime. Run along. Don't keep Bart and the abbot waiting."

THE TOUCH OF GAMALIEL

Cami and Max Meriwether were confused as they walked down the main aisle of Bethel Hall. It was abandoned.

"Miss Lucille? Mr. Bartimaeus?" Cami called out, searching among the display cases for the people who seemed to live at the museum.

"Where could they be?" Max asked, spinning his wheelchair around to face his sister. "Maybe we should go."

"No. We've got to tell them what we've seen. Will isn't going to. So that leaves us to—"

"To 'tell' what, dear?" Aunt Lucille said, walking into the hall from the gaping hallway that opened to the other galleries.

"Oh, Miss Lucille. It's Will. He's acting very strange and there are some things I thought—"

"Will is not the only one acting strange today," Lucille

said, quieting Cami with her lowered tone. "Why don't we go upstairs to my office. We'll have privacy there. Let's take the lift for Max."

"You're just trying to get out of climbing the stairs, Miss Lucille," Max said, peeling out in front of her with a glimmer in his eye.

The trio, in silence, passed through the door marked PRIVATE, around the spiral staircase, into the hidden, gated elevator and cruised upward.

On the ground level of the north tower, Will found the only sarcophagus in the main hallway. It lay at the end of the hall, past several solemn statues of robed men, explorers, and angels interrupted by the occasional potted plant.

The pink marble casket was among the oldest Will had ever seen at Peniel. The top edge of the sarcophagus was badly gouged, like someone had taken a pickax to it. Aside from the sculpted circular medallion of a bearded man holding a book and a cross on the front, it was unremarkable. Beneath the figure, Will read the Latin inscription:

EX-S-M-CASINO.

"Buckle up, little man. Time to fly," Bartimaeus said, hastening down the hall on his two crutches. Abbot Athanasius was close behind him.

Will started to step into the stone casket. "Nope. Get on out of there," Bartimaeus said, waving him away. "I go first. That way I can be waiting for you on the other side. We don't need you wandering around Monte Cassino without a chaperone. You're liable to make off with St. Benedict's bones or sumpthin'—and they won't know who the heck you are, anyway. Move aside."

Will backed off. Bartimaeus handed his crutches to the abbot and slowly lowered himself into the sarcophagus. "All right, lay 'em on me," he said, once in recline.

The abbot returned the crutches, which Bartimaeus wrapped in his arms. "See ya in Monte Cassino," Bartimaeus whispered with a wink to Will. Then after slowly announcing, *"Nex ut vita,"* he was gone in a flash.

"Your turn, William. Make sure to seek out Abbot Gamaliel. He knew your great-grandfather and me. He may also know something of this Asmodeus." The abbot lowered the strap on Will's pith helmet so it was beneath his chin. He then clapped him on the shoulders.

Will threw himself into the pink casket, crossed his arms over his chest, and just before he uttered the phrase that would initiate the *sarcophagal peregrination,* he asked the abbot: "We just have to get my great-grandfather's diary and then we can come back, right?"

"Correct. Find out how he dealt with this creature. And do make sure you ask for Gamaliel. He possesses powerful gifts."

"Sure thing." Will shut his eyes tight, lay back in the sarcophagus, and mouthed *"Nex ut vita."* The floor of the casket fell away and he hurtled through space. It felt like being aboard a turbulence-tossed airplane, without the benefit of the wings. He never got used to the shock of traveling by "sarcopha-bus." And just when he thought he couldn't handle it anymore, just when he felt like he was going to be sick from the speed of the journey, he stopped moving. Will blinked open his eyes to find a faraway white, vaulted ceiling. He was surrounded by bookcases and it smelled dusty.

"Well, you got here in one piece, little man," Bartimaeus said, leaning over him. "Lucky for us, this is the library. And it seems pretty quiet."

"Ahem," someone said from behind him. Will stood up to find a rotund, black-robed monk staring at them through tiny black spectacles. "You come-uh from where-uh?" he asked in Italian-accented English.

"Uh-Mer-EE-Kuh," Bartimaeus said slowly, as if that would bridge the language gap. "Peri-Luss Faahhhls."

The hard expression on the bald monk melted into a smile. "Pero-lis-uh Falls-uh . . . Jacob-uh Wilder town. Ah, *sì, sì, sì.*"

Will nodded uncertainly to the monk.

"You got it. Jacob Wilder town," said Bartimaeus, laughing. He looked back at Will. "Ma Italian's gittin' better." Then back to the monk: "We're looking for one of Jacob's diaries. A few of his books are here." He was slow talking again, loudly. "We need some information."

"Informazione . . . uhh . . . Jacob-uh Wilder?" The monk

pinched his fingers together, painting indecipherable word pictures with his hands. "Abbot Gamaliel-uh. He will-uh help-uh you. *Avanti. Avanti.*"

"I think that means 'let's roll,'" Bartimaeus said, galloping after the plump monk. Will, with some trepidation, did the same.

In Jacob Wilder's office at Peniel, Cami told Lucille everything she'd seen over the last few days, from Will's "unbelievable" performance on the football field, to the way he confined three football players in a makeshift jail, to the bewildered state of the people in town, to the cheerleader that Will had suddenly taken an interest in. "He practically ignores Simon and me. The only reason he gives Andrew the time of day is because they're on the football team together," Cami went on, clearly upset by what she shared. "He's changed. He's different."

"I'm glad you all came to me, dear," Lucille said, worriedly straightening the silk arms of her jacket. "His newfound ability on the field is coming from the amulet he wears. The locket of Samson." She pointed absently to the empty case in the corner. "I know it's hard to love people when they're not loving you. But it's often the moment when our friends are not treating us well when they need us most." She eyed Max and Cami with pity. "Will is fortunate to have friends like you."

Aunt Lucille clapped her hands suddenly and went to one of the crammed shelves along the office wall. "Will's having some difficulty *seeing* the things that we rely on him to see. I had thought of giving this to him, but I'm not sure he's in any condition to use it properly."

She held a dented, conical metal helmet in her hand.

"Is that the Joan of Arc helmet you told us about the other day?" Cami asked.

Aunt Lucille nodded, placing it down on the desk. "Only one who is pure, one who is truly concerned about others can make use of this relic."

"Really?"

"Really. I think you need to use it, Cami—for Will's sake and perhaps for the sake of all of us."

"But what can I do?" Cami asked.

"Wearing the helmet, you will hear and see things others cannot. Until Will's sight is restored—and only he can do that—we need other eyes on the ground." Aunt Lucille inhaled and drew both her lips into her mouth. "And frankly, from what you're telling me, and from what I know, I worry about the safety of this town." She handed the helmet to Cami.

Wide-eyed and unsure, Cami balanced the helmet on her knees.

"Don't worry, Cami," Max said, reaching toward her. "I saw somebody wearing the helmet in a dream last night. Will was punching and there were ugly people around. Horrible people. One of them had horns like a bull. Somebody had that helmet on next to Will. I couldn't see the face. It must be you. You're part of this."

"We're all a part of this," Aunt Lucille said, coming around the desk and bending down to Cami's sight line. "Put the helmet on your head when you fear something is amiss. Now, you can't go down the street with the thing on your head, but find times to wear it when you're not likely to be spotted or when you are indoors. My mother always claimed to hear a voice when she wore it. She saw some things too."

Cami slowly lifted the helmet and put it over her head. It was heavier than she expected.

She stared at Lucille and then over at Max, but saw nothing out of the ordinary. As she went to take it off, a tiny voice with a slight French accent filled her ears. *"Don't be afraid,"* it whispered. *"You were born to do this."*

Cami pointed to the helmet, excitement exploding on her face. "It's working. I think it likes me."

The bald monk led Will and Bartimaeus out of the monastery, into the night. They followed the flickering light of the monk's candle down several darkened staircases and onto a gravel path near the foundation walls. "This-uh abbey looks very different-uh from when Jacob-uh Wilder was here."

"So that's his nice way of saying the United States leveled the place during World War II," Bartimaeus tried to whisper. "They thought Nazis were holed up inside, so they dropped bombs on the abbey. A whole lotta bombs."

"We are-uh here." The monk held the candle toward a thin stone staircase that led to a hole in the side of the foundation wall. "Abbot Gamaliel." The monk pointed. "He up-uh there."

Will and Bartimaeus looked at each other for a moment before Bart started climbing the steps. A faint light illuminated the opening in the wall, diffused by a thin gray curtain. Bartimaeus was the first to go in, ducking his head to enter.

On a cot at the far side of the dwelling, he discovered a figure wrapped in covers. "Abbot Gamaliel?" Bart said gently.

Will pushed the curtain aside to enter the crude room. "He's sleeping. Maybe we should come back later." Before he could speak again, a hand like a baggy baseball mitt covered his face, knocking his pith helmet off balance.

The hand belonged to an ancient-looking, rail-thin man lost in faded black robes. He lay sideways on a platform just above the entryway and had a great pumpkin head covered with brown splotches. Will started to pull away.

"No, no. Hold still." The monk with paper-thin skin and deeply sunken eyes continued to hold Will's face, his arm extended from above. His expression changed from delight to concern as he held Will's face. "You see less than I do, boy. For a Wilder, that is disgraceful." He released his hold.

"What . . . how do you know what I can see?" Will said indignantly.

"I know what I feel. The eyes can lie—and mine are of little use to me these days—but the spirit never lies." His eyes were like slits and Will was unsure if Gamaliel could see anything at all.

"The decoy over here is pretty smart," Bartimaeus said, amused by the blanketed mannequin on the cot.

"A good example of people seeing what they want to see. I have always slept above the doorway. That way I know who has come. And who I wish to let go." He dropped from the ledge with astounding ease for an old man and turned toward Will. "The eyes of your soul are dulled. You see the surface, indulging your eyes, gobbling up what pleases you and missing what is essential. What a waste of a gift. You'll never progress that way." The old man's mouth never really closed, but hung agape even when he wasn't speaking. "You see only for your own pleasure and that will jeopardize us all."

Before Will could respond, Bartimaeus stepped between them. "Abbot, I'm Bartimaeus Johnson. And you were right, this is a Wilder. Dan Wilder's boy, Will. Sorry 'bout barging in on you, but we have an emergency."

"I didn't imagine you came for a tour. . . . Dan Wilder's son, hmmmm. No wonder he sees nothing. What do you seek, Bartimaeus?" the abbot asked, ignoring Will.

Will started to speak, but Bartimaeus shushed him with

a scowl. "One of Jacob's diaries has some information we need. A demon has risen in Perilous Falls: Asmodeus."

"The Wilders have always had difficulty with that one," Abbot Gamaliel said, falling to his knees. He reached inside a hole in the rocky wall. Within moments he produced several leather-bound books, warped by age and weather. "Most of Jacob's writings are at Peniel, no? These are the only things I have. If a diary exists, it will be among these volumes."

Bart held the books close to his face, one at a time, until he found one that looked familiar. "This is the ticket." Bartimaeus anxiously leafed through the pages. The *W* etched on the cover, like the one on Jacob Wilder's desk, was the giveaway.

Abbot Gamaliel opened his big palms to Will. "Jacob's writings are only part of the reason you are here. I trained with your great-grandfather, Will. Give me your hands."

"I'd rather not," Will said, crossing his arms, still stung by the comment about his dad. "Mr. Bart, I'm going to wait outside."

"As you wish." The abbot shuffled aside to permit Will room to exit. "You may as well step into the darkness— you're already halfway there."

"What?" Will spun around.

"Your insolence, your selfishness . . . you're clouded by the *Darkness*. It has a hold on you."

"I don't know what you're talking about," Will said.

"Then give me your hands." Gamaliel once again presented his palms.

Bartimaeus stopped flipping pages. He looked over at Will. "Go on."

Will hesitantly offered his hands, stiffly laying them on the old man's palms.

Abbot Gamaliel rolled his oversized head as if trying to relieve a kink in his neck. Then he tightened his grip on Will's hands. "Your strength is not your own."

"I have the relic of Samson," he whispered. "On me."

The old man's eyes opened like two dark caverns, filled with pinpoints of light. "You are so alone, Will Wilder. The dead surround you—black, black arts," he raved, still holding Will's hands tightly. "There is not much time. Not much time."

CHAPTER 17

THE INCENSE RECIPE

After contorting his face for several moments, Gamaliel bellowed, "Ahhh" and threw Will's hands aside in disgust. "The situation is dire. He sees nothing. If he can't even see demons, how will he ever progress to the spirits of the dead or angels—"

"Angels?" Will asked.

The abbot thrust his hands into a stone basin in the corner, washing them. "He is so compromised—what did you say your name was?"

Bart looked up from the book. "Bartimaeus."

"Of course, Bartimaeus." He smiled as if a fond memory had resurfaced. "The boy is attached to the *Darkness*." Drying his large hands, he returned to Will. "Do you know what I am speaking of?"

Will nodded guiltily, though in fact, he didn't know what Gamaliel was getting at.

"You must break free of this thing. Death. I see death all around you. Does that make sense?"

"Not really." Will was more frightened than he had been all day. He nervously started looking behind him. And what did Gamaliel mean when he said Will would see dead spirits and angels?

"If I can get in here for a minute . . ." Bart shook the old warped book at Will. "I think I found somethin' we were looking for." He motioned for Will to come closer.

Abbot Gamaliel lowered himself onto a box along the wall and rested his face in his hands. Will read the diary over Bartimaeus's shoulder.

"This could be the 'death' the abbot has been talking about," Bart said, pointing to the middle of the page. "That's Jacob's handwriting."

Will studied the page.

In Paris, but also later in Rome, we discovered the way Asmodeus uses the dead like puppets to enact his will. The Nazis at the Louvre utilized the black arts to summon the demon via a blood rite. In each case, the donor of blood became the demon's vessel—for a time. Eventually, the beast returned to claim the donor's life, moving on to a new host. In Rome, Brother Felix found spoiled graves and coffins slashed open by Asmodeus.

The demon reanimated the corpses, which it promptly possessed. I am certain this is what the prophecy means when it references the "many masks" this demon wears.

"So now we know why those bodies went missing from the old de Plancy Cemetery," Bartimaeus told Will. The boy took the diary from Bart, lost in the deluge of information.

This Marquis of Iniquity is among the most powerful and elusive demons I have ever encountered. It is also one that I had persistent problems identifying. For a time I lost all view of it. . . . Since we escaped Paris, my Sarah has been transfixed by a peculiar tune. She's hummed it ceaselessly. When I asked her the origin of the lilting lullaby, she curtly informed me that it was something Colonel Von Groll, one of her Nazi coworkers at the Louvre, played on a music box while they worked. I have since heard the same tune on the streets of Rome, in New York, Jerusalem, and Hong Kong. This was no coincidence. I began to see a pattern. In each instance individuals were drawn to the music—obsessed by it. At first I thought it was just a distraction or a fad. But I've since learned that the song is of a diabolic origin. It targets those who desire things not theirs to have. They become obsessed with their cravings, lusting for unattainable things, situations, or people. Those already focused on satisfying their cravings are particularly susceptible to the music. Over the last few weeks, the Brethren have worked to destroy the recordings of the tune played on the wireless and stamp out all distribution of it. But mass communications make this a difficult task.

The music had a maddening effect on Sarah, leaving her listless and hostile toward me and even her closest friends. Those addicted to the music go into a walking trancelike state. But it has an even worse effect on those who love them. I saw couples divided and men go mad—families destroyed by this hellish music. The melody itself creates an insidious isolation that produces seeming "miracles" for those who listen. The music actually fuels their dissatisfaction with life and pulls them into a realm of fantasy. The Sinestri add to the illusion by creating real-world assistance. In Sarah's case, it was romance that she desired. Invisible imps delivered flowers to her throughout the week with flattering notes. She became obsessed with discovering who her "secret admirer" was—even though I told her there was no such person. My explanations only made her more indignant. Without Sarah's assistance I was lured in and deceived by a songstress named Tamara Malvagio. She performed at the Palazzo Modo, a club outside of town. . . .

"Modo?!" Will asked Bartimaeus. "Just like Cassian Modo? Could it be the same family?"

"Family! Ha." Gamaliel lifted his great head. "There is no 'Modo family'—only the horde of minor demons and the possessed who go by the name of their master: AsMOdeus. Modo." The old man held his stare.

Will nervously returned to the book, searching for more answers. Was there a way to stop Modo? Could Cassian be Asmodeus, even though all the world could see him?

"Now this is pretty interesting." Bartimaeus pointed to the lower portion of the opposite page. Will's eyes followed Bart's finger.

Confronting the beast was no easy task. Tamara led me to a villa on the outskirts of Rome, on the Old Appian Way, occupied by a high-ranking SS officer. Brothers Charles and Gamaliel were already embedded there as undercover servants. They had discerned weeks earlier that this place was a den of evil activity and possibly the home base of Asmodeus. Beneath the home were the ruins of a pagan temple where ritual sacrifices and other black arts were common. I might have been killed that night had it not been for dear Gamaliel. When I entered the party, two Nazis struck me on the head and dragged me down to the pagan temple. Upon awakening, a hideous thing—a creature with three heads and a withered leg with lethal talons—approached me. Among the twenty or so people in the room was Gamaliel. Unbeknownst to me, he had devised an incense that, when burned, incapacitated and stunned the demon. By the time I awoke, Brother Charles had broken the chains that held me captive and incense filled the chamber. Without

Charles and Gamaliel's incense, I might have never
survived, nor defeated the beast. It took time and was
truly a communal effort. . . .

"Abbot Gamaliel?" Will looked over to the shriveled man seated along the wall. "Was this you? Do you remember how to make that incense? How to defeat this demon?"

"I told you I trained with your great-grandfather." He brushed his hands atop his legs and stood. "Now I suppose you'll want my incense recipe."

Nightfall plunged the main corridor of the north tower of Peniel into near darkness. From the courtyard, Baldwin barged into the hallway, heaving. He flattened himself against the nearest wall and made sure the passage was empty before he moved again. Shards of moonlight glinted off the heavy sledgehammer he lugged to the end of the hallway. Baldwin stood silently before the pink sarcophagus, the one Will and Bartimaeus had used to reach Monte Cassino. Sweat glistened off his forehead as he scanned the casket. Then in a fit of anger, he dropped the hammer to the floor and turned to leave. In the middle of the hallway he balled his hands into fists and struck his stomach in anguish. "No, no, no," he moaned, muttering, as if arguing with some unseen figure. A sharp pain in the palm of his hand forced him to hold it up to the moonlight. A nasty purple gash appeared where the witch of Wormwood had cut him weeks earlier. The edges of the cut held a touch of green and stung horribly.

"No! I don't care what you do to me. I must do this," he hissed, glaring at his palm. At once, he turned and ran toward the sarcophagus as if his mortal enemy were inside it.

"Jacob gave me more credit than I am due," Gamaliel said, indicating the diary. He handed Will a scrap of paper and a pencil. "The incense was something I came across during my Scripture readings. It's in the Old Testament Book of Tobit. Did you know that Tobit's son, Tobias, battled Asmodeus? An angel instructed him to catch a fish and set aside its heart, liver, and gall."

"A fish?" Will asked, puckering his lips the way he did when he was unsure of something. He wrote furiously.

"Not any fish. A sheatfish. What you in America call catfish. The heart and liver of the fish must be burned on embers so that the smoke fills the air. This will weaken and repel the demon. For whatever reason, Asmodeus cannot stand it."

"Is that how my great-grandfather beat him?"

"No. That's how we weakened the thing. This one is wily. The demon has many faces and it will take more than you, as it took more than Jacob, to repel it. It's exceptionally strong—a Marquis of Hell. You will need allies to assist you. Each will play a role." He scratched at his brown-splotched head. "Right now, you are very alone and that worries me."

Bartimaeus took the notes Will had scrawled and slipped them into his hip pocket. "We'll get Brother Godfrey to rustle up some sheatfish and I'll bet Philip can build us an incensor to spread the smoke around."

"Good, good. And save the gall of the fish. It has healing properties," Gamaliel whispered, pointing at Bartimaeus's eyes. He then approached Will. "May I lay hands on you?"

Will nodded without conviction.

"You have fallen bit by bit—through a succession of bad decisions. I will pray that your attachment to the *Sinestri* will weaken."

"The *Sinestri*? I'm not attached to the *Sinestri*," Will said.

"Quiet," the old man barked. He lowered his head and began to whisper to himself, hands gripping Will's shoulders. After several seconds he shook Will urgently. "The *Darkness* is passing away, Will, and the true light is already shining. You have only to open your eyes to find it. Look to your friends. Look to your family. The light is there. It'll be up to you to rekindle it. Do you understand?"

"I think so."

"Good. Good. You must both go now. Time is very short and Asmodeus grows bold." He scampered out of the dwelling, ahead of them. Will and Bartimaeus raced to keep up with the old man. They hastened up broad stairs, through a pair of cloister yards, and past an octagonal well. The old man opened a thick wooden door and they found themselves inside an abbey hallway.

Approaching the library, Gamaliel jabbed a finger into Will's chest, stopping him. "There is something else. This demon wants you. But to accomplish its end, it will mark and torment an innocent female—one whom you care about."

"The prophecy said something about that. That I had to protect an 'innocent maiden.'"

"Jacob misunderstood that part of the prophecy. The demon was after him but targeted Sarah, your great-grandmother. She was the one who could have saved him."

"Saved him from what?"

"From his demise." Gamaliel's mouth hung slack, but he said nothing else.

"Did Asmodeus kill my great-grandfather?"

Gamaliel shook his enormous head. "No. Just remember the innocent maiden could protect you sometime near or far."

"How did he die?" Will demanded.

Gamaliel looked at Bartimaeus, who silently looked away. "We must get you both to the sarcophagus before it's too late." And he dashed into the library.

"Abbot Gamaliel. How did my great-grandfather die?" Will's voice bounced off the outer walls of the monastery.

Baldwin swung the hammer high and smashed the face of the pink sarcophagus in the north tower. With each blow, chunks of the front panel and broken bits of the carved monk figure fell to the ground. Within minutes only jagged pieces, no more than a few inches high, remained attached to the base. He stepped into the remains of the casket, adjusted his stance, and began slamming the hammer against the head of the sarcophagus. After three strokes he had reduced it to dust and rocks.

"Baldwin! Stop!" It was Tobias Shen, screeching in a tone no one had ever heard from him before. "Will and Bartimaeus are at Monte Cassino!"

"I'm saving him," Baldwin yelled, raising the hammer once more. Before he could lower it again, Tobias Shen charged at him. With a hand flat as a knife, he struck Baldwin in the middle of his shoulder blades. Seized by pain, Baldwin dropped the hammer and crumbled to his knees. In a lightning assault of elbows and hands, Tobias flattened Baldwin and began to yell for help.

Moments later, Abbot Athanasius and Brother James Molay were standing over the ruined sarcophagus.

"Why, Baldwin?" the abbot asked. Then he turned to Tobias. "I thought he was locked in his cell."

"He was," Tobias answered.

"I broke the lock on my window. He mustn't return," Baldwin groaned.

"Who? Will?" Tobias spat.

"Yes. Whatever's inside of me wants him gone," Baldwin whimpered.

The abbot motioned for Tobias to step away. Athanasius

touched the forefingers and thumbs of each hand, closing his eyes. A slender blue ray radiated from the abbot's
fingertips. He trained the beams on the back of Baldwin's
neck.

"We will not come out, ATHANASIUS," Baldwin yelled in
a high-pitched voice not his own.

Despite Baldwin's pleas, the abbot only recited Latin in
a monotone and refused to speak with the vicar. The hook-
nosed man started to sing the bewitching lullaby familiar
to everyone in Perilous Falls. He writhed on the floor for
several minutes, his body twisting into positions no gymnast had ever attempted. The display was so fearsome, that
Brother James joined the abbot, touching his index fingers
and thumbs together. He also directed the blue ray issuing
from his fingers at the back of the tormented vicar's neck.
At one point Baldwin's head and heels touched, making
Tobias think that Baldwin might snap in two.

After several minutes, Baldwin's head lunged forward as
if something had hold of his chin. His mouth dropped open,
and a foul purple cyclone of mist spewed from his quaking
body. The mist spun upward, evaporating into the air.

Baldwin fell to the floor, unmoving. The abbot and
James pressed their palms together and the blue rays were
no more. When Baldwin began to stir, the abbot knelt beside him. "Why did you destroy the sarcophagus?"

"To spare the boy," Baldwin blubbered. "If he returned,
the voices inside urged me to strike him . . . hurt him . . .
kill him. I couldn't risk it."

"You should now be free of the voices. But why didn't you come to us?"

"How could I come to you? I visited a witch, Athanasius. In Wormwood of all places. I invited the *Darkness* in—into me, into this sacred house."

Tobias glumly picked up the broken pieces of the sarcophagus that he knew barred Will and Bartimaeus from returning to Peniel. "How will Bart and Will return to us? It could take a very long time."

"I don't know, Tobias." The abbot clutched his long white beard with two hands. "Take Baldwin to the old isolation room. Stay with him."

"I was envious of Will," Baldwin cried while Tobias lifted him by the arm. "I resented his being the chosen one. My cousin Lilith told me about this woman in the swamps of Wormwood who knew the future. A woman with powers . . ."

"Who is your cousin?" Tobias asked. "How old is she?"

"She's about my age—in her fifties. Lilith is a barmaid in Sorec. A confused but good person."

Tobias knitted his brow but said nothing as he and James escorted Baldwin down a brightly lit staircase.

Gamaliel tapped his foot impatiently. Will grew more troubled by the moment. Bartimaeus was still lying in the pink sarcophagus in the Monte Cassino library, staring at the ceiling. He had been in the sarcophagus for fifteen minutes, repeating the line that usually transported him after only one mention.

"Something is wrong." Gamaliel flapped his big hands in the air, motioning for Bartimaeus to rise. "The portal must be broken."

"Never seen nothin' like this," Bartimaeus said, sitting up.

Gamaliel stalked away, his large head bent. "Well, you've seen it now. There is a problem with the sarcophagus on the other end."

"How do we fix it?" Will asked.

"There is no fixing it." Gamaliel spun around, shoving his hands into his armpits. "But there is another way to get you home. It's risky, but it will work."

"I try not to do risky," Bartimaeus said, standing.

"It's the only option." Gamaliel stomped off into a canyon of bookshelves.

"Where are you going?" Will asked, helping Bartimaeus out of the marble coffin.

"To the crypt. Keep up."

CHAPTER 18

INTO THE DEEP

"**D**an, I'm sorry to trouble you," Lucille said into the phone when she heard Will's dad pick up.

"Aunt Lucille," Dan said, clearly annoyed. "What is it?"

In the background, Lucille could hear the thrum of Cassian's music.

"I'm calling about Will."

"Is he all right? He hasn't been hurt?"

"He's fine, dear. Perfectly fine. Working away here at the museum. I just didn't want you to worry. He and Bartimaeus are laboring away on a project that is taking more time than any of us thought it would take."

"What project?"

"They're trying to locate some old book. You know how Bartimaeus is once he begins a project. There's no stopping him. Just wanted you to know that I'll drive Will home later."

"Good, I don't want him out with those . . . uh . . . With everything happening in town."

"What do you mean, Dan?"

There was a marked silence on the line.

"I've seen . . . Just please bring him home or I'll come get him. I don't want him out with that music. It's everywhere."

"I think I get your drift. I saw Deb the other day. She didn't seem herself. She looked very taken with Cassian Modo's music on her show the other night."

"That music is ripping us apart," he whispered sharply. "Not only us, the whole town."

"You're right. It's audio poison. I went out to Dis. I met with Cassian Modo. Now, I know you don't want to hear it, but it's the work of the *Sinestri*, Dan."

Lucille could hear Deb screaming out, faintly in the background, "Who are you talking to? Who is that?"

"Was that Deborah?" Lucille asked.

"Hold on," Dan whispered. It sounded like he had gone into a smaller room and closed a door. "It's transformed her. All she wants to do is listen to a loop of Cassian's music and she is extremely protective of it. The city council is putting speakers all over Main Street to blare that junk into the ears of the few people who aren't already hooked."

"Ava Lynch's doing, I imagine?"

"Yes . . . yes."

"We may need your help, Dan. The *Sinestri*—"

"No. I can't . . . I can't. I don't want to talk about the *Sinestri* and your . . ."

"My what? My what? I know you're still shaken by what you endured. But that was a long time ago. We all suffered, Dan—to protect you. You may have to do the same for your family. For your son. They're targeting Will and he's not even resisting."

"Bring him home, soon."

"Can I count on your help?" Lucille was stern.

"They're installing the speakers on Main Street tonight. I'm sure one of your sidekicks can frustrate that. Sheriff Stout told me he's been getting calls from homes all over Perilous Falls. Objects are appearing out of thin air. Things and people are levitating. Good, sane people are fighting, turning violent. Doing crazy things. I asked him about the music. He told me the music was playing in every house he and his deputies visited. Every one. We've been invaded . . . invaded."

"Invaded by what, Dan?"

Deborah called out again. "I've got to go," Dan said. "Let me know if you need me to pick up Will."

And the line went dead.

Passing into the darkened cathedral at Monte Cassino, Gamaliel led Bartimaeus and Will through the marbled and gold colossus until they reached a latticed metal door along a side wall. He pushed it open and urged them to go down the tunneled stairway. Along the walls were figures of knights and women in veils, kings and young people seemingly making their way down the stairs. A mosaic firmament of stars twinkled overhead. But nothing prepared Will for what awaited him below. The gold mosaic of the crypt ceiling set the room ablaze.

Leading them around a corner, Gamaliel opened a knee-high black metal gate. On the other side of it sat a marble altar. Behind it, two statues were set into the rear wall. They were black-robed figures, a bearded man and a woman with gold hands and faces staring heavenward.

"This is the tomb of St. Benedict and his sister St. Scholastica," Gamaliel enthused. "Do you recognize those two medallions beneath the statues?"

Will did. They had the same cross-within-a-circle design as the emblem on the pink sarcophagus that had taken him to Monte Cassino.

"Those are St. Benedict medals. They are known to ward off evil," Gamaliel said, touching one of the gold medallions set into the black rear wall. "Now, there on my left"—he pointed to a sculpted effigy of the saint lying in a niche above them, on the side wall—"is St. Benedict. And over there, on my right, is St. Scholastica. They were brother and sister, so it's fitting that they would reside here together. Bart, get in front of that Benedict medal over there. And, Will, you come here by this one."

He instructed them to place their right hands on the medallions embedded in the back wall. "You must press them at the same moment." They did exactly as he said. To Will's amazement, the marble wall to his left, beneath the resting figure of St. Benedict, scraped open.

"Wow," Will uttered.

"No time for 'wows.' Come quickly and watch your step," Gamaliel advised, crouching through the opening.

They walked down a narrow passage to a crude metal gate. Gamaliel pulled it open and then pushed at the ancient wooden door behind it.

"Where are we?" Will asked.

"The oldest part of the abbey. This section survived the bombing during the war."

Will stared at the piles of rubble, cracked dishes, and broken statues on either side of the hallway. "If it survived, what is all this?"

"After the bombings, the Brethren salvaged what they could and piled it in this passage. They are mementos of our past, but the real treasure is down here."

After several minutes they reached a bronze door covered with squares containing individual robed figures. Gamaliel pulled a huge key from his habit and jammed it into the lock. He then reached up and, in succession, pressed his hand against each of the four robed figures on different corners of the door. At his touch the figures receded.

"So in the Middle Ages, this must have been like typing in a security code," Bartimaeus said, chuckling.

The tall door quivered and the clunks of the locks unlatching filled the chamber.

"What's all the security for?" Will asked.

"*Hooold on.* I know where we are," Bartimaeus said slowly, tightening the grip on his crutches. "Are you taking us to the Living Waters, Abbot?"

"You shall walk into them this day, Bartimaeus."

Will looked to Bartimaeus for some reaction, but he only shook his head worriedly and followed after Gamaliel. "Looord help us. Come on, Will."

Cami and Max moved quickly down Main Street on their way home. With the twinkling lights in the oak trees and the big streetlamps aglow, it had a festive air. Shoppers milled about and people wandered into restaurants. Some of the stores and businesses were closing up for the evening. Max remarked on the dozen or so uniformed city employees perched on ladders. They were busily working near the overhangs and storefront canopies, up and down the street.

When the siblings reached the Milk and Honey Bistro, Cami had an idea.

"Max, turn into the alley here."

"Why? I want to go home."

"It'll just be a minute. I want to try something."

Max gave her a sour look but did as she requested,

steering his wheelchair into the shadowy alley beside the restaurant. Cami lifted the metal helmet off Max's knees and placed it on her head.

It fit snugly around the sides of her head, and the opening for her face seemed custom made, just for her. She approached Main Street and, avoiding the lamplight, hid in the shadows of the alley. Across the street, a group of high school girls came out of a dress shop with their newly filled bags, giggling and humming *that* song. DJ Cassian's song.

Max watched Cami's face go blank. Her hand covered her mouth.

"What's wrong?" asked Max.

"Will was right. There are little black devils next to everyone on the street. They're everywhere." She frantically looked to her right at the people leaving the bistro. "They're very hazy, but I can see them when I wear the helmet." Like huge rodents, the imps covered the street and some even crawled onto the people they accompanied.

A city workman on the ladder in front of the dress shop spoke into his radio. "Okay, Joe. We're wired on half the block if you want to test the audio."

Seconds later, Cassian's music spilled from a few stores on the other side of Main, including Bub's Treats and Sweets. The cluster of high school girls started singing the tune monotonously, and they were no longer laughing. It was as if the music had drugged them somehow. More imps gathered around them as they sang.

A couple, yelling at one another, ran out of the bistro.

The man tried to calm the woman, but she pushed him away. A pair of small black creatures rode on the woman's shoulder, whispering into her ear. Cami was so spooked by what she saw, she began to pull the helmet off.

"No. You were born to do this. Don't be afraid," the French-accented female voice said inside the helmet. *"You are a crucial part of this mission. You must go to the cemetery. Take down the names of those whose graves have been violated, so that you all may understand."*

Cami froze in place. "Understand? Okay, okay," she said, afraid to move.

"You are not safe where you are. An evil one approaches. Flee him. Return home, and later, at your first opportunity, go to the cemetery," the voice responded.

"Cami, what's happening?" Max asked, troubled by the perplexed look on his sister's face.

There were three loud taps on the back of the helmet. Cami spun around, lifting it off her head.

Max shifted the controls on his wheelchair so he could turn to see who was standing beside them.

"What's the matter, you don't like good music?" Cassian Modo stood in the shadows, playfully holding the walking stick that he had just struck against the helmet. "Why are you the only girl in town who can resist my songs, Cami?"

"You're DJ Cassian." Cami glanced at her brother fearfully. "We have to go home."

"What is that you have there? Some kind of noise canceler?" He tossed his ponytail over the shoulder of the floor-length leather coat he wore. "May I see it?" He tapped the dented metal of the helmet with the jewel at the end of his walking stick.

"No," she said, hugging the helmet to her.

"I wasn't going to take it, Cami. I only wanted to see what it was." He began to bop his head in time with the music resounding on Main Street. Cassian started to echo the tune "La-dee-dah-dee-dee-dahhhh." He watched Cami intently, waiting for a reaction.

"We're going home," Cami said with false boldness.

"Hmmm. You intrigue me. Why don't I take you and your brother for an ice cream across the street? I have a new tune that I just came up with. No one has heard it before. You'd be the first." He flashed his bright, white teeth. "If you give my music a chance, it'll change you forever."

"No thanks."

"Don't you want to be like the other grown-up girls?" He pointed at the group of high schoolers still swaying in dazed unison on the other side of Main Street. They suddenly looked at Cassian as if he had called their names. The pack of them started crossing the street. "Why do you think your friend Will is so sweet on that cheerleader from Sorec Middle School? She's cool. She gets it. All the grown-up girls are listening—"

Max rolled his chair onto Cassian's foot.

"AAAAAHHHHH. You little—You're on my foot." He struggled to push the mechanized wheelchair away, but it was heavy—like a small car on his toes.

"She doesn't want to be like your girls. We're going home!" Max shouted. He sped out of the alley, all but pushing his sister onto Main Street.

Cassian jumped out after them, but for whatever reason he did not give chase. Running alongside her brother's wheelchair, Cami kept imagining all the imps surrounding them—all the invisible devils brushing their legs while they moved. She looked back to find Cassian clutching the corner of the building. He lowered his sunglasses and winked at her. A chill ran through her body. At that moment, the sound of raised voices and the crashing of furniture and glassware broke out along Main Street.

But Cami blocked all of it out and picked up the pace. She had to catch up to Max, get home safely, and tomorrow pay a visit to the de Plancy Cemetery.

The low-slung chamber's ceiling was covered in green and blue bits of glass. Along the edges were mosaic depictions of bearded old men and a few women in black veils. At the center of the space, a rounded pool of churning water ran to a tunnel on the chamber's far side. In niches along the walls were statues of dead monks, lying atop the tombs where their remains must have been. The whole scene freaked Will out.

"Are these 'the waters' mentioned in the prophecy?" he asked.

"The very same. The Living Waters," Gamaliel announced, the deep lines around his mouth accommodating a smile. "Abbot Anthony the Wise wrote the prophecy not far from where you are standing. His grave is just there." Gamaliel's eyes shot to a simple niche near the ground, occupied by a sleeping statue of dark marble.

"How is this going to get us home, Abbot?" Bartimaeus asked in a hush.

"The waters connect the past, the future, and the present. You must know that the waters run in Peniel as well."

"Yes, I do," Bartimaeus answered.

"Then it's very simple. You'll plunge into these waters, focus your minds on Peniel, and when you emerge, you should be returned."

"Should be?" Will puckered his lips, pushing them to the side nervously.

"Should be," Gamaliel said, snatching Jacob's diary from Will. "I'll keep that here. It'll only be destroyed in the waters."

"If the diary can be destroyed, how are we going to make it?" Will asked.

"This is ink and paper. You are flesh and spirit." He lightly swatted Will's pith helmet with the diary. "Do not fear! Focus on your destination and you will get there." His voice turned serious. "When you arrive, there is only one question that you need concern yourself with: On what have I set my heart? Ask yourself that and all will be made plain. You are still tangled up in the *Darkness*, Wilder. Find your attachment to the *Sinestri* and root it out—or it will overwhelm you and devour what you have been created for."

Will was so confused, so worried about what awaited him back home. He stared out at the ominous waters. "What do we do now? Do we just jump in?" he asked.

"Go out into the deep. Only by entering will you find your way." Gamaliel extended an arm toward the waters. The pool suddenly grew choppy. "Accompany him, Bartimaeus. Remain focused on Peniel as you go beneath the waters. Oh, and you should keep your eyes closed. The images of the past, present, and future are not something any of us should look upon."

"C'mon, boy," Bartimaeus said, dropping his glasses into his front pocket. He trudged forward without enthusiasm.

"What's wrong, Mr. Bart?"

"I've heard stories about the Living Waters," Bartimaeus whispered. "They can do unexpected things. But I'm on the ride with you, Will. We'll make it—together." He took Will firmly by the hand.

The moment they stepped into the waters, they pulsated with brilliant colors. Magenta and green, red and blue swirls filled the pool. Then a straight line of water leading to the tunnel on the other side of the chamber stilled before them, as if showing them the way. All the while, the waters on either side of the quiet stream splashed and bubbled more violently than before.

It was warm as they waded into what seemed thicker than water. Will felt like he was swimming in warm gel.

And it smelled clean, like spring air carrying hints of flowery scents. *Like fabric softener! Smells just like Mom's fabric softener.* Will's smile melted into a frown as the Living Waters got hotter and Will wasn't sure if the temperature would stabilize. His stomach ached as he thought about boiling to death in the waters.

"Do not fear, Wilder, only believe," Gamaliel shouted from across the pool. Then with a laugh he added, "A teacher once told me, 'Man is an abyss; what will rise out of the depths, no one can see in advance. Go your own way.'"

"That's what I'm worried about—going the wrong way!" Will yelled back.

Gamaliel made a steeple with his big hands. "On what have you set your heart?" He beat out each word with his hands.

"You thinking about Peniel?" Bartimaeus asked Will.

"Yep," he said in a shaky voice.

Will waved to Gamaliel, exchanged a look with Bartimacus, and within moments the pair were sucked beneath the surface of the Living Waters.

CHAPTER 19

MIGHT MAKES FRIGHT

It was the strangest sensation Will had ever experienced. Beneath the waters, it was no longer hot, but cool. And though he knew he was moving, he felt as though he were inside a bubble. All the while, Will tried to keep his mind focused on Peniel, and home, and his family.

He desperately wanted to open his eyes. Where were they exactly and for how much longer would this continue? He held Bartimaeus's hand tightly. After several minutes Will could no longer resist.

I'll just take a quick peek. One eye. Only one eye.

He lifted his right eyelid and gazed out at the twinkling, colored water. It blurred past like colored lights seen through the window of a speeding car. But as he focused, the colors formed shapes.

There was a man in a pith helmet. It was his pith helmet.

That must be my great-grandfather.

Jacob was screaming in terror. He ran toward a woman. She held a knife above her head. She too was screaming, struggling with something . . . no, with some*one*. A boy. She held a boy by the arm and she was slashing at him, trying to cut him with the knife. Jacob grabbed her. They fought until she dropped the blade. Her face filled with anger, like that of a mad dog. She broke free of Jacob and lunged for the boy.

Will was too frightened to keep watching. He snapped his eye shut and tried to forget what he had seen. What did it mean? Who were the woman and the boy?

The next thing he knew, he was bobbing atop the waters in a dark place.

"I think we made it, Will," Bartimaeus said.

Will was still stuck in the memory of the violent images. He had seen just enough to rattle him and summon a hundred questions.

They were in a crypt, much like the one they'd left. Only here, there were no decorations, no mosaics. Just raw stone and tombs cut into the niches on the walls. The only light—with a flickering gray quality—came from the other end of the huge cavern. Will rubbed his eyes and saw what appeared to be a cloud, a swirling mass across the waters. It dully flashed, as if thunder lived within the smoky column.

"What's that?" Will asked, breaking away and paddling toward the cloud.

"Ooooh no," Bartimaeus said, grabbing Will by the collar

of his shirt. "We made it back to Peniel in one piece—and I want you to stay that way. Let's go. Out of the water." Bartimaeus directed him to the edge of the pool.

When Will stood, he was astonished that his clothes were not wet in the least. He ran his hands up and down his arms, over his pith helmet, and through the back of his hair. All bone-dry.

"This is so cool." Will laughed to himself.

Bartimaeus slowly climbed the low steps out of the pool. "It is cool. They used to call this Perilous Chapel. Your great-granddaddy would spend a lot of time down here. Still does." He pointed a crutch toward the sleeping carved figure near Will's feet—a sharp-boned man with a pith helmet over his chest.

"He's here? He's buried here?" Will asked, taking it all in.

"Sure is. He liked to come down to the crypt to think, to prepare for battle. A lot of your relatives are down here—and a lot of my old friends."

"Why's the cloud over there, Mr. Bart?"

"I'm tellin' ya, boy, don't go near that. It's too powerful. I know you did ya thing with some of the relics up in here. But that cloud is *serious*. So keep ya distance, ya hear?"

Will couldn't take his eyes off the slowly twisting column of smoke in the corner.

"Come on. It's late. We've got to get you home. Your grandfather Joseph had an elevator installed years ago. I hardly ever come down here. But it's over this way some-where." He felt along the wall near Jacob's tomb. "Here it is." Bartimaeus found a light switch. An elevator with a re-tractable metal gate illuminated. "Take this upstairs and get your aunt Lucille, right quick. I know she's worried about you. I've got a little business to attend to." Deflecting Will's questions, Bart pressed the only button inside the elevator and sent Will on his way.

Once the elevator was out of sight, Bartimaeus returned to the edge of the pool. He leaned on his crutches, opened his palms, and shut his eyes tightly.

"Jacob, I need some help here. This demon's got his hooks into your great-grandson. I need to see how you took this thing down and what we can do to help Will. Let me see. *Ut Videam. Ut Videam.*"

The cloudy column spun to the middle of the Living Waters. At the center of the column, images began to pulsate in the haze. Then the fog that obstructed them slowly cleared and Bartimaeus could discern the images. He looked like a child seeing a movie on a big screen for the first time. There was wonder and then terror in his milky eyes.

Friday was the day of the big game. Immediately after school, Cami, Simon, Andrew, and Will were planning to meet at Bub's Treats and Sweets for a quick snack. Will would then grab a bite at home and get ready for the game. But the afternoon didn't go that way.

Cami, Simon, and Will sat at the chrome-edged table

by Bub's front window. Andrew was late. Will told them nothing about his visit to Monte Cassino, but he did offer glimpses of what he learned there.

"Be real careful, guys," he said conspiratorially, leaning across the table so others could not hear. "There're little devils everywhere." (He could faintly see a few crawling about as he came into the shop.) "I know everything seems normal, but all over town, bad stuff is happening beneath the surface."

"Oh, bad stuff's always happening beneath the surface, hon," Miss Ravinia said, breaking in on their conversation. "Life's a lot sweeter when you ignore the negativity and focus on the positive. Here's your Puffer Fluffs, kids. How's that for something positive?" She cackled as she dropped the plates of smoking hot treats in the middle of the table.

The kids reached for the fried bloated squares filled with cinnamon cream like they had not eaten all week.

"Tonight's the big game. Are you all coming?" Will asked, with half his mouth full.

"We'd love to come," Simon said, "but Cami and I have to—"

Cami kicked him hard under the table. "We have to go to some event for Max. But why don't we meet at Burnt Offerings after the game? We can celebrate your win!"

Simon adjusted his glasses and resumed reading his paperback.

"I hope we win," Will said. "It's all about the team and we don't exactly get along. That Caleb is a really bad dude."

"Not him again. . . ." Simon never looked up from his book.

"I'm telling you, he's a demon!" Will said a little too loudly, drawing some looks from people in the shop. He whispered, "He's a demon. He enjoys hurting people. And every time he's around, my nose goes crazy."

The sight of Andrew running past the window, red-faced and panting, stopped all conversation. The boy threw open the front door and darted to his friends' table.

"Oh, am I glad to see you here, Will-man," he huffed. "There's trouble in the locker room. Everybody's been look-ing for you."

"What happened?" Will asked.

"Todd, Harlan, and Boyd—they were hurt. They were in the locker room with Caleb and—"

Fire lit Will's eyes. "Caleb hurt them? What was I just telling you guys? What did he do?"

Andrew shook his head. "Caleb didn't do it. They think *you* did. Caleb, Todd, Harlan, and Boyd were dressing early to run some drills, and they say they heard your voice in the locker room. You started razzing them."

"But he's been with us from the moment class ended," Cami said.

"It was definitely not Will," Simon said, eyeing the last Puffer Fluff just as Andrew saw it. Simon jammed it in his mouth. "Will couldn't have doooon aaaaht."

"And you say I'm a pig," Andrew said, dismissing Simon.

"I was here the whole time." Will was getting louder. "It's

Caleb. I'm telling you, he's either possessed or he's Asm—Modo."

"You think he's Cassian Modo? My brother and I ran into him the other night. . . ." Cami was now thoroughly confused.

"The guys said they heard your voice, Will-man, and then three of them were slashed. Their legs. Their arms. There was blood everywhere." Andrew ran two hands through his mop of red hair.

"It's the demon. He's hurting his own friends. That's what it does. It creates vessels; then it destroys them!" Will shouted.

"Kids, let's try to keep it down," Miss Ravinia said, rushing to the table. She picked up the empty plate. "Y'all are scaring people." Even the cats nuzzling the legs of other customers started to mew. "The animals are getting spooked too. Let's try to talk quietly." She put a finger, like a corn dog, to her mouth and bounced away.

"There's something I don't get—they're saying they saw me slash those three oafs?" Will jumped out of his chair. "Caleb saw me do it? Is that what he's saying?"

"No, no, no. Calm down." Andrew blocked him from running out the door. "They all heard your voice, but Caleb was on the other side of the lockers when this went down. Boyd, Harlan, and Todd said it happened so fast, they didn't see *anybody*. I told Coach that I thought you'd be here—and I'm glad you were."

"The coach is involved?!" Will asked.

"Oh yeah. He was real angry. Said whoever did this would pay and they'd be off the team forever. There was blood all over the place. . . . It was pretty spooky. Those guys won't be able to play tonight."

"Caleb won't be able to play tonight either." Will punched his own hand in a show of force—and instantly shook the receiving palm, wincing in pain. "It's Caleb. He faked my voice or something and then hurt those guys."

"I'd be very careful if I were you, William," Cami warned. "Are you sure this guy is possessed or is a demon?"

"Yes, I'm sure."

"You'd better be." She got real close and patted the talisman under his shirt. "Because with your little power enhancement, you could hurt people too. And you don't want to hurt the wrong people."

"How do you know about that?" Will pulled away.

Simon piped up, flipping open his book. "King Arthur says something interesting here. . . ."

Will rolled his eyes. "I didn't know this was a meeting of the Blabbingdale Book Club."

"Here it is." Then Simon read, "'Why can't you harness Might so that it works for Right?' He suggests here that Might resides in bad people, but that it could be directed toward something good. Maybe you can do good with your fists of fury?"

Cami blinked, trying to make heads or tails out of that. Will headed for the door. "I've got to go see the coach—and find Caleb."

Andrew ran after him, attempting to share all that he had seen in the locker room.

Simon threw his book on the table, watching Will and Andrew charge up the block. "Jerk. I was trying to be helpful."

"I know." Cami patted his bony arm. "But you can help me. We've got to get over to the de Plancy Cemetery before the sun sets."

"Fine. But I'm not going to his game. Forget about it. In Will's case, Might makes Fright!"

Cami lifted her shopping bag with the Joan of Arc helmet from the floor and Simon grabbed their book bags.

"What's the hurry, hons?" Miss Ravinia asked, pursuing them to the front door. She tugged on Simon's book bag and lowered her voice. "Look, anytime you want a Puffer Fluff, you don't have to fight those kids for scraps. You just come ask Miss Ravinia, and I'll get you the biggest Puffer Fluff in the kitchen—on me."

Simon thanked her and in his nasal tone said, "I may just take you up on that, Miss Ravinia." She closed the door behind him and shooed away the hissing cats gathering at her feet.

Brother Godfrey LeFleur, the stoop-shouldered, shy brother who spoke only when spoken to, under obedience, spent most of the day on the Perilous River. It was hardly a chore for Godfrey. He loved the solitude and spent as much time outdoors, and at the river, as possible.

When Bartimaeus informed the community that they needed to catch sheatfish to repel Asmodeus, the abbot lifted his head and uttered one word. "Godfrey."

The brother shuffled forward, and in his light French accent said instantly, "I shall be on the water before sunrise. Before sunrise." He had a habit of repeating himself.

Early Friday morning, he took his fishing poles, a net, and a cooler and loaded them all on a gray flat-bottomed boat the Brethren kept at Lucille's pier. They used it whenever they had to go out along the river.

At nearly five o'clock, Godfrey, still in his waders, walked into the refectory—the dark-paneled dining room where the Brethren ate all their meals.

"Pardon my intrusion," Godfrey said, his droopy eyes sparkling. He held a large ziplock bag in his hands. "I've caught enough sheatfish for our purposes. They are large— rather large. I had to go out beyond Dismal Shoals." He laid the bag with the silvery pink fish on the table near the abbot.

"Why so far?" the abbot asked, wiping his mouth. "I've seen you catch plenty of fish near Lucille's house."

"When I cast off, the banks of the river were choked with dead sheatfish. They weren't only dead. They were all blackened bones—all bones. The *Sinestri,* it appears, used their black arts to kill many of the poor fish. Not a bit of flesh remained—not a bit. This is why I went downriver."

"So you got enough of 'em?" Bartimaeus asked.

"Hundreds and hundreds. Whatever the *Sinestri* did had no effect downriver."

"Now for the hard work," Athanasius said, examining the fish in the bag. "Who is going to separate out the hearts and livers?"

The double doors of the kitchen instantly swung wide and Ugo Pagani, his potbelly covered by a leather apron, appeared wielding two twelve-inch knives. "This kitchen's going to look like a fish trauma unit by the time I'm finished. Somebody better get me some good sheatfish recipes, because we're going to be eating these fillets for the next decade." He guffawed and leaned against the door frame. "In a half hour, there'll be enough fish organs for you to have an underwater recital. But how are we planning to smoke their innards? The fumes have to reach the demon—and he could be anywhere."

"It's under control," Philip, the community builder of gadgets, said out of the side of his mouth. "You just give me the assets. I've already set up grills that'll create lots of smoke all over town. At night people won't suspect a thing."

"They won't suspect fish guts stinking up the neighborhood?" Ugo asked.

"You take care of the organs; I'll take care of the distribution. I'll give you a hint." Philip looked to the left and the right, as if the brothers were suddenly spies. "Think storm drains. So long as we don't get rain, and there's none in the forecast, we'll be fine. I also have a mobile incensor that we can quickly deploy if necessary."

Athanasius looked down the table at Pedro Montaigu, the compact Spanish brother with dark green eyes. "You'll be taking care of the speakers along Main Street."

"Yes, sir," Pedro said with a sharp nod. "I have rerouted the music source from city hall to an antenna at the library. Meaning, I can play whatever we want to play—from here." He held up his smartphone.

"How 'bout some Sinatra?" Ugo Pagani deadpanned.

"I've always liked *Th-eline* Dion," Brother Amalric, the rotund bookkeeper and attorney of the group, suggested.

"Can't we work in some Celtic music?" Brother James asked.

The abbot raised his hands in exasperation. "That is enough. This is not your personal playlist, gentlemen. We are discussing a serious mission."

"I was going to play flamenco music anyway," Pedro said dismissively.

"And what if the city discovers your rerouting scheme, and Cassian's music fills the streets again?"

"Eet is no problem." Pedro pulled out a pair of wire cutters. "I will jump along the roofs and snip-snip the speakers. It will take them days to reattach."

"Sounds like a plan, gents," Ugo said, pushing open one of his kitchen doors, mischief in his eyes. "Now, if you all could bring those little fishies in here. The operating theater is open."

Most of the guys were already warming up on the field by the time Will got there. Some of his teammates fell silent when they saw him and Andrew approach. He could tell from their glares that they all thought Will had injured his teammates. Their stares burned. How were they going to win a game this way? Coach Runyon was relieved to find that Will was with his friends at Bub's and nowhere near the bloodied locker room earlier in the day. He gave Will permission to play. Still, the atmosphere on the field unsettled Will.

His nose started itching the moment he neared the locker room. Renny Bertolf sat on the bleachers near the entryway.

"When they took those kids away on stretchers, I told them it wasn't you, Will." Renny spoke quickly and with a touch of hysteria. "I knew you wouldn't do anything like that to those kids. It's the same thing he did to me. He gets you when you're alone." His wide nostrils flared and he pointed to the locker room ominously. "Caleb just went in there. Be careful."

"It's okay, Renny." Will squeezed Renny's shoulder to reassure the boy. "My friend Andrew is in there changing." But his nose was now tingling something fierce, and just as he spoke, Andrew stepped out of the locker room, fully dressed in uniform.

"See you on the field, Will-man," Andrew said, attaching his helmet strap.

"See you on the field," Will said half-heartedly.

He inhaled deeply, then turned toward the locker room doors.

"Be careful, Will. Be careful," Renny kept repeating as Will walked away.

With every step, his sinuses burned like crazy. He thought about going back and asking the coach or Andrew to come to the locker room with him. He thought about waiting until Caleb came out. But his feet kept moving forward and he convinced himself that there was nothing to fear.

AH-CHOO! AH-CHOO! AH-CHOO!

CHAPTER 20

A LITTLE GAME

There was no sign of Caleb or anyone else in the locker room. Between sneezes, Will quickly slipped into his uniform, his mind racing:

Caleb has to be Asmodeus. But how do I stop him? He's hurting people. He beat Renny twice, busted a hole in the band room, changed into some monster— What did the prophecy and Gamaliel say? "This commander of legions has many faces." Now he's cutting guys on the team—his own friends. I should have packed some fish hearts and livers . . . darn it! Then there's that creepy Cassian dude's music. Imps are all over Perilous Falls. Mom and the whole town are going nuts. This all has to be related. I'm missing something here. . . .

The feeling of chains wrapping around his arms jolted Will from his thoughts. Caleb tightly held the ends of the chains, pressing them into Will's back. "Not so strong now, are you?" Caleb whispered. "You took my teammates out and I guess you thought I was next. It's not happening."

Will was sure the beast was about to slash him. He grabbed the middle of the chain at his chest and popped it apart like it was made of daisy stems. Caleb, his tiny eyes suddenly wide, stared at the slack chains in his hands. "I thought this was supposed to keep you . . . stop you." He was genuinely terrified.

"I know who you are, Caleb, and you're not going to hurt anybody else," Will said.

"It was your voice, Wilder. I was right over there. I don't care what the coach says—I heard it." Caleb started backing away, his eyes darting around the room. "Three of my friends are in the hospital because of you. Three of 'em. Keep away from me, Wilder. Keep away." He dropped the chains, grabbed his helmet, and bolted out the door.

Will stood still for a moment, pondering what had just happened. *It's a little game. The demon is trying to bait me into hitting him. Then I'll be off the team and he'll be able to go on hurting people. I've got to be smart about this. . . . Maybe might can make right, Simon.*

Will tied up his shoelaces and ran onto the field. Buses filled the school lot and crowds were moving into the stands for the game. But the only person Will saw as he walked onto the sideline was Lilith Lorcan. She was finishing a routine with her fellow cheerleaders, her thick black hair catching the purple of the dying sun. She turned just in time to intercept Will.

"I didn't know if I'd get to see you before the kickoff," she said, standing a little too close. "So you think you can whip them?" she whispered, so the others couldn't hear.

"I'm going to try. It's my first game and . . ." Over Lilith's shoulder, at the top of the stands near the end zone, three women in gray uniforms were testing a console with two huge speakers on either side. Standing behind the console was Cassian Modo.

"Are we still going for milkshakes after the game? I told my dad to pick me up at Bub's later, so we could talk," Lilith cooed. When she got no response, she gently tugged a piece of Will's hair hanging over his ear. "Hey, I'm over here."

He looked back at her. "What?"

"I asked if we were still going to Bub's after the game?"

"I guess we can . . . yeah. Sure. Uh . . . I did promise some friends that I would see them—"

The first chords of Cassian's music, the droning beat that had become the soundtrack of Perilous Falls, blared from the big speakers. A cheer went up.

Will couldn't take his eyes off Cassian, who raised his arms above his head and started gyrating.

"So are we going or not?" Lilith playfully hid her pom-poms behind her back and batted her eyes.

"Yeah, I want to. It's just that I told my friends—"

"Come on. It'll be fun. What are you afraid of, Will?" She giggled, gave him a quick hug, and added, "Good luck and see you at Bub's."

She bounded off before he could say another word.

Cassian's music blanketed the field. Many in the crowd started swaying in unison. Some were amused by the display. But Will wasn't. Neither was Dan Wilder, who tried to convince his wife to sit down. She loudly refused and kept right on jigging with the others.

Suddenly the music stopped and the voice of Mayor Ava Lynch intruded. "Is this on? Oh, yes, there I am," she said, hearing her voice bounce back to her across the field. "We are honored tonight to have with us for both the halftime entertainment and for the playing of the national anthem, DJ Cassian Modo!"

Wild applause rang out. Will could hear his mother whistling.

"As excited as we are to have DJ Cassian with us, let's remember we are here to support our middle school teams. So have a wonderful game, fellas. Go on, Cassian."

The teams assembled on the sidelines, Sorec Middle on one side, Perilous Falls Middle on the other. Cassian's adaptation of the national anthem was strange and ploddy. Not that any of his fans in the crowd or along the sidelines felt that way. They all began to sway to the slow, rhythmic beat. Will kept his hand over his heart and the amulet. Something in his peripheral vision made him turn toward the stands behind him. As if summoned by the music, hordes of imps climbed the bleachers and scattered through the crowd. Before the anthem was over, laughter began to explode from different sections of the stands. Guffaws and high-pitched squeals sounded everywhere. Will focused on the people chortling. The creatures were tickling them, causing the laughter. By the time the anthem ended, the place was in hysterics.

Will didn't know what to do. So intent was he on the action in the stands that he missed the coin toss and the start of the game. Will caught sight of his father, whose head was popping back and forth, worriedly scanning the crowd. Leo and Marin waved at Will—and seemed the only normal people in the stands that day. Will's nose burned.

"Let's go, Wilder. Wilder!" the coach yelled, pushing Will onto the field. "Come on, we've got possession, son."

He was to be a receiver on the play. The ball snapped and Caleb threw it to the other side of the field for no yardage. On the second down, Caleb searched for a free receiver as the linebackers surrounded him. With nowhere else to throw the ball, he angrily hurled it toward Will. Will grabbed it with one hand, as the kid next to him turned to make a tackle. The Sorec player wrapped his arms around Will and got dragged for 5 yards. That's when Will stopped running. Clutching the ball, he shook his torso and sent the Sorec kid backsliding to the middle of the field. The boy landed so hard and skidded so far that he took the four feet of green turf with him. It bunched under his backside like a displaced rug. Will resumed running toward the end zone. Two guys were getting close. He gave one the stiff arm and bounced the other back with his hip. The coach shook his head in delight as Will passed the 20-yard line, the 10, the 5, and sauntered into the end zone for a touchdown.

The Perilous Falls crowd exploded and Cassian started playing a jubilant version of the same song he always seemed to play. Will's initial enjoyment faded when he faced the stands. At first he thought they were cheering his score. But he quickly realized they were fighting, bickering, yelling at one another. Even his mom was now shouting at the top of her voice at his dad and the kids.

Perilous Falls Middle scored the field goal. Andrew congratulated Will, who was too busy checking on Lilith across the field to notice. She gave him a big thumbs-up.

On what have I set my heart? On what have I set my heart? Will kept thinking to himself, smiling at her. Sitting on the sidelines, he looked over his right shoulder to the very top of the stands.

Cassian, perched behind the console, pointed at him with two hands, swaying to the music.

"Will Wilder, this one's for you," he purred into the microphone. Then he unleashed the obnoxious lullaby that made some in the crowd swoon. Many began a trancelike dance while others argued with those around them. The imps crouching on shoulders and perched in the stands did their best to stoke division: pulling at hair and swatting the unsuspecting. Across the field, Lilith stared straight at Will and began jamming to the music. He watched her intensely.

She may be the maiden I have to protect. The girl who could save my life . . . Or am I being "conquered" by beauty?

Will dropped his face into his hands, helplessly confused.

"This headstone is no help at all. It's too old and the name is scratched off. Is that an 'n-e-y' here at the end?" Simon asked, squatting next to the marred, crooked gravestone beside an open pit.

"Let's find the next one," Cami said, shining a flashlight on the unreadable headstone. "The voice in the helmet said I had to take down the names on the graves that had been violated. There's got to be others."

Simon looked at the gravestones and tombs down the row beside them. Shadows lengthened across every path. It was his idea to start at the back of the cemetery and work their way forward. "All right. Why don't we go down each row, together. Quickly. It's getting dark, Cami, and we don't want any trouble."

"It'll be fine. Come on." She lugged the brown bag with the St. Joan helmet. Simon walked ahead of her, hoping he could speed up the search. Attending Will's game didn't seem like such a bad idea anymore.

Simon halted unexpectedly. He couldn't walk any farther for some reason. "Uh, Cami. We have a problem," he squealed.

"What's going on?" she asked nonchalantly.

Simon couldn't lift his feet. He was stuck. "My feet won't move."

"Just lift one up and then the other," Cami tried to assure him. "You'll be fine."

His face flushed from the effort to move. He hopelessly gyrated, even flapped his arms like wings, but his feet were stuck in place. "It's like something is holding them down. Come over here and help me."

Cami shone the flashlight at his feet and saw nothing but Simon's tennis shoes. While he moaned and cried for help, Cami slipped St. Joan's helmet onto her head. When she cast the light back toward Simon's feet, she saw the outlines of four imps, paws wrapped around the boy's ankles, staring directly at her.

"What is it? I can see from your face that something is— What are you seeing, Cami?"

"Not good—what do I do?" Cami said to herself.

"For what? What 'do you do' for what? Tell me what's going on." Simon was swiftly approaching panic mode.

The tender French voice filled Cami's ears. *They fear the helmet. Or rather, the one who gives it power. Move closer to the creatures and they will scatter.* She did exactly as she was told and took Simon by the hand. Cami saw faint outlines, like holograms of the pint-sized devils, scuttling away.

Simon could again lift his feet.

"How did you do that?"

"I'm not sure, but let's get moving," Cami said. Up ahead she saw what appeared to be more imps, lurking behind gravestones and in the trees. "Stay close to me, Simon."

"Don't worry," he said, tightly holding her one hand with both of his own. "I'll be right here—you know—to protect you."

"Go to the front of the graveyard. At the open grave you will find answers for your friend. Hurry." Cami picked up her pace, with Simon clinging to her for dear life.

With much of the town at the football game, the Brethren fanned out across Perilous Falls, doing what they could to weaken the power of Asmodeus. Philip had set up circular grills beneath most of the storm drains in the city. In pairs, the Brethren descended into underground tunnels to light the grills and fill them with fish hearts, livers, and incense. Lucille and Bartimaeus were assigned to light the incensors downtown.

"Once we fire up these last four burners, we should be good," Bartimaeus said, dumping the fish organs from a plastic bucket into one of the pits.

"This is a rather curious way to weaken a demon," Lucille said, a blowtorch in her gloved hand. She lit the brightly colored pebbles in the pit and stepped back. "Though I have to say Philip's incense mixture does conceal the fishy smell rather well."

"I know it's weird but we had to do it. It's how your daddy whipped the thing."

"Is that what the diary said?"

"The diary said it was a group effort. But I saw what happened when your daddy faced Asmodeus."

"You *saw* it?" Lucille lifted the front of the welder's mask she wore. "You mean in a vision?" Bartimaeus was a *Sensitive* who could sometimes intuit or feel things before or after they occurred.

"When we came up in the crypt the other night, the Column of Fire was there just spinnin' away, so I went up to it and asked to see how Jacob beat this demon." He moved on to the next pit, bucket in hand. "Well, Jacob could see the creature, but hard as he tried, he couldn't defeat it. Somethin' was wrong. All of a sudden a whole band of Brethren moved in. They were kickin' and prayin' and slayin'—all pitching in to make up for Jacob's shortcomings. They beat it together."

"The prophecy did say only in weakness would Will find his strength—and he would have to vanquish the thing through self-giving."

Bartimaeus had a faraway look in his eyes while he poured the fish organs into another pit. "When it was over, when they'd beaten the thing, there were victims. I saw 'em."

"You mean some of the Brethren died in the fight."

"More than some—"

The walkie-talkie on Lucille's hip crackled to life.

"Lucille. Bart. Come in." It was Brother Pedro's strained voice. "I need you here right away. I'm on the roof at city hall," he sporadically yelled. "We have a situation. Ahhhhh. Come now!" And the walkie-talkie went dead.

CHAPTER 21

IMP INVASION

Simon had the sickening feeling that he and Cami were being watched as they weaved among the gravestones and cracked mausoleums. Tree branches like witches' claws reached toward them. In the distance, they could see the off-kilter wrought-iron gate that fronted the cemetery.

"Let's start over there." Cami pointed to the far side of the graveyard, near the charred remains of the Karnak Center. "We'll check all the graves along the front gate."

"Fine. Just let's be quick about it." Simon still had Cami by the hand, making her his human shield, cowering behind her whenever he was spooked by a shadow or the rustling of trees.

Tyler Dirksen. Zeb Lynch. Felicity McFadden . . . None of these names, etched into the headstones, provided the kids with any "answers."

"This is a waste of time," Simon complained. "We should get out of here or come back with adults. A lot of adults. Adults driving cars with power locks who could drive us around the cemetery without having to—" Simon suddenly sounded as if he had just inhaled a pigeon and was choking on it. He pointed his flashlight to the open grave and headstone to their left and released Cami's hand. "Do you see the . . . the . . . It's the kid's name!"

Cami read the name on the square gravestone next to the open hole. "I see it." Seeing the name carved in the stone took her breath away. "We've got to tell Will. I can't believe . . . Do you think it's the same person?" Just as she leaned down to confirm the name, to make sure that she hadn't lost her mind, a voice like brakes screeching made her jump.

"What are you young'uns doing here?"

Simon went white with fear.

"We . . . we're . . ." Cami was too shocked by the tall, old man's face to formulate a sentence. It looked like that of an emaciated horse, if the horse had been rolling in dirt or soot for days. His clothes were ratty and as filthy as his face.

"Can you two not understand English? Name's Lemar James. I'm the night watchman here. Be interested to know who in creation you two are."

Simon strained to think of something to say or do. He nervously glanced up Dura Lane, hoping that someone would come along and help them. That's when Simon saw a third open grave, two places over from where they stood.

When he shone the flashlight on the face of the tombstone, he and Cami mouthed in quiet terror what was written there: LEMAR JAMES 1934–2002.

On the freight elevator in the back of city hall, Bartimaeus Johnson's hands were extended, his eyes tightly shut. "We're walking into something baaaaaaad, Lucille." He lightly shook his head. "Somethin's up there. I don't see anything, but I sure can feel it."

"Is it a demon?" Lucille pushed back the silky arms of her jacket, readying herself for whatever awaited them upstairs.

"I don't think it's a demon. Feels more like some lesser form of evil—maybe some *Fomorii*." The elevator dinged and the door slid open. "But I have been wrong before."

The sound of Brother Pedro screaming greeted them as they stepped out onto the roof. Pressed up against the short wall surrounding the roof, Pedro writhed. He struggled against some unseen force, involuntarily rising up toward the top edge of the wall.

"Bart, as much as you can, I need you to tell me where these creatures are," Lucille whispered, pounding across the roof.

"I'm on it," Bart said, closing his eyes and leaning forward on his crutches.

"Free him," Lucille called out, flinging holy water from a

vial in her right hand. One of Pedro's arms, along with his long hair, was being pulled upward. His two legs were twisting off in the other direction. After Lucille doused him with the water, Pedro fell to the floor. She could hear scratching sounds all over the roof—growing louder by the second.

"Whatever they are, they're very powerful," Pedro warned, rubbing the back of his head.

Lucille bent her knees, assuming a fighting stance. She touched her forefinger and thumbs together, pulling her hands close to her chest.

"They're imps, minor demons. We're surrounded, Lucille," Bart said, without opening his eyes.

"Both of you: over here," Lucille ordered.

Pedro cartwheeled to her side and Bart hobbled near as quickly as he could.

"Get behind me," she whispered, "and move as I do."

Without another breath, she extended her arms and from her fingers shot a red and white ray that lit up the rooftop. She turned in a tight circle, blasting every inch of the tarred roof around them. As the ray burned through their scaled bodies, the creatures were momentarily visible. In brief torched poses of pain, the imps bared claws, gritted teeth, and grimaced in horror before vanishing from sight. Lucille continued her assault, making three full circles.

"Back up. Toward the elevator," she barked over her shoulder. Pedro and Bart inched backward, hoping Lucille had taken out most of the creatures. At the control panel, Pedro repeatedly punched the DOWN button. After nearly a minute, the door squealed opened. The trio backed in. For good measure, Lucille continued her light spray until the door began to close. The second it shut, thuds, like baseballs hitting the metal door, shook the car.

"You came just in time. They were going to dump me off the roof," Pedro exploded, bracing himself in the corner of the elevator. "My legs were like lead. I had no control over my body."

"The important thing is you're okay now, dear. Did you disable the speakers?"

Pedro pulled a series of cut wires from his pocket. "I not only disabled them, I crossed so many lines it will take a week to get them working again."

"Good." Lucille exhaled, wiping the perspiration from her forehead with the back of her hand. "Then we got everything done. That'll buy us some time. Let's get to Peniel and meet the others."

The halftime show at the Perilous Falls Middle School game looked more like a concert. All eyes were on Cassian revving up the crowd with his peculiar remix of the same tune. Dan Wilder could not understand how the audience, even his wife, could dance nonstop to variations of one song. Marin wore a set of noise-canceling headphones over her ears. She couldn't stand listening to Cassian's tunes around the house. When she heard from her mother who would be playing at the game, Marin asked to borrow her dad's noise cancelers. She grimaced at the people jamming around her.

"This is nasty music," she lisped to her brother repeatedly.

Leo too was disturbed by the display. "Can we leave? I mean, Will's team is going to win anyway," he said, pointing to the scoreboard. At halftime, the score stood at 46 to 3, in Perilous Falls's favor.

"We are not leaving until the game is over," Deborah droned, shaking back and forth in front of her seat.

When the second half of the game started, the crowd remained raucous. Coming onto the field from the locker room, Will hesitated when he saw even more imps crawling around than before halftime. They mobbed the stands and gyrated in time with the music along the sidelines. Forty or fifty of them were scattered around the field.

Cassian and his uniformed Amazons had cleared out, but the beguiling music continued to quietly throb from the speakers at the top of the stands. Will considered racing up there and disabling the console. With his strength, it would be easy to demolish the speakers and maybe disperse the imps. But before he could move, his team took possession of the ball and the coach told him he'd be replacing Caleb on this drive as quarterback.

Caleb, who was already on his feet, threw his helmet to the ground and flopped back onto the bench. He glowered at Will as he took his place on the field.

The other guys on the team were so spooked by the

speed and power of Will's passes that they let two fly by without even trying to catch them. On the first throw, the entire ball sank into the turf, creating a hole near the end zone. The other hit a cooler on the sideline, busting it wide open, sending blue liquid spraying in all directions.

Will came up with his own play for the third down. At the snap, he threw the ball straight up into the air. Shoving aside the linebackers with ease, he cleared a path to receive his own pass. No one else even reached for the ball. The opposing team had been so brutalized by Will's prowess that, though they initially ran toward him, one glance was enough to stop them in their tracks. Huge Sorec players raised their hands in surrender and offered no resistance at all.

Unopposed, Will charged toward yet another touchdown. His only obstacle: the scores of pint-sized devils now flooding the field before him. Like wild dogs, those at the front of the pack leapt onto his legs. Others scaled the backs and shoulders of their fellow imps to create a demonic wall, blocking Will.

As if practicing kung fu moves in midstride, Will kicked his legs off to the sides. Then he punched his arms out spasmodically, trying to knock the imps away.

The coach took his hat off and swatted his knee with delight. "Have you ever seen a kid do anything like that?" he asked his assistant coach. "I don't know what all the shaking's about, but man—is it working." To the eyes of the coaches, and the rest of the crowd, Will jabbed and mule kicked his way across the field in a display that was, to put it mildly, bizarre.

Approaching the end zone, he tucked his head low, drew the ball to his chest, and barreled through the wall of demons. Will flailed and spun into the end zone to cheers from some in the stands.

The coach embraced the players near him with joyous laughter, until he realized that Will was still kicking and throwing roundhouse punches at the edge of the field.

"Now what's he doing?" the coach asked no one in particular.

Dan Wilder stood and hustled the children out of their row. He took his wife by the shoulders, and despite her protests pushed her toward the exit. In horror, he continued to watch Will thrashing away in the end zone.

"Let's head home. All of you, we're going home," Dan ordered his family. At the bottom of the stair, Dan started toward Will, who was no longer flailing at the air. "Are you okay, son?" he yelled.

"I am now," Will said. The imps had apparently taken enough punishment and retreated to the stands.

"Come home. Come with us now," Dan demanded.

Will glanced up at the console still pumping out Cassian's sickening melodies. "I've got something to do first." He ran to the top of the stands. Dan started to follow Will. But hearing the calls of Leo and Marin, who were trying to keep their mother from returning to the bleachers, he joined the rest of the family. Pushing them toward the parking lot, Dan watched with concern as Will reached the console at the top of the stands.

Crouching behind the console, he examined the locked cabinet doors that housed the circuitry and fed the speakers music—that horrible, monotonous music. Will punched through, then ripped open the aluminum doors in seconds. Inside were stacked hard drives, furiously blinking in time to the music. He smashed them with his fists. Plastic and metal bits flew from the cabinet. Wispy smoke leaked from the wreckage. The music slurred and finally stopped altogether.

To his left, in the very last row, sat the old lady in the green shawl who had warned him about Baldwin. She wore headphones and stroked the head of the golden retriever standing at her feet. She gave Will a thumbs-up and smiled. Will nodded, but as he went to ask why she was so interested in him, she started down the stairs with so many others.

Mayhem reigned in the stands. Those who were previously swaying now complained angrily, demanding the music they had become addicted to. Family members and friends tried to restrain the afflicted. But they hysterically begged for the music to be restored. Some of them pushed their way toward Cassian's console. Will could see the imps fleeing the stands and most of the crowd seemed to be following them. The referee made an announcement that given the unruly audience, both teams had decided to end the game early. He asked everyone to "calmly" leave the field.

Rather than descend the stairs, Will thought it best to escape detection and drop over the back side of the stands. He threw himself over the railing and climbed down the metal framing on the rear of the bleachers. When he reached the bottom, he dodged the oncoming crowd making their way to the parking lot.

A fog had rolled in. It covered those returning to their cars or heading out onto Main Street. But Will knew it wasn't fog. He could smell the spicy hint of incense in the air. Those walking through the smoke seemed to be regaining their composure. Will's mom had even stopped shoving her husband and children away. The arguments of the stadium had quieted and Will knew the Brethren must have engineered the "smoke screen."

He was making his way to the locker room when Renny Bertolf ran up beside him. "I told you you were better than Caleb, better than Andrew—and all those guys."

"I'm not," Will said gravely, avoiding eye contact with the smaller boy. "I'm not, Renny."

"You are!" Renny jumped in front of Will and kind of ran backward so he could hold his attention. "You just killed Sorec Middle School, you're the hero of Perilous Falls, and the hottest cheerleader anywhere is having milkshakes with you tonight. Lilith told me that you all were meeting. She was really excited—"

Lilith! I've got to meet Lilith.

Will thanked Renny for coming and ran to the locker room. Andrew had been searching for Will inside the room to congratulate him. But Will entered and changed so quickly into his khakis, he was headed out the door, pith helmet in hand, by the time Andrew caught sight of him.

"Hey, Will-man!" Andrew yelled to no avail. "Will-man."

Will didn't even hear Andrew's calls. He ran out the locker room and sped toward Bub's, thinking only of Lilith and protecting the "maiden" who might protect him.

CHAPTER 22

SURROUNDED BY DEATH

"What do we do?" Simon whispered rather loudly to Cami as they faced the decrepit old man at the front of de Plancy Cemetery.

"I don't know," Cami said, smiling weakly.

"His name is on the tombstone," Simon squeaked, sheltering behind Cami. "He's dead. He even looks dead."

"What y'all so sceered for? What are ya doing here?" Lemar James asked, his mouth cracked and ashy.

"Run," Cami told Simon, pulling him along. "We're going to run—to Peniel."

And they did. The pair charged down the path and rounded the front gate, high-stepping it to Dura Lane.

The bewildered old man stood alone in the middle of the path lined with nothing but headstones and crabgrass. He was so confused. Since that flash of light, he hadn't seen anyone for days, until he happened upon the two kids. Lemar James wanted to go home. Only he couldn't remember where home was. "Keep everyone away. Keep everyone away," he repeated to himself, echoing the voice inside his head. He wandered down the path in his confusion, hoping the execution of his duties would bring him clarity.

Cami and Simon were halfway up High Street and far enough from the cemetery to stop and catch their breath. "The game is probably almost over. Maybe we should head over to Burnt Offerings and wait there for Will?" Simon said.

"I think it'd be better to tell Miss Lucille what we saw," Cami said, trying to regain her composure. "And then we'll go meet Will. Peniel is not that far away."

"Doesn't Will deserve to know that he's been socializing with dead people?" Simon exploded.

"Okay, I'll call him," Cami said, removing the helmet and returning it to Simon's shopping bag.

Will's phone rang, but he did not pick up.

"Keep walking," Simon said, pushing Cami up the street and checking behind them. "We don't want Count Dracula catching up with us."

Cami dialed Andrew's number as they walked, hoping he was with Will. After several rings, Andrew's voice broke through. "Where are you guys?"

"Simon and I are headed to Peniel," Cami said. "I need to talk to Will."

"Peniel? Why are you all going there?" There was noise in the background. "I'm sitting in our room at Burnt Offerings. I thought we were all meeting here after the game?"

"We didn't make the game. Simon and I went to the cemetery and we've got to tell Miss Lucille what we saw. Where is Will? I need to talk to him."

"Unless you're that cheerleader, Lilith, I don't know if he wants to talk to you. I heard he was going to Bub's to meet with her. He didn't even say goodbye to me when the game was over. After making like seven touchdowns he was acting all—"

"Go to Bub's and tell him to come meet us at Peniel," Cami demanded into the phone. "Carry him if you have to, but bring him there. That kid Renny Bertolf that he's been hanging around with—he's dead. One of the open graves at the cemetery has a headstone with his name on it. He died two years ago!"

Andrew jumped to his feet. "How can he be dead if he's walking around?" He grabbed a roll from the table and headed for the door.

"Just go to Bub's. Call me when you get there." Cami hung up just as she and Simon neared the gates of Peniel.

At Bub's, Will drummed his fingers on the front table, his eyes trained on the door. Every table was filled but one. A steady stream of people pushed through the glass door, but no Lilith. Will had already inhaled a milkshake and was losing patience. "Where is she?" he asked quietly, checking the faces at the tables.

Just as he was about to leave, Renny Bertolf passed by the front window. He was staggering—bruised and bleeding from his mouth. Will ran to the door and all but caught the boy as he stumbled in.

"What happened to you?" Will asked.

"Caleb," heaved Renny, wiping the trickle of blood from the corner of his mouth. His jacket arm was ripped and there were cuts on the side of his face. "I was walking over here with Lilith. He found out you were coming to meet her and went crazy. I tried to stop him, but . . ."

"Where are they now?" Will yelled. People at nearby tables stared in their direction.

"The cemetery. He said something about the cemetery," Renny struggled to answer.

"The CEMETERY?" Will's face turned red with anger. *Of course a demon would head for the cemetery. A place of death . . . surrounded by death . . . It would have more power there.* "We've got to go save her."

"I'm scared, Will." The small boy looked as if he'd been running in traffic—and got to know each car intimately.

"You'll be fine with me," Will said, adjusting his pith helmet. "I can take care of Caleb—whatever he is." Will stormed out the door of Bub's, with Renny hobbling behind him.

Aunt Lucille sat at her father's desk and deliberately dialed Dan Wilder's number, with Simon, Cami, and Abbot Athanasius surrounding her. "Dan, I've just learned something disturbing and I need your help."

The kids couldn't hear Dan's response, but one side of the conversation was enough to get the meaning.

"We don't know where he is. Cami and Simon were just at the cemetery. It turns out that Renny boy that Will befriended—he's been dead for two years. . . . Dead. Yes, dead. His grave was one of those disturbed." Aunt Lucille grimaced and stared at the receiver for a split second. "Hello, Dan? Are you there? Oh, good. He may be with Will now. . . . We don't know. . . . Your son's life may be at stake. . . . That's what we do when a member of the family is in danger; we step in to protect them! . . . I might need Leo and Marin's help. . . . I understand that, but Will is in danger NOW!"

While she argued with Dan, Cami's cell phone rang. It was Andrew. She retreated to a corner and took the call.

"He's not here," Andrew said, standing in the doorway of Bub's Treats and Sweets. "I don't know where he got to. Hold on." Andrew went over to the first table nearest the door, one of the three against the front window. "Excuse me, have you all seen a kid with dark hair in a pith helmet? Seen where he went?"

A rotund man in overalls, with the remains of a doughnut in one hand and powdered sugar covering his thighs, looked up. "Sure, he was here a few minutes ago, right, Harry? The Wilder boy."

His emaciated tablemate in a seersucker jacket nodded, continuing to sip his coffee.

"Couldn't a been more than a few minutes ago. He shot out of here with some other little kid who was all busted up." The fat man stuck his tongue out in mock disgust.

"What did the kid look like?" Andrew asked.

The thin man in the seersucker jacket smirked, raised his gray eyes to meet Andrew's, and deadpanned: "Looked like the Phantom of the Opera's son."

The fat man giggled. "He did look like the phantom's son. Haa haaaaaa. Only this kid was messed up, like he'd been hit by his daddy's falling chandelier." He swatted his friend for a reaction and got none.

"Did . . . did you see which way they went?" Andrew stammered.

"The Wilder boy screamed something about the cemetery. 'Spect that's where they went. Right, Harry?"

The other man took a swig of coffee and silently nodded.

"Thanks," Andrew said, running from the shop. "Will went to the cemetery. And Renny's with him," he blurted into the phone.

Cami relayed the information to Lucille Wilder, who resumed her heated call with Dan. "He's at the cemetery. Go there with the kids. . . . Dear, I know all that. . . . Where did they lure Daddy and your father? Exactly. Their power is strongest there. This demon is playing for keeps. If you care about Will, you'll meet me at the cemetery with the children, Dan, or I'll come get them myself." She slammed down the phone and turned to Athanasius.

"It's a *Sinestri* trap—one the Wilders keep falling into." Lucille rose, flexed her fingers, and headed for the staircase. "I was too late to help my father and my brother, but I'll be darned if I fail Will." Her blue eyes went misty. "We can't."

"I'll run up ahead. Join me there when you can," Athanasius advised. Without another word, he gathered up Cami and Simon and raced after Lucille down the spiral staircase—all of them intent on reaching de Plancy Cemetery as quickly as possible.

CHAPTER 23

DUST TO DUST

Will and Renny crouched next to a cracked mausoleum in the middle of the graveyard. When they heard Caleb screaming, they ducked behind the nearest structure—a bricked family tomb—which unbeknownst to Will was emblazoned with the name MODO.

Ten yards off, Caleb held Lilith by her arms and seemed deranged. He spoke quietly, then burst into yells, making it hard for Will to understand what was being said. Will could hear the yells, but Caleb's whisperings were unintelligible.

"You said to meet you here. I met you here," Caleb said intensely. "You said to get the other guys to jump him. We jumped him. You said to wrap him in chains. I wrapped him in chains. IT DID NO GOOD." Caleb wore an expression of anger and frustration that Will had never seen before. He strained to hear what was being said, to no avail. But his nose itched and he fought back a sneeze.

Caleb gripped Lilith's arms tighter. "You said you'd tell me! So what is it? Why the quiet act all of a sudden?"

Will grabbed at the corner of the tomb, ready to sprint and knock Caleb into next Tuesday. Watching the scene, he gripped the wall tighter, bits of the brick turning to pebbles in his hand.

"Don't go. You don't know what he'll do," Renny warned.

"I can take him," Will spat out. "I just demolished him on the field. I have to protect her." Will never took his eyes off Lilith, whom he could tell, even from a distance, was panicked. She struggled to break free of Caleb's grip.

Renny held Will's arm. "If he's a monster or whatever, he'll destroy you."

"He won't. I'm stronger than he is," Will said, sneezing into his hand.

"How, Will? How are you stronger than him? Look what he did to me."

"You don't have to worry." Will touched his chest. "I wear this amulet." He pulled it out of his shirt so Renny could see. "Don't tell anybody. But so long as I have this, I'm like invincible. It has the hair of Samson inside, and it gives me incredible power." He tucked it back into his shirt. "Everything's going to be fine."

Caleb raged at Lilith in the clearing. "I've had it with you! When do I get my strength? You promise, and you promise, and you tell me nothing. I thought you liked me!"

Will had heard enough. He got to his feet and rushed Caleb.

Abbot Athanasius stepped out of the shadows, blocking his path. "William!" he hissed. Will skidded to a stop.

"What do you see?" the abbot asked.

"He's a demon." He pointed at Caleb. "He's a demon. He's going to hurt her—Lilith."

"I didn't ask that. What do you SEE?"

Will blinked in anger and confusion. "I don't see anything," he hissed at the abbot. "But I know he's a demon. I can feel it."

"Feelings are changeable," the abbot said, situating a thick purple ribbon around the back of his neck. "Your gift was never your feelings but your sight. I hope it is not too darkened. Stay here." He turned to Caleb, arms at his side, touching his forefingers and thumbs together. The abbot intoned Latin as he pointed three fingers of each hand squarely at the boy. Caleb backed away from Lilith with a look of sheer terror. A thin blue light radiated from the abbot's hands and reached toward Caleb.

"What are you doing? Who are you?" Caleb screamed.

"Discede ergo nunc, discede, seductor. Tibi eremus sedes est. Tibi habitatio serpens est: humiliare, et prosternere."

"What do you want? Are you her dad?" Caleb stumbled over a gravestone and Lilith hid behind a tree.

"Silence, spirit! You answer my questions alone," the abbot said. "Your name? And how many of you inhabit this boy? YOUR NAME?"

"I . . . I'm Caleb Gibbar. I . . . I . . ."

The abbot trained both the blue rays on him and moved closer. "Your name, beast? Not the boy's. YOUR name?" Caleb tucked his head to his chest and covered it with his arms.

In front of the de Plancy Cemetery, Dan Wilder pulled up just in time to catch Aunt Lucille approaching with Cami and Simon, who was still holding the brown shopping bag with the St. Joan helmet inside.

"How's that for perfect timing, dear? Thank you for coming," Aunt Lucille sang out. "Simon and Cami, run ahead and find Will. I'll be right behind you with the kids." She opened the back door of the station wagon and Leo and Marin climbed out.

"Stay close to Aunt Lucille, okay, guys?" Lucille turned sternly to Dan. "You're not coming?"

He clutched the wheel of the car and shook his head. "I can't . . . I can't . . ."

"Well, I haven't time for a debate, dear. And neither does Will." She took Leo and Marin by the hand and marched them into the darkness of the cemetery.

Dan sat in the car, the window rolled down, listening to a boy shrieking in the distance. It wasn't Will, but it was a boy. He reluctantly stepped out of the car and slowly walked toward the cemetery gates when he was startled by a dog leaping at his pant leg. It was an old golden retriever. *It couldn't be . . .*

"Raphe?" The dog yipped and licked his hand. "I thought

you died a long time ago, boy." He dropped to his haunches and found himself suddenly laughing as the dog lapped at his face. When Dan was younger, Raphe was his constant companion. They went everywhere but to school together. He hadn't seen him since that horrible day when he was twelve—the day he lost his father and mother. Dan was like a boy again, nuzzling his old friend in the shadows. Tears, which he could not explain, spilled from his eyes.

"Danny."

He turned toward the huge oak tree that grew along the cemetery fence. There stood a figure in the dark, beneath the tree's broken shadow. She called his name again. Dan wiped his eyes and stood warily.

"Yes?"

Into the light stepped a woman with white hair and high cheekbones. She yanked at her green shawl, brushing tears away from her eyes.

"Danny. That's actually not Raphe; it's his son. I never quite got over Raphe either."

Dan inched closer, with wonder and trepidation. There were sprays of wrinkles around the woman's eyes and she was much smaller than he remembered her being. Slack-jawed, as if encountering a ghost, he slowly mouthed, "Mother?"

In the cemetery, the abbot relentlessly demanded the name of the demon inhabiting Caleb. Over and over the boy kept muttering his own name, until he finally passed out.

The abbot dropped his hands in frustration. "This is useless. He's not possessed."

"He is," Will protested. *AH-CHOO! AH-CHOO!* "He is. I know it. The demon has to be right here."

"He's right," Renny called out from the edge of the Modo tomb. "I saw him with my own eyes. Caleb's the demon. You've got to kill it."

Cami, Andrew, and Simon came running up the path. "Don't listen to him, Will," Cami yelled.

"He hurt me badly—three times," Renny said hysterically. "He'll kill us all if we don't stop him."

"Renny Bertolf has been dead for two years," Cami told Will, pointing to the open pit nearby. "His grave is over there. I don't know how he's walking around, but he is."

Will sneezed madly. He was dazed with confusion. *How could Renny be dead? He's standing right there. Caleb has to be Asmodeus. He has to . . . Where did Lilith go? Lilith knows Renny. I've got to protect her. She "must be protected."* "Lilith? Lilith?" Will screamed.

"What do you see, William?" the abbot asked. "We need your eyes."

Will panted, looking all around him. Renny was still standing by the tomb. Andrew, Simon, and Cami were walking toward him. He saw nothing out of the ordinary. No extra shadows. No glimmering lights. No creatures.

"Nothing," Will bleated helplessly. "I see nothing."

Cami put an arm around him. "It's okay, we're here for you."

"I'm here for you too." Renny shuffled forward. He was

so alone and pitiful. "They're trying to separate us. They're jealous that we're friends."

"I'm going to just stand behind you if you don't mind," Simon whispered to Andrew.

"I was the only friend who cared when they were ignoring you," Renny said. "They don't understand us."

"Stay where you are," the abbot ordered Renny.

"Tell him I'm your friend," Renny pleaded with Will. "Don't let them hurt me too. How can I be dead? I'm right here."

"He's dead, Will. That's Renny Bertolf's body, but there's no kid in there," Cami said, staring the small boy down.

"And who do you think is in here?" Renny spoke in a smooth, sultry voice, eyeing her hatefully. "Why don't you come over and see who's inside. What are you afraid of, Cami?"

"Don't converse with it," the abbot said, stepping between the kids and Renny.

"Step aside, superstitious shaman." With a flick of Renny's hand, the abbot flew into the side of a tree and was out cold.

Cami took the shopping bag from Simon and slipped the Joan of Arc helmet over her head.

"Since you're wondering, why don't I show you who's in here." Before the kids' frightened stares, Renny Bertolf's head turned to putty. It then molded into a succession of faces, beautiful and horrible: fat old men, fine-boned women, a stoic man with different-colored eyes, a wrinkled woman with a hook nose, and finally—after a string of children—the tanned features of Cassian with his pony-tailed black mane emerged. Renny's small body stretched and grew before their eyes to six feet. "How's that for power?" He snapped his leather coat and started humming his familiar tune.

Will spotted Lilith, shivering near the tree where the abbot lay. He raced to her side.

"Stay away from me, kid," Lilith barked at him, sashaying toward Cassian.

"But I think I'm supposed to protect you," Will whined.

Inside the helmet, Cami heard the clear, strong voice of the maiden. *"Now Will knows who the demon is. But it is you the beast desires. Take your friends and flee from it."*

"Guys," Cami whispered to Simon and Andrew. "We've got to run. Come with me, now."

Lilith stood before Cassian. "I brought him here. I did as you asked. I get to stay like this forever? That was the deal. I'm free, right?"

Will tried to process everything he was hearing while Cami urged him, "Run! Come with us now!"

But I'm supposed to protect the maiden. Unless she's not the . . .

While the thought was still forming in his head, Cassian laid a hand on the side of Lilith's face. When he lifted it, her cheek was wrinkled and saggy. "Poor Lilith. You failed. You couldn't figure out the source of Wilder's power or where the relic was. I had to do it all myself."

Will reached out to touch Lilith's arm but recoiled as her face and entire body withered with age. And then for a brief moment, she looked back at him, quaked, and turned to a statue of ash. Before he could speak a word, she collapsed to the floor: a cheerleader's uniform in a pile of soot.

Cami, Simon, and Andrew ran down the path, still pleading for Will to follow.

"For you are dust and to dust you shall return." Cassian threw his long ponytail over his shoulder and regarded the pile of ash before him with a smirk. "She was Baldwin's cousin. A helpful pawn for a time. But the old girl was not bright. Hardly worth your energy. Did you think you could save her, Will?" Cassian laughed quietly. He lowered his sunglasses, waiting for a response.

Will knew better than to speak with a demon. He backed away slowly. *Wrong maiden!* Will thought. Over Cassian's shoulder, he could see his friends vanish down the grave-lined pathway. *It's Cami. I have to protect Cami!*

"We can be friends, Will Wilder. We were already such close friends. Give me the amulet and I'll let you and the others go." Cassian held open his hand.

Will didn't move. He needed the talisman to strike down this demon—this "clawed hellion." *Why did the prophecy call Asmodeus the "clawed hellion"?*

"No amulet for me? Then I'll have to gain strength some

other way." Cassian smiled and spun around. A sharp, black serpent's tail sliced the leather coat in two from the inside, then slithered out onto the dirt. From the top of its tarlike, misshapen back, the thing sprouted three heads: one of a bull; one of a man with changing features; and one of a ram, complete with turned-up horns. Two slick, ebony arms with pincers blossomed from the demon's torso.

No sooner had it appeared than it awkwardly galloped down the path in the direction of his friends. Will chased it with all the energy he could summon. With each stride, he could see the rest of the ungainly demon more clearly. One leg was that of a huge panther and the other a spindly, rooster-like limb with a sharp claw protruding from the calf.

Will felt a pang in his gut.

I guess that's why they called it a "clawed hellion."

CHAPTER 24

ASMODEUS

"Mother? Where . . . where . . . have you been? I thought you had died . . . ," Dan stammered to the woman in the shawl. For a moment he wondered if he was seeing a vision of some kind.

"I was scared, Danny. When I saw what the *Sinestri* did to your father—my pitiful, deluded Joseph—I was terrified. After I escaped, I hid inside a dead tree for days with Raphe. He protected me from those awful creatures. We survived as best we could, living in an abandoned shack near the old Wilder mine. I knew you were safe with Lucille. And for all these years, I've hidden in Wormwood—vowing to get back at the *Sinestri*. I tracked the one who bewitched your dad. I know who she is now, and I have seen her wicked ways." Marian Wilder embraced Dan, burying her face in his chest. "I'm so sorry, son. I was scared for me—for you."

Dan said nothing. Marian jabbered away.

"Lucille took such good care of you. From across the river, I watched her train you. I so wish I could have been here. Every time I attempted to come back, every time I got in the boat, something stopped me. The *Sinestri* infest that place. I thought they'd follow me over—or she would. I've spent my life studying the *Darkness*—running from it. I know things, Danny. I've seen things."

"Why are you here?"

"Because they are after your Will. When I saw what she was doing, I had to warn him. And you! Once I made that decision, I didn't look back. Raphe and I outran the creatures in the caverns and made it to the old dock. Once we were on the water, the fear just evaporated even though they pursued us into the river. Still, we made it. I thought the old hag restricted herself to Wormwood." She violently shook her head. "She doesn't. She's here in Perilous Falls."

"What do you mean?"

"The Witch of Wormwood. She's here. I've seen her." Marian fell quiet and craned her head around, peering into the darkness. "I'll tell you more later. Go to Will now. He needs you."

"Aunt Lucille and the Brethren are with him."

"Danny, my poor scared boy." She took him by the hands and kissed them. "I have spent my life like you, watching from the shadows—terrified—petrified by what I saw that day. It's no way to live. We have to act—to bring light. I see that now. It's not enough to observe evil. We have to risk everything—even our lives—to *fight* the *Darkness*. I'll tell you what I know soon, but right now we have to fight."

"I . . . I . . . I don't want to lose any more of my family."

"You will if you don't go into that cemetery now." She tenderly wiped a tear from the corner of his eye with the knobby joint of her forefinger. "I know how scary it is. I have only my wits and Raphe. You have gifts, Danny. Use them."

He touched the scar on his left cheek and sharply inhaled through his nostrils.

Up Dura Street, moving at forty miles an hour, a three-wheeled vehicle, with what looked like a great black tuba attached to the front, rumbled onto the cemetery property. Brother Philip sat behind the wheel; Bartimaeus and Tobias were in the back. They pulled up next to Dan Wilder.

"Where's Lucille?" Bartimaeus called out.

"She's . . . she's with the kids. In the cemetery. She went in with the kids."

"What'cha doin' out here?"

"I was waiting for you." Dan climbed aboard to the astonishment of Tobias and Bartimaeus. He turned to say goodbye to his mother, but she was already gone, as was Raphe.

"I guess miracles do happen every day," Bartimaeus said, ogling Dan Wilder. He clapped Philip on the back. "Let's go, Philip. We got a demon to bring down." Tobias nudged Dan and held his gaze with a look of respect and gratitude. Dan smiled back weakly. The off-road vehicle sped through the front gates and down the main aisle of the cemetery.

Cami, Andrew, and Simon stopped running and checked behind them. They could hear the pounding of feet, like a team of horses approaching. But the path was empty.

Aunt Lucille stuck her head out from behind a nearby tombstone. Marin and Leo were on either side of her. "I'm glad you all made it. Where is Will?"

"He's back there. He was talking to Cassian," Cami said.

"Cassian Modo? Oh dear."

Suddenly Simon looked up the trail. "Wait. There he is. There's Will. Why is he running so fast?"

"You kids should come back here," Aunt Lucille instructed.

Will motioned for them to move forward. "Go! Keep running," Will yelled as he approached. Just in front of him he could see what they couldn't: Asmodeus closing in on the lot of them. Just as disturbing, hundreds of imps were crawling over the tops of headstones and around the edges of the tombs, spilling onto the pathway. They seemed to be gathering around Asmodeus.

The demon awkwardly jumped off the ground and extended its serrated pincers toward Cami. Will had only one choice. He too leapt high and grabbed the back of the demon's tail, yanking it hard. The beast whimpered, its pincers making holes in the gravel. "I'll have the maiden," Will heard it rasp.

Cami, Andrew, and Simon stood shell-shocked, staring at the lengthening grooves in the ground before them. "Will, what are you doing?" Simon yelled incredulously.

"I've got Asm—this *demon*—by the tail." Will flew back

and forth, up and down in midair—struggling to restrain the demon invisible to his friends and family. He refused to let go. "Run! He's right here. And there are imps everywhere!"

The kids didn't realize that Asmodeus's pincers had come within inches of their heads.

Aunt Lucille stepped in front of Cami, Andrew, and Simon, pulling up her sleeves. She trained her red and white rays on the area just in front of Will. The way the rays spread on impact showed that she had clearly hit something.

"All right, Leo," Lucille screamed over her shoulder. "Show them what you've got." Leo moved next to her, placed his hands together at chest level, as if in prayer, and closed his eyes.

Will pulled hard on the demon's tail. Under Aunt Lucille's blast, it seemed more pliable, if not exactly weakened. Asmodeus spun around and faced Will, who held fast to its tail. The horror of the three heads: the angry bull, the enraged ram, and the constantly morphing human face in the middle, caused Will to tremble for a moment.

"I will devour you and all you love, Wilder," all three heads said in unison. "Don't worry, I'll save you for last." The demon turned back toward Aunt Lucille and started to run at her until Will lugged the tail over his shoulder like a rope, dragging the demon back. The thing clawed at the ground, but it could not find traction.

Simon shook Cami and Andrew in a panic. "Shouldn't we go now? Didn't you say we should run?"

Cami didn't move. "No, the voice says now is the time for us to stay and fight."

"With what?" Simon asked. "Your helmet?"

At that moment, Brother Philip's mobile incensor came bouncing over a bluff to Will's right.

"Turn it on, Bart," Brother Philip ordered through the side of his mouth. Given Will's position and the focus of Lucille's blast, Philip figured the demon had to be nearby, so he steered the vehicle between Will and Lucille.

Plumes of smoke billowed out of the funnel on the front of the three-wheeler. The beast let out a ferocious roar and recoiled from the incense. It doubled over and had to lean on a tall monument to steady itself. Will straddled the tail to try to weigh the beast down and keep it away from the others.

"Stop them, my little ones," the demon bellowed to the imps on all sides.

Hordes of the slick black creatures ran at the vehicle, Aunt Lucille, and the kids. Will tried to warn them, but his cries came too late. The imps hit Philip so hard, the mobile incensor swerved into a tree. Bartimaeus was saved by his seat belt, but Tobias and Dan went flying into the air.

As if struck by an invisible wave, Lucille fell to the ground. Will watched her helplessly drown in a crush of tiny black devils. "Leo," she cried, sinking beneath their weight. "Now. NOW!"

Leo, who had been standing perfectly still, parted his hands. A piercing white light issued from his body. As his flesh became incandescent, Will's friends and Marin gathered close to the boy. The tiny black creatures nearest Leo smoldered and disintegrated. His light rippled outward like a slow-motion nuclear blast. As it touched the imps, they became visible for a brief moment and then evaporated.

White smoke continued to spew from the dented and bent funnel on the front of the three-wheeled vehicle. Asmodeus thrashed about on all fours, clearly disoriented by the fumes covering the path. Then suddenly the creature unsteadily rose to its full height and yelled, "I want the power you possess, Wilder, and I will have it."

Asmodeus raised its tail, with Will aboard, and smashed it into the mobile incensor. Will sailed into a gravestone, snapping it in two. The three-wheeler flipped several times across the path. Leo, Marin, and Will's friends saw it coming and dove to the ground. Aunt Lucille, who was just regaining her feet, had her back to the oncoming vehicle. The rear tire hit her across the shoulder and sent her skidding into a statue of a veiled woman with a snake beneath her foot.

Will saw the terror on the faces of his friends and siblings as he rose from the dirt. They knew something malevolent was present but had no idea where. The demon crawled in their direction. It intended to devour Cami and the rest of them. Aunt Lucille wasn't moving and the abbot was out cold down the road. There was no one to vanquish this thing.

Will had to do something. But what? His fists clenched,

he started running at the beast. He'd fight the demon, use the amulet to beat it down, and save his friends.

"Hey!" Will called out to it.

Then he recalled the prophecy: *"For only in weakness shall he find his strength and only in self-giving shall he vanquish ASMODEUS."*

The demon turned his way, weary but powered by fury. Its heads grunted and yowled even as its body reacted more slowly.

Will ripped the amulet from inside his shirt and held it high. "You want my power? You want the power of Samson? Here it is. Go get it!" Will pitched the thing as far away from his friends as he could, high into the air. But the chain snagged on a tree limb only a few yards away. Without the amulet, his throwing arm wasn't so great. To everyone's amazement, Will's hair retracted and his upper body and arms visibly deflated.

The three heads of the demon laughed. "La-dee-dah-dee-dee-dah," it sang in Cassian's voice. It struggled to stand upright, using the huge oak trees to steady itself. "For centuries we have sought this. To have it given to us by a Wilder is a treat." Asmodeus easily reached up with its pincers, snapping off the branch that held the chain of the amulet.

"Will, come over here," Cami said, loudly enough for him to hear. Her face, partially hidden by the Joan of Arc helmet, was as serious as Will had ever seen it. She stood behind Leo, who remained aglow—Marin, Andrew, and Simon quivering beside her. Will backed up toward his friends.

"We will destroy this trinket and absorb its power." Asmodeus's three heads stared at the relic dangling from the branch it held. Will knew no demon could directly touch a relic, which is why Asmodeus clawed the branch and not the chain or amulet itself. "You're not so strong now, are you little *Seer*? Soon the people of Perilous Falls will turn on one another and destroy themselves. Then we'll rise against Peniel and all the other crumbling citadels the Brethren have erected. Asmodeus will rule over this plane—forever—all due to you, Will Wilder."

The beast ambled toward Will and his friends. "You know I wear many faces, Will." The faces of the middle head shifted at an alarming pace, transforming into anguished expressions of different people. "I crave more faces—more souls. I claim them with this." It slowly raised its massive, black rooster leg, turning it slightly to show off the metallic single claw at the back of the leg. "They were once identical, my legs. I injured this one in the fall from heaven. No matter. It does the trick." The talons dug into the earth, flicking soil in their direction.

Will had reached his siblings and friends. He pushed them all behind him. Leo's light continued to shine.

All three demon heads laughed as Asmodeus advanced toward them. "This display of bravery is so sweet. The little boy's light show is impressive. Sadly, it works only on minor demons and I am a major Marquis of Hell." Asmodeus's heads scanned both sides of the path. "Look at old Lucille, down for the count." She lay unmoving, splayed out next to a monument. "No one around to help the kiddies. They can't see me, Will, and you can't vanquish me. So I suppose, as we say in the casino business, the house will now take its *cut*."

"I think we should run," Will whispered to his friends.

"The voice in the helmet is telling me to stay here," Cami whispered back. "Don't move."

"What if the voice in the helmet is in your head?" Simon sputtered.

"What if I knocked you upside your head?" Andrew threatened Simon.

"The good news is, your friends won't see the final cut coming," Asmodeus said to Will. "Like those stupid boys I smacked around in your locker room: It happened so fast, they didn't know what hit them. And I'm so good at doing your voice, they thought I was you. 'Imagine that?'" the demon said in Will's voice. "Haaaaa. I had you believing that fool Caleb was a demon. How stupid you were. I only wish you'd struck him. I wanted to see you punished. To watch you suffer. Never mind. Making you watch your friends and family die will be much more satisfying."

Will could not have felt more defenseless—more useless—at that moment. This demon was closing in on his brother and sister and best friends, and even with all his training, with all he had learned, he was out of options. The prophecy talked of finding strength in weakness. But what did that mean? Then he made a lightning decision.

"Guys, we're going to spread out," Will whispered. "We're

going to run in different directions and confuse the demon. It can't run after all of us at the same time. Simon and Andrew, go try and wake Aunt Lucille. Cami, you take the kids and go hide over there behind the gravestones. I'm going to run out and distract him."

"I don't think you should, William," Cami said.

"I've got to. I'm the only one who can see it. It'll give you all a fighting chance."

"You ARE the only one that can see me," Asmodeus growled, whipping its tail under Will's legs. The boy fell to the ground, his pith helmet spinning away from him. The demon then laid the heavy tail over Will's torso, immobilizing him. "And you will be the last one to see me!"

"Not the last." Dan Wilder, looking stunned and dusty, his glasses off-kilter, stepped between the demon and the kids. "I see you, Asmodeus."

"Dad?" Will smiled for the first time since he got to the cemetery. "You're a *Seer*?"

Dan Wilder wasted no words. He formed a triangle over his chest with his forefingers and thumbs. From that finger-triangle he projected a red-and-white ray that cut into Asmodeus's tail.

As the creature's tail recoiled and flopped in pain, Will scrambled free, picked up his pith helmet, and raced over to Aunt Lucille. He lightly tapped her cheeks until her eyes fluttered open. "We've got a little demon problem we could use your help with."

She rolled her left shoulder back into place, wincing, and

with Will's help made it to her feet. They joined the others in the middle of the path as Dan continued to blast Asmodeus with his ray.

Aunt Lucille shook off her pain, touched her fingers and thumbs together, and joined Dan in his assault on the demon.

"I'm glad you're back with us, dear," she told her nephew with a hint of pride.

Will stood just behind them, helping direct his aunt Lucille's rays to the head and chest of the demon. To the outsider it sounded as if Will were offering play-by-play of a game.

"It's moving to the right. It just grabbed that big limb on the oak tree and is pulling its body up. It's lifting the rooster leg, the leg with the—*Run!*"

Asmodeus raised its lethal talons, the ones that presumably cut open coffins and could rip through human bodies like a buzz saw. Hanging from the lowest tree limb, the demon proudly displayed the three talons at the end of its foot and that single metallic claw on the backside of its leg. Asmodeus drew up the leg and prepared to strike Dan, Lucille, and Will with a single blow.

CHAPTER 25

TAKEN

Will's scream to "Run!" sent the kids scattering in separate directions—all except Marin. She remained where she stood, her hands clutching the sides of her dress, her mouth open, and a look of fright mingled with determination in her eyes. The girl released a piercing scream that caused even the demon to flinch.

The moment the sustained shriek hit its ears, Asmodeus knew what it meant. All three heads of the beast stretched heavenward, searching the skies for what would inevitably follow. The *Summoner* had issued her call.

Aunt Lucille and Dan did not stop pounding the creature with their rays, but to Will's astonishment, the rooster leg and claws never descended. Wrapped around the leg, he could vaguely see the glittering outlines of hands, like floating white Christmas lights. As he stared, the light sharpened. Hands of angels—strong, powerful angels—held the leg back until, all at once, they ripped it away from the demon's body.

Asmodeus moaned and cursed in anguish, falling to the dirt as the sparkling spirits carried the leg away.

Philip and Shen righted the three-wheeled vehicle, which was still spewing smoke where it crashed. Together, they pushed it back up the bluff.

"Will, where's the demon at?" Bart asked from the driver's seat.

Will pointed to the ground, beneath the oak tree's broken limb, an area lit up by Lucille's and Dan's rays. Bart turned the vehicle so that the funnel pointed to the spot where the ray's light splayed and splattered.

The combination of fish incense and the relentless red and white light literally shrank Asmodeus. The shriveled demon clawed at the dirt; dropped the branch holding the amulet; and in three strangled, small voices warned, "You restrain one of us and more will rise up. We have taken Wilders before and we shall again. We already have the hearts of your selfish people. The Brethren will fall." The three shrinking heads glared at Lucille, Dan, and Will. "It's good that you're afraid." With that, a flash of lightning exploded, illuminating the cemetery path, and Asmodeus was no more.

"You did it," Will said, laying his hands on the warm shoulders of his dad and great-aunt.

"We did it, son." Dan threw his arms around Will and

held him tightly. Down the path, in the darkness, Will saw the wispy, gray outlines of several people. Among them was Renny and an old man, thin as a pool stick. Renny waved and with the others, dissolved like smoke before his eyes. *Spirits of the dead. They're free of the demon.*

"Will, you look like you've seen a ghost," Lucille said, collecting the amulet of power from the pathway and dropping it into her pocket.

"I think I might have."

"I saw them earlier," Dan said quietly.

"Ya vision's gettin' stronger, Will," Bartimaeus said, ambling over. "'Member what Gamaliel said about your vision? That you'd see spirits of the dead and angels. You're growing into your gift. That's good."

"You met Gamaliel?" Dan asked. "The one who trained Jacob?"

Aunt Lucille leaned in. "There are a few things we've kept from you—during your absence. Are you back for good, Dan?"

"I may be." Dan touched Lucille's arm. "I saw my mother tonight, here at the cemetery."

"Oh, your vision is still refined. That's wonderful, dear. Was her spirit at peace?"

"Not her spirit. HER. She was here with Raphe . . . a new Raphe."

Lucille ran her knuckles along her jawline. "It can't be. I saw the *Fomorii* chase Marian down. I thought for sure she'd died in Wormwood after they killed your father."

"She survived. She's been over there all these years, hiding."

Lucille blinked in confusion. "She's been living in that evil pit? For decades? Why? I don't believe it. Are you sure it was her?"

While Dan pondered the question, Caleb stumbled up the path with Athanasius leaning on his shoulder. "Can you all help us here? The old guy is bleeding."

Philip, Tobias, and Lucille ran to look after the abbot, who despite a gash on the side of his head, was otherwise fine. "It's a flesh wound," he kept saying. "Don't be dramatic, I'm perfectly fine." He was more concerned with the whereabouts of Asmodeus.

Will tried to apologize to Caleb. But the boy was so spooked, he instinctively backed away from Will. "I just want to get home," he said. "Where's Lilith?"

"She . . . um . . . left," Will told him.

"All right," Caleb said, nervously checking out Leo, Marin, Cami in her helmet, and all the others. "I guess I'll see her later, then. I musta blacked out when that old guy with the beard started yelling at me and— What happened? He was lying next to a tree when I woke up. Next thing you know, he started to get up and we saw some kind of red lights over the hill. What was going on?"

Will and his friends alternately shrugged. "It's complicated," Will said, looking over at the beat-up three-wheeler, smoke belching from its front.

Caleb ran a hand through his hair and nervously took in

the entire group staring at him. "I'm going to head home," he said.

"You want company?" Andrew asked.

"No, I'm cool," he said, backing away. Caleb ran out of the cemetery, not wanting to spend another moment with Will Wilder or any of the other strange people standing around in the dark.

"You were mighty brave tonight," Bartimaeus whispered to Will. "Took guts to throw the amulet away. I mean, had the demon made off with it, we coulda all been killed. But it was still a pretty gutsy move."

"I shouldn't have taken it out in the first place. I thought with more strength I'd have control over things. . . ."

"Well, did ya?"

"Not really. I was only thinking about the things I wanted. I wanted to make the team and once I did, I wanted to keep feeling special, and there was Lilith. . . ." He grimaced and stared at the ground. "Then I thought I could use the power to protect other people. But to do it, I put everybody at risk and almost lost my sight . . . and the most important thing—you all."

"So you learned somethin' from your mistake. That's what mistakes are for, Will." Bart brushed the soil from the sleeves of his loud coat. "Keep looking beneath the surface. Most important thing is that question Gamaliel asked you. Get that right and everything else will follow: On what have you set your heart, my man? On what have you set your heart?"

Cami walked up and squeezed Will's deflated biceps,

which made him flinch. "Even without your muscles you saved us." She smirked through the opening of the metal helmet.

"Not really," Will said. "Had you not tipped me off to Renny being a zombie, you'd probably be digging my grave right now."

"Teamwork," she said, giving him a friendly shove.

"Teamwork." And he flicked her metal helmet just like she always flicked his pith helmet. She started to remove the medieval hard hat just in time for Aunt Lucille to take it in hand.

"I'll bring that back to Peniel now, dear," Lucille said, passing it to Tobias. "But you know where it is if you ever need it. You did very, very well, Cami. It's nice to find a young person who knows how to follow directions." Lucille cut her eyes at Will and laughingly walked away.

On Saturday morning, Will rode his scooter to Burnt Offerings for his regular brunch with the gang. There were no Cassian Modo tunes blaring from the storefronts on Main Street, and Will felt that everything had returned to normal—even the Wilder home was peaceful again.

When he came down into the kitchen that morning, his mom and dad were laughing in the breakfast nook. "Where are you off to, Will?" his mom asked with a sparkle in her voice she hadn't had in days.

"Going to meet the gang at Burnt Offerings."

"Of course." She got up with an empty breakfast plate and came toward him. When she placed her face right next to his, he flinched a bit—given the way she had been yelling at the entire family recently. "Have a great time." She planted a kiss on Will's cheek and straightened his pith helmet. "Tell the kids I said hello."

Dan followed Deb to the kitchen sink with his own plate. "It's good to have Mom back, isn't it?" he whispered to Will.

Will bugged out his eyes and nodded. Then he got serious. "It's good to have you back too, Dad."

Dan adjusted his glasses and proceeded to the sink. Will blew past his siblings, who were fighting over a board game in the den, and headed for Main Street.

As he chained his scooter to the tree in front of the café, he watched a group of ladies passing a newspaper around their outdoor table.

"Isn't that just awful?" a woman with sunglasses that wrapped around the sides of her head told her well-coiffed friends. "That's the fourth child that's gone missing in the last three weeks." She pointed to a picture of a smiling boy of about ten on the front page.

"Were they kidnapped?" a fragile lady with a flutelike whimper of a voice asked.

"Read the paper. They weren't kidnapped, Polly," responded a woman whose loud, deep voice sounded just like Dan Wilder's old lawnmower. "Says right there, 'There were no ransom notes or any indication of kidnapping or foul play.' They just disappeared. That's what's so weird. They were there one minute, gone the next."

The woman with the wraparound specs pushed her coffee mug aside and leaned forward. "It's not just kids. Last year, my friend Jackie—y'all remember Jackie." There were nods around the table. "Well, Jackie's family stuck her in that retirement resort over in Ekron. I went to visit her a couple of months ago. Vanished! She ain't there no more."

"People don't just vanish," Polly, the squeaky-voiced woman, said. "They have to go somewhere. I hope the police are working to find those poor kids. Jackie too."

Will's stillness and knitted brow revealed how riveted he was by their conversation. But after making eye contact with the human lawnmower, he broke away with some embarrassment and hustled into the café.

Simon was at the back table, lost in a slim green paperback written by someone named William Golding. Andrew was already halfway through his eggs. "Muffins haven't come yet, so you're right on time," Simon said, laying the book down.

"Settle a bet for us," he said, looking toward Andrew. "Are you staying on the football team?"

"Probably not. I got on by using the amulet and without it I'm not all that good."

Simon opened his palm to Andrew. "Pay up, lummox. I told you he wouldn't stay. I hope that means you'll be returning to the Scouts, Will."

Andrew slapped a dollar into Simon's hand. "Will-man,

you played strong. That last game was amazing. But I think you're right; without the relic juice, you're gonna get creamed."

Max came rolling into the room with Cami running behind him. They were both distressed, Cami out of breath. "You won't believe this, guys," she said. "Tell them. Tell them."

Max tilted the seat of his wheelchair forward so he could see them better. "I've been having this dream. . . ."

Andrew buried his head in his hands. Simon sat back and rolled his eyes. Will felt a pinch in his gut.

"I hope I wasn't in this one," Will said.

"No, but my friend Zachary was." Max spoke with effort, working to make sure every word was understood. "Zachary is in class with me. He uses a wheelchair too. A few days ago I started seeing him and other kids in my dreams. They're laughing and eating and all of a sudden this blackness comes over them." He used his one mobile hand to make a fluttering motion. "Little black dots come in and cover them and then the kids are gone."

"I wasn't one of the kids, was I?" Simon said.

"What did you see next?" Will asked.

"That was it. It was the same dream every night. Zach and other kids I can't make out disappear and people go out looking for them. Last night, I woke up screaming," Max said, shaking. "Cami came in and I told her about Zach and the others. Zach was so clear."

"Then on the newsstand, just down the block, we see

this." Cami held up the front of the *Perilous Times* news-paper, her hand shaking. It was the ten-year-old boy the women outside were talking about. "That's Zachary. That's Max's friend. He's missing."

Aunt Lucille stomped down the pier in front of her home. She opened the door to the boathouse and jumped into the *Stella Maris*, the sleek, baby-blue speedboat she used any-time she went out on the river. She checked the gauges and reached for the rope holding the boat in dock.

"I wouldn't go over there, Lucille."

She snapped her head to the corner of the boathouse to find a woman her age with a dog at her feet. "Marian?" It was Dan's mother. Lucille could not believe what she was seeing. "How did you survive the *Fomorii* attack? I saw them chase you down."

Marian knelt near the boat. "I promise to explain every-thing soon. It's not a pretty story, Lucille. I figured you'd try to head to Wormwood after Dan told you that I had re-turned. But you can't go there now."

Lucille folded her arms defensively in front of her. "Why not?"

"Because she's here. The Witch of Wormwood is here."

"Where is she?"

"Right HERE."

The golden retriever's features turned snakelike before

Lucille's eyes, and soon its whole body became smooth and reptilian. The thing slithered onto the floor of the boat.

Lucille backed away and attempted to press her thumbs and forefingers together. But the snake, in a shot, wrapped itself around her hands—making contact impossible. When she looked up, the kind-faced woman kneeling at the prow was no more. Marian's eyes had gone black as night, and her face was now long and hollowed out.

"You have obstructed us for the last time, Sarah Lucille."

The woman opened her mouth and emitted a choked, guttural sound. She vomited out a steady stream of flies, maggots, and gnats. They covered Lucille's body and dragged her flailing and screaming to the floor of the *Stella Maris*. The struggle lasted all of three seconds.

After a prolonged silence, Lucille Wilder's boat cut through the waters of the Perilous River and headed downstream, a hooded figure at the wheel, a snake peering over the rail.

❖ AUTHOR'S NOTE ❖

I have received countless letters and emails from readers of the series asking whether the relics mentioned throughout the books are real. The answer is: most of them are. Here is some background information on a few of the relics and where you can find them. This might appeal to readers, young and old, who wish to have their own adventures. Although, I will repeat what Aunt Lucille and Bartimaeus are forever telling Will: look, but don't touch!

The Helmet of Joan of Arc (Will Wilder #3): According to legend, this helmet, which dates from 1375–1425, was given by St. Joan to the Church of St. Pierre du Martroi in Orléans, France. It hung over the main altar until it somehow came into the possession of the Metropolitan Museum in New York—where it resides today (when it is not at Peniel). For more information, visit: metmuseum.org/art/collection/search/21988

The Ark of the Covenant/St. Mary's of Zion Church, Axum, Ethiopia (Will Wilder #2): The second Will Wilder book opens with a flashback to Axum, Ethiopia. Hundreds have written to me asking if there is any validity to the claim that the famed Ark of the Covenant is actually in Axum. I did extensive research on the region and St. Mary's of Zion to make sure that the opening scene accurately reflected the original spot where the Ark would have been kept at the time Jacob Wilder visited Axum. The Ethiopian Christian community there claims that the Ark was brought from Jerusalem to Ethiopia by the son of King Solomon and the Queen of Sheba. According to *Smithsonian* magazine: "It arrived nearly 3,000 years ago, they say, and has been guarded by a succession of virgin monks who, once anointed, are forbidden to set foot outside the chapel grounds until they die." Since no one is allowed to see the Ark, save for the Guardian, curious adventurers will have to settle for a view (through the fence) of the chapel where the monks say it is stored today. For more information, visit: smithsonianmag .com/travel/keepers-of-the-lost-ark-179998820/

The finger bone of St. Thomas (Will Wilder #1): The bones of Doubting Thomas can be found at the Basilica of St. Thomas the Apostle in Ortona, Italy (where the opening of the first Will Wilder book takes place), as well as at the San Thome Basilica in Chennai, India. Thomas was martyred in India, but most of his remains were transferred to Edessa in the fourth century. Hundreds of years later, most of his bones were moved to Ortona. But if you want to see his finger bone, it is on display at the Santa Croce in Gerusalemme (the Basilica of the Holy Cross in Jerusalem), which, despite the name, is a church in Rome. The story goes that Constantine's mother, Helena, established the church in Rome with dirt she brought from Jerusalem. Thomas's finger bone may have been housed in this church since the fourth century. (Perhaps the finger bone in Perilous Falls is one of the other nine digits of the saint.) For more information, visit: santacroceroma.it/en/features-3/reliquie.html

Monte Cassino Abbey (Will Wilder #3): This abbey is one of the oldest monasteries in the world, and Jacob Wilder's base of operations during World War II. Founded in the sixth century by St. Benedict, the father of Western monasticism, the abbey has been home to generations of Benedictine monks who continue to live and work within its walls. The crypt, library, and grounds described in this book are accurate descriptions of the monastery today. In 1944, the abbey was leveled by Allied forces who suspected that the Germans were housing artillery units and troops on the monastery property. Within a few decades, Monte Cassino was rebuilt where it stood prior to the bombing. For more information, visit: abbaziamontecassino.org/abbey/index.php/en/

There are many more relics and sarcophagi, which appear in the series, that are housed in museums, churches, and libraries around the globe. For the time being, I'll leave it to you to separate the real relics from the ones that I have reimagined for my own purposes. Happy hunting.

❖ ACKNOWLEDGMENTS ❖

Will and I owe a great debt of gratitude to my wife and my rock—the lovely Rebecca—who makes this and all my stories possible. And to the three adventurers who started me down this path: Alexander, Lorenzo, and Mariella. Thank you for giving me a reason to return to the "dark wood" of the desk and to stay there until I understood the entire tale. I love you all.

To my friends and collaborators at Random House, I think we finally have this thing down. Special thanks to Emily Easton, my editor and publisher at Crown, who I believe may well be a *Seer* herself. She never fails to spot my missteps and lead me back to the path. My dear Phoebe Yeh and the brilliant Barbara Marcus, president of Random House Children's Books, have made this house at Random a warm home for Will Wilder and me. I cherish you so.

Dominique Cimina and Mary McCue in publicity; John Adamo in marketing; Ken Crossland, our talented designer; Samantha Gentry, who kept every stage of production moving along; and the entire sales force have labored not only to create a beautiful book, but also to make sure Will's latest adventure reaches readers. With the Random House team at my back, who needs an Amulet of Power? Thank you. Thank you. Thank you.

Jeff Nentrup has topped himself with his latest Will Wilder cover. It is even more dynamic and fun than I imagined, and the interior illustrations make the story pop in unexpected ways. Thanks, Jeff.

Francis "Chip" Flaherty, my friend, consigliere, and agent on the entire Will Wilder series, has been a godsend. Three down . . . many more adventures to come. So grateful to have you on this ride, Chip.

For their inspiration and support, I must thank my friend and co-conspirator Laura Ingraham; Niko, Dima, and Maria Ingraham; Christopher Edwards; Jim Caviezel; Dean Koontz; Randall Wallace; Ron Hansen; Kyle Zimmer; Umberto Fedeli; Ryan Milligan; Monica and Kevin Fitzgibbons; Stephen Sheehy; James Faulkner; Cristina Kelly; Carla Turnage; Michael Paternostro; Mary Matalin; Msgr. Christopher Nalty; Terry and Kathleen White; and Pat Cipollone.

Special thanks to my EWTN family, especially Doug Keck, Michael Warsaw, Peter Gagnon, Lee South, Dorothy Radlicz, the Franciscan Missionaries of the Eternal Word, and the sisters of Our Lady of the Angels Monastery.

To my Fox News family: Thomas Firth, Alexis Papa, Elisa Cipollone, Robert Samuel, Nick Robertson, Andrew Conti, Kayvon Afshari, Tyla Tyus, Lauren Woodhull, Shannon Bream, Tucker Carlson, Sean Hannity, Meade Cooper, Amy Sohnen, Ron Mitchell, John Finley, and Suzanne Scott—it is a joy to collaborate with you all, seen and unseen.

Waves of gratitude to my parents, Raymond and Lynda Arroyo, and my brother Scott, who encouraged the madness early on with no assurance that a good story would emerge. Love you all.

To the kids, parents, teachers, librarians, aunts, uncles, grandparents, and all who have entered Perilous Falls, you are so appreciated. The older I get, the more I believe that a story is the most precious gift we can give a child—and each other. Thank you for making Will Wilder a part of your story.

I need to also thank all the students, reading specialists, teachers, librarians, and merely curious who have visited my reading initiative, Storyented.com. I founded it in 2015 to introduce readers to incredible authors and their stories. Nobody can excite a reader to open a book the way an author can. To all those who ventured to "find your story and find your way" via Storyented, thank you. I hope many others will join us there for compelling interviews and tips for getting reluctant readers to dive in.

Finally, I must thank Dublin, Ireland, for providing me with a crucial bit of inspiration for this series when I needed it most. During a visit in 2012, I learned that a relic had been stolen from the Christ Church Cathedral in Dublin. The 800-year-old heart of St. Lawrence O'Toole, the patron saint of Dublin, had been snatched by thieves. My first thought when I learned of the theft was: Who would steal a relic, and why? Any reader of my series knows where that question led. . . . I am happy to report that in the spring of

2018, the relic was recovered in a Dublin park and returned to the cathedral. In some ways that story reflects how this series has impacted me. I put my heart into the Will Wilder saga, and through many visits with and letters from readers, it has come back to me—fuller and better for having been embraced by you all. Thank you, my friends. There is much more to come.

❖ ABOUT THE AUTHOR ❖

Raymond Arroyo is a *New York Times* bestselling author, award-winning producer, and Fox News contributor, as well as lead anchor and managing editor of EWTN News. As the host of *The World Over Live*, he is seen in nearly 300 million homes internationally each week. He is also the founder of Storyented, a large-scale literacy initiative. When not in Perilous Falls, he can be found at home in New Orleans with his wife and three children.

RaymondArroyo.com